THE TRUTH THROUGH THE STORM

Danny Book 2

REG QUIST

Published in the United States by Wolfpack Publishing, Las Vegas

CKN Christian Publishing
An Imprint of Wolfpack Publishing
5130 S. Fort Apache Road 215-380
Las Vegas, NV 89148

cknchristianpublishing.com

Paperback ISBN: 978-1-63977-408-1
eBook ISBN: 978-1-63977-407-4
LCCN: 2021951042

THE TRUTH THROUGH THE STORM

THE FIGHT THROUGH
THE STORM

Also by Reg Quist

Prologue

The band was clearly in its element, playing piece after piece. But the dance was a spontaneous affair, totally unplanned. When a full and fun one-half hour had passed, the pianist called a halt and leaned towards the microphone he had placed beside the piano.

No one had seen it, but Box, again taking charge, had signaled that it was time.

"Well, folks, we could play all afternoon and into the night and love every minute of it. But looking at the bride and groom I'm guessing they're about ready to make their escape. So, before you go, this last one's especially for you kids."

With that, the band, again led by the fiddle, swung into a slow, pleasant, but somehow nostalgic waltz. Everything about the music caused the listener to long for that home of their dreams, or, perhaps, of their memory. Or, in the case of the newlyweds, the home they were determined to establish, a happy home, a Godly home.

There's nothing quite like the country fiddle, well played, to draw the listener's melancholy to the surface.

No one said anything. Even Box knew to be silent as Danny swung Syl back onto the floor. She nestled her head against his chest as they danced expertly to the slow swing of the somehow wistful music. Music that reminded everyone in the room of how they would like to imagine life to be. Danny, in the silence of his mind, was looking forward to the day their home and life would fulfill that dream.

After a couple of minutes, he whispered into Syl's ear, "How would it be if I danced us towards the door?"

"Do it. It's time."

The crowd parted, sensing what was happening. The space they vacated was soon filled by other dancing couples. Everyone loved a last dance. A keen observer may have noticed three or four young cowboys directing special attention towards an equal number of young nurses.

As they neared the door, Wes draped Syl's winter coat over her shoulders, without breaking the rhythm of the dance. Lifting one hand free, Danny accepted his coat from his brother.

Momentarily going their separate ways, they moved to their own parents, with hugs and handshakes and then exchanged places while they did the same for their new in-laws.

Turning to the crowd, they waved their thanks for the love and good wishes and stepped out the door.

The .32 was gone. Ted had put the top up and

driven home earlier, taking his son Hal, along for the ride. Christie had taken the girls home at the same time.

Beside the curb a well-dressed man stood beside a vehicle, holding the door open. With Danny holding his Stetson with one hand, against the still blowing chinook wind, they walked to the car. They settled into the rear seat and the driver closed the door. Without a word, the driver swung away from the curb, and they were soon around a corner and heading to the highway.

Once on the highway, the driver glanced into the rear seat through the mirror.

"Name's Bryson, folks. About an hour to the city. The chinook cleared the roads off. Should be no trouble at all. Sit back and relax. Let me do the work."

Danny found no reason to comment.

They sat silently, but closely for the first half hour. Finally, Danny quietly said, "Well, Mrs. Framer, are you ready for married life?"

Syl squeezed his hand firmly and responded, "More than ready, Mr. Framer. And I'm hoping you are as well."

"You needn't wonder, Mrs. Framer."

Chapter 1

Danny and Syl had planned their honeymoon trip around warm ocean beaches and quietness. They found what they wanted on one of the smaller Hawaiian Islands, with the assistance of a travel guide. Neither one was drawn to the busyness of the big tourist cities.

Not being seasoned flyers, they were both exhausted after the flight to the island, but two days later they were feeling fine and looking forward to what the lodge and the surrounding area had to offer. Preferring some separation from other lodge guests they had chosen one of the smaller cabins that was slightly removed from the main lodge buildings.

They either took their meals at the lodge restaurant or made the short walk into the adjacent town, where there was an abundance of dining spots and shopping choices.

The first day spent on deckchairs nestled under the overhanging branches of a shade tree neither knew the name of, was a great pleasure for the newlyweds. The second day, regardless of the warm breeze and the novelty of watching the small sail boats rise and fall on the slightly rolling sea was a little less so. The third day, Danny's mind went back to his ranch and the little cabin that was being renovated to welcome them home, on their return. He wasn't sure what Syl was thinking, or dreaming of, but he thought it may be unwise to mention home, with its November winds, the snow, and the several months of winter yet ahead of them.

But by noon of that third day, he found he had to confess to his wandering mind.

"Syl, I've been thinking of something. I've thought of it before but didn't act on the idea."

"You're thinking of home, aren't you?"

Danny tried to mollify his new wife with a lop-sided grin, a grin she had seen many times, and was to see many more times.

"This is lovely and all. And I'm totally enamored with the fact that I have you as my wife, sitting right here beside me. But we have to be honest. This is for three weeks. Home is forever."

Syl reached across the few inches of sand that separated their two chairs and wound her fingers through his.

"You might just as well talk about it. You never know. I might be having the same thoughts."

"Well, you might. But I think you'll find this a bit offbeat. What I'm thinking of is the winter ahead and the years after that, and the winters recently past. For each of the three winters that I've lived in that cabin we've had power outages in the entire area. The wind whips up and knocks branches off the trees, dropping them across the power line. Could happen miles away. Doesn't matter where it happens, but with a great flash, out goes a transformer or at least a safety drop switch, and along with that, the lights. And the furnace. I never suffered overly much because I had the wood stove, but many neighbors didn't do so well. I've thought for two years or more that I should have a power plant installed. You know, a generator that would supply just our ranch. I hesitated because of the cost and also because no one else seemed to be doing it, which is a really poor excuse. But, in spite of my broken leg and the extra labor costs, we had a good year with both the haying and the cattle. We can afford a generator."

Syl squeezed his fingers, as if to gain his attention to the facts.

"Well, my loving husband, you will remember that we are in Hawaii and the generator suppliers are several thousand miles away, with an ocean, a mountain range and hundreds of miles of prairie between us. Could you just relax and enjoy, and deal with the generator when we get home?"

"Just a couple of phone calls, Syl. I promise. I won't get fixated on this. Just a couple of phone calls."

Syl laughed and said, "Do what you need to do. You might want to figure out what time it is at home before calling."

At nine the next morning, when he figured Willy would just be finishing up his lunch, Danny dialed his home number from their ocean front cabin. Before leaving home, he had asked Willy to answer any calls and take notes.

Willy picked up the phone after three rings.

"Willy, Danny here. I've got something I want you to do for me, but first, how is the job going?"

"Job's nearly done, my friend. Two more days and I'm out of here."

"That's good news, Willy. But what I really need to do is talk to your electrician. Can you give me his number?"

"Don't have to. I just have to pass the phone to him."

The electrician came on the line, introduced himself as Colin, and gave Danny his business phone number. Danny quickly outlined what he wanted done.

"Call me in two days. I'll have it priced out for you and you can make a decision."

"Thanks, Colin."

He hung up and grinned again at Syl.

"There, now that didn't take long, did it? Let's walk down to town and find something gooey and full of calories to snack on."

The lodge concierge was a wealth of information about things to do on the island. At his suggestions, Danny and Syl snorkeled, went for a long ride in a guided sailboat, rented horses for several after-noons and walked on the trails that bordered the beach. And all the time Danny was thinking of home. Syl recognized the signs and chuckled inwardly without letting on to Danny that she saw through him as easily as looking through a recently polished window.

It was three days before the end of their scheduled stay that they rented horses for the entire day. Having proven themselves to the stable owner that they were competent and trustworthy riders, they were allowed to venture out without the customary guide. With map of beach side trails in hand, a bottle of water for each and a lunch purchased from the restaurant, they were ready for their last Hawaiian adventure.

Plotting out a route, with the assistance of the stable hostler, that would show them some attractive areas to ride through while keeping them away from road traffic, they set out in mid-morning. The trail was everything they were told it would be. It skirted a small residential area before leading into a lightly treed park and a half mile later, pointed the riders down a slight grade, to the wide, sandy beach.

Almost a full mile ride along the beach took them to an opening into the treed area again. Meandering at a slow, walking pace, they found themselves again facing the beach. But this time there was no way down. At the top of the cliff that separated them from the sand and water was a picnic table and fire pit. They would have no use for the fire pit, but the picnic table was put to use. A slow lunch on this slow, melancholy day, thinking of the snow and cold they would return to in just two days, put them in a reflective mood. They found themselves discussing hopes and dreams in details they had not opened themselves to before. The very preliminary plans for a new house were laid out verbally. They had no paper to draw on. Plans for accommodating the horses in the big barn and even thoughts of a chicken coop brought smiles and laughter. The thought of a family crossed Danny's mind, but he said nothing of that. Finally, Syl said, "Why don't we ride some more?"

Riding from the isolated, cliff top rest area, leaving the picnic table behind them, Danny and Syl pointed their rented horses onto the partially bushed trail. As they rode, there was a periodic peek-a-boo look at the glistening Hawaiian waters. They saw no one and heard nothing until they ventured onto a two-track route that meandered through a heavier growth of trees. A half mile of this meandering lay behind them when they entered a small clearing and saw a car sitting at a strange angle, its front passenger side bumper touching the ground. Still a half mile away, it was impossible to be sure what the problem was. But it seemed obvious, even from the distance, that trouble surrounded the vehicle.

Cautiously they rode forward, not knowing if the broken-down car had been there for an hour or a month. Danny suggested that Syl wait behind until he saw what was going on. She would hear nothing of the sort. Together they approached, seeing no one. As they got closer, they could see that the driver had misjudged the corner, had driven into the shallow ditch and damaged one front wheel. Even if the car was pulled out of the ditch it lay in, there was no hope of it going anywhere. The bent wheel was no longer serviceable.

They were almost right upon the car when they saw an elderly couple sitting on a downed log, in the shade of the roadside trees. At first, no one spoke. Not knowing what to expect, they simply stared at each other. Danny finally took the initiative.

"Looks like a problem with that wheel. Have you called for help?"

"There's nowhere to call from. So far as I know we're miles from help. We thought we were on the road marked on the tourist map. But apparently, I chose the wrong corner, and here we are. I'm sure we drove five or six miles down this wrong trail before that happened," he said, pointing at the broken wheel assembly. "And, unfortunately, I'm in no shape to walk that far. The wife wanted to walk out herself but I'm not comfortable with that. We've been hoping someone would come along."

Danny and Syl looked at each other, passing unspoken questions between themselves. Syl asked, "You said five or six miles back down that trail. What's back there? Is it a store or a garage or something else?"

"Naw. The road was pretty barren since the last small settlement. All we saw was some kind of a shanty with three barking dogs and several surf boards leaning against the shack. Didn't see any folks. Might not even have a phone. There's just no telling. Could walk all that way and still be nowhere."

Danny took a bold approach towards the man with, "You say you can't walk well. What's the problem? Can you walk at all?"

"Thank you for being polite, young man. But the truth is that I'm sure you can see the problem. Oh, yes, I've got some arthritis in my knees and a troublesome back, but the real problem is right here," he said, as he gripped his belt and jiggled his corpulent belly. "There, and with my lungs, which is a bad combination, I know, but there it is. Facts are facts."

Danny rode the rental horse closer and dismounted. He studied the couple for another moment before making his decision. The afternoon was moving along, and night falls early and quickly in the tropics. Something had to be done for this couple and there was no time to waste.

"Well, we can't leave you here. And by the time we ride back and send help, dark will be upon us. Then, to complicate matters, we would have no idea where to send the help to. All we've ever seen are these shoreside trails. So, on your feet, the two of you. Let's go for a horse ride." He tempered that statement with a grin.

Syl pulled her animal closer and dismounted, as well. The woman stood and stepped towards Syl.

"I'm Sonja Gable. My husband is Terrence. We're very thankful to see anyone at all come along but I don't know about this horse thing."

Terrence struggled to a standing position and offered his hand to Danny. Danny shook it and introduced himself and Syl. He followed that with an explanation of his rapidly put together plan.

"This horse won't make it back with both of us riding so we're going to get you into the saddle and I'm going to walk along, leading him. All you have to do is sit there. It's going to take some time and sundown will soon be upon us, so it would be best if we could get this show on the road."

"Danny, that's kind of you, I'm sure. But I only ever sat a horse the one time in all my long years of life. That was at my sixth-year birthday party when the folks hired a man with a Shetland pony to give all the kids a ride. That single experience left me a slight bit short of meaningful horsemanship. Besides that. I'll never get up into that saddle, without someone coming along with a winch truck."

Danny was surprised at the man's good nature, but time really was becoming important, so he rushed it along. Glancing behind himself he saw that Mrs. Gable was already in the saddle. He surmised that Syl had helped her up while Danny had his back turned, to save any chance of embarrassment for the lady, who was decked out in a beautiful, flowing, Hawaiian flowered dress. Syl stood with the reins in her hand while Mrs. Gable had taken a two-handed grip on the horn. Syl had to show her how to put her feet in the stirrups and explain that she would do better if she could sit up straight.

Studying Mr. Gable, Danny knew the man was correct. There was going to be a problem mounting the saddle. He finally said, "Mr. Gable, I want you to come to the car. I'll open the door and you step up onto the floor frame beside the seat. Hold the steering wheel or the roof edge for support. We only want to do this the once so put your all into the effort. Now come on, let's get it done."

Knowing that turning down their only hope of help would be foolish, and somewhat embarrassed that his wife was already in the saddle, Terrence waddled towards the car. Gripping the steering wheel with his right hand and standing as if he was going to bend and take the driver's seat, he looked at Danny as if to ask, 'now what'?

"Good. Now lift yourself up and stand with your right foot on the bottom door sill."

With great effort, along with some lifting from Danny, and moving his grip from the steering wheel to the windshield trim, the elderly man managed to do as instructed.

"That's great. Now bring your left foot up and swing your weight onto it."

Mr. Gable had to turn his back against the car to accomplish that instruction, but he got it done and then looked again to Danny. Danny braced himself, leaning his shoulder into Mr. Gable's girth. He didn't dare move away knowing that if he did, the man was in danger of falling forward, and away from the car.

Danny held firm while he said, "Syl. How be if you tie that horse off and come give us a hand."

When Syl arrived, Danny said, "Now, Syl, if you could lead my horse as close as you can to the car door and back him against the car, we'll finish this operation."

Danny could feel the man trembling with effort,

and perhaps some fear. Silently he thought, *Hurry, Syl, we're going to lose him in a few minutes.* Syl clearly understood, and in less time that Danny had hoped for, the horse was in place, appearing to be calm enough for the next step.

"Mr. Gable, listen carefully now. The door prevents the horse from getting as close as we would like, so you're going to have to reach out with your right foot. Syl will hold the horse steady and I'll guide you into the stirrup. Then, using all your strength and transferring your weight to the stirrup, you are going to lean that way and reach for the saddle horn. I'll move out of your way, but I'll be right here beside you the whole time, giving you balance. When you get a grip on the horn, I'll hold you as best I can, but I can't carry your entire weight. You keep your right leg strong, pull with all your might on the horn and lift your left leg over the horse. You'll be mounting from the offside and the horse could balk at that. If he moves or steps sideways a bit just go with the horse. Don't reach back for the car. Syl will help, and I will be right here to help too. Ready Now?"

"It might be easier to just shoot me, son, but I don't imagine you have a gun any more than you have a phone. Alright, here goes."

With an enormous effort from all three participants, which almost came to disaster when the horse took a small sideways step, the rider had an off-sided seat on the saddle and a grip on the horn, along with a startled look on his face.

Danny, pushing and encouraging, managed to

maneuver the man squarely into the saddle. Syl tugged until his left foot found the stirrup. Everyone took a deep breath and silently gave thanks.

Mrs. Gable, looking on from her seat in the saddle on the other horse, said, "Well done, my dear." It didn't sound altogether like a strong expression of admiration.

Mr. Gable said, "I didn't think it would be this high."

Danny lightened the moment with, "If we had known you would be here and needing help, I could have brought a shorter horse."

Mrs. Gable laughed but her husband sat silently, staring at the ground.

Danny picked up the reins and Syl did the same from her own horse. Side by side they moved down the trail, back the way they had come. Just once Danny gave a warning. "Use your stirrups to keep straight on the saddle. Call out if you feel yourself slipping. If either of you slide off there's no telling how we'll get you back up there."

Hours later, the two tired walkers, leading the two exhausted horses carrying the two, saddle sore and fatigued riders, walked into the stable yard.

Twice, along the way Mr. Gable gasped out, "I can't go on." Neither Danny nor Syl responded. The second time Mr. Gable had cried out, "Just let me drop off this beast and leave me here. Take my wife along and leave me. I'll just lie in the grass and perhaps tomorrow you can get some help out here." Again, he was ignored.

The short evening was about to fall into the

darkness of night, but the stable yard lights were their guide for the last few hundred yards. They were met by a startled hostler who was leading up to a question about where they had been, when he saw the Gables aboard the horses with the young couple he had rented to walking and guiding the animals. He was struck into silence at the sight, only staring without comment.

Thinking about the two riders dismounting and knowing he could not hold Mr. Gable's full weight, Danny was out of ideas and nearing despair, wondering if the old gentleman would simply have to fall off and drop to the stable yard. The hostler, seeing the problem, remembered a seldom used step ladder that was stored in the outdoor shed.

Mrs. Gable was more afraid of the ladder than she had been of the horse. But with the hostler steadying the ladder while Syl guided her feet onto the steps with Danny providing strength for her balance, she carefully made her way down the three steps to the ground. Everyone was forced to ignore the fact that her flowery summer dress was in no way the appropriate fashion for ladylike riding, especially dismounting. Danny and the hostler studied the floor of the stable while Syl helped Mrs. Gable get her leg across the animal's back and onto the ladder. Happy to be back to civilization and at the end of the long horse ride, it was not clear that the grateful rider even cared about propriety at that point.

Placing her two feet on the ground, she simply folded into a heap and slowly settled down, taking her rest on the grassed yard. Maintaining a semblance of her sense of humor she looked up at Syl and said, "Thank you, dear. Now don't bother me again until morning."

Syl chuckled when she said, "You did admirably well, Mrs. Gable. I only wish we had taken a photo. Think how proud your grandchildren would be when they see the visible proof of your story."

Mrs. Gable didn't bother to respond to this thought.

With Syl holding the horse while the hostler and Danny provided the required strength and balance, Mr. Gable was soon down the ladder and lying on the ground beside his wife. He was totally spent. He had nothing left of whatever feeble strength his overweight body normally held. But he too, showed the tag end of a sense of humor when he raised one hand, pointing at the horse, and said, "I have never had occasion to kiss a horse, but I wish I could think of something to let those two beasts know how grateful we are for the rides. Perhaps I'll think of something after my worn body recovers. If it recovers, I should have said. And Danny and Syl, what can we say?"

Mrs. Gable finished his thought with, "Tomorrow, my dear. We'll think of something tomorrow."

The hostler called a taxi, and with another great effort, first rolling onto his side and then up to one knee, followed after a time by the other knee, and with both Danny and the taxi driver helping, the reluctant horse rider was loaded into the waiting car. Mrs. Gable made an easier job of rising from the comfort of the grass. Soon they were whisked out of Danny and Syl's life.

Although none of the events of the afternoon were truly humorous, they found themselves laughing outrageously after the taxi was out of sight. The hostler joined them in laughter that he didn't fully understand before he asked, "Now, do you want to explain this to me? The boss is going to be asking questions."

On the way back to their lodge Syl squeezed Danny's hand and said, "My love, you are like a magnet to the needy and desperate."

Danny, not really sure that was a good thing, said nothing.

Chapter 2

The final two days of their honeymoon passed uneventfully while Syl planned their last couple of dining experiences and packed their bags. While this was going on, Danny was pacing the hotel room floor and thinking of all he had to do at home. They heard nothing at all from the Gables.

The pilot came on the speakers as they were nearing Calgary, advising everyone to gather up their personal belongings and prepare for landing. Along with that admonition he gave a brief weather report.

"The weather on the ground, folks, is fairly typical for this time of year. That is to say, awful. The temperature hovers around ten below, Fahrenheit. The wind is gusting between twenty miles per hour, and you don't want to know. There was a major snowstorm a few days ago but that may have all been blown into Montana by now.

"We here on the flight deck, as well as your

cabin slaves wish to thank you for flying with our airline. Now, just so you know, we will be returning to Hawaii in the morning. If any of you wish to go back, after sticking your noses out the door, I'm told the lounge chairs in the terminal are quite comfortable for sleeping.

"We sincerely hope your vacation was a great one and we look forward to the next time you choose to fly with us. Good night."

Danny had phoned from the lodge before leaving Hawaii, giving Bryson, their driver, their flight number and landing time. He promised to meet them and bring along the heavy coats and boots they had left in his care.

The man was as good as his word. As Danny and Syl were waiting for their luggage, he stepped up behind them with a greeting and a 'welcome home'.

When the carousel delivered their luggage, Bryson reached in front of Danny and grabbed both pieces. With a simple, 'follow me', he led them to the nearest exit. The airport wasn't large, so the choices were few. Somehow Bryson had managed to park his car in the 'taxis only' section without having it towed away. The engine was running and Syl was sure the heater would be doing extra duty to welcome the sun hunters back home on a blistery evening. None of that prevented them from shaking with shock and cold when they stepped out the door. Their heavy coats were lying on the rear seat. In just a flash of time they put them on and snuggled into the warm car. The driver closed the door and moved quickly to his own space.

The car rocked and shook as wind gusts grabbed it, while they moved down the almost deserted highway, at a safe and conservative speed. On occasion, the blowing snow came close to blocking out forward vision altogether.

Danny waited a discreet length of time and, hoping he didn't sound doubtful of the man's driving ability, asked, "Is this wise, my friend, or would you rather go back to the city? We could get a hotel room and try again tomorrow."

"The road actually isn't slippery. There's no sign of ice. It's just the blowing snow that's causing a bit of a slowdown. But we're in no particular hurry. This is a good heavy vehicle. The wind won't do more than just make a bit of a nuisance of itself. We'll take our time and keep it safe. Give you the chance to acclimatize back into your home turf. Mentally, at least."

The trip took longer than usual, but they did arrive back in Riverside safely. Instead of the usual well-lighted streets with all the brightly colored signs, and the cheerful homes and businesses, they drove into a city wreathed in total darkness.

From the front seat came a comment that expressed nothing but the obvious truth, "Looks like a blackout, folks. I wonder if you'll have light or heat at your place."

Danny, remembering the electrician's assurance when talking about the generator, answered, "We'll be fine. I'm sure of it." Even as he said the words, he was thinking of his beloved wood stove.

They made their way along the darkened streets and onto Sugartown Road. After a few miles through the still drifting snow, they saw the yard light of the D-F ranch standing out like a lone beacon in an otherwise deserted land. They had seen no other lights along the road, or in the city.

The drive from the airport had presented no insurmountable problem, right up until they reached the driveway into the ranch. There, with a callousness that never failed to frustrate Danny, as well as many others along Sugartown Road, and throughout the district, the county snowplow driver had filled the entry to the driveway with a two-foot-high mound of snowy road scrapings. Danny would have smashed right through, or at least tried to, with the old truck, but the newer sedan they were riding in wasn't the vehicle to tackle a challenge like that. The chauffeur pulled to a stop and sat silently, obviously wondering what to do.

Danny slid forward on the rear seat and held out his hand. In it were a couple of folded bank notes, the cost of the hiring, plus a generous tip.

"Take this my friend and open the trunk. We'll get our luggage out and hoof it in from here."

"I hate to leave you standing on a snow-covered road on a cold night, with the wind blowing. Our service is advertised as door to door. This hardly qualifies."

"Well, it qualifies tonight. We'll be fine."

Danny told Syl to wait until he broke a trail before she stepped from the vehicle. He had buttoned up everything that would button on his clothing before he left the car. Finally, tucking his pants into the knee-high, lace up boots, he walked to where Bryson had the trunk open and lifted out the luggage. He set it in the snow beside the driveway entry and said, "Just hold a minute please, until I break this down so Syl can get across." He had to lean into the wind a little just to maintain his position.

With that, he kicked and stomped and swung his foot sideways, scattering snow in every direction, until the plow-made hillock was flattened out enough to get through. It seemed as if half of the snow he shunted aside was wind-driven back into the space it had just vacated, while much of the rest flew into his face. But the opening would have to do for a single passage.

He then reached for the door handle and Syl stepped out. With a last wave to the driver, Danny picked up the two suitcases and said to Syl, "Let me go first. Try to stay in my path. Hold on to my coat if it would help."

Again, kicking and sliding his feet, through the foot deep snow, hoping to make a usable path, Danny led the way. Full darkness had fallen on the land during the drive from the airport, but the yard light was brightening the snow just enough to see where they were going. Along with that were a couple of shaded lights in the rental house.

Bryson turned his car crossways on the road to allow his headlights to shine down the driveway, assisting the yard light which was further into the empty space between the cabin and the barn.

When Danny turned towards the cabin porch, he dropped one suitcase and waved his thanks to the patient Bryson.

Along with the renovation, Danny had asked Willy to install a good lock on the door. With a twist of the knob Danny confirmed that job had been done. But he had no key. Again, Syl waited in the cold while Danny made his way to the rental house. Two firm knocks brought Ted to the door.

The two men greeted one another quickly as Danny explained about the key.

"Got it right here. Willy left both copies with me."

With the keys in hand Danny was soon back at the cabin, the door was opened, and the suitcases placed on the kitchen floor. He had done this while purposely blocking Syl from the doorway. Once his hands were empty and the interior light was turned on, Danny said, "Now, Mrs. Framer, welcome to your new home."

With that, he bent and picked her up, with one arm under her knees and the other around her shoulders. With the bulky clothing both were wearing, his grip didn't feel all that secure, but Syl helped with a firm, one arm hug around his neck. Still, he didn't delay in carrying his bride into their home and out of the wind and cold.

He set Syl down on the kitchen floor, which was a bit slippery with the snow clinging to the bottoms of their footwear, and steadied her until she found her balance.

"Carrying the bride across the threshold is a bit of a strange old custom, my dear, one I know absolutely nothing about, nor could I explain, but we don't want to enter into a lifetime together having missed any of the markers along the way."

Syl answered with a gloved hand on his cheek and a quick kiss, before starting to unbutton her heavy coat. Danny said, "I'm going to go check out that generator. I'll be right back."

The house was reasonably warm but the first thing Syl did was turn the thermostat to a more satisfactory temperature. The first thing Danny did when he returned from looking over the generator was light a fire in the wood stove.

"No matter what the furnace is doing, there's just no comparison to the wood stove heat."

With the coats hung up and the luggage laid out on the bed Danny said, "Your folks will be wondering. I'll put the coffee on and look around the kitchen to see what's available for dinner if you want to give them a call. Then I'll call my folks. You'll want to find out how your folks are making out in the power outage. I can go pick them up if it's necessary. Or if they could make it through one night, I can go for them in the morning. With the new couch and chair, we can manage with the four of us here until their power comes back on."

The phone calls were made, and a simple dinner was spread before them.

Danny had felt somewhat at ease with the simplicity of the controls on the generator, thinking he could figure it out if need be. And he took pure delight at the comforting throb of the diesel engine.

Following Syl's conversation with her parents

she had said little. Now, with enough time passed to think what to say to Danny she turned with a somewhat shy smile; "Honey, I don't like to think of my folks sleeping under every blanket they own, in a cold house, but they promised they were alright. Anyway, Mom was insistent. Clearly, she understands, without saying anything directly.

"I don't want to share our little cabin with anyone but you on our first night home. That was her thought too. I know her well enough to say that. We'll call in the morning. If the power doesn't come back on you can drive in and pick them up. We'll manage, as you said before."

A phone call confirmed that there was still no sign of the power being restored the next morning. Danny promised to get the old truck started and somehow make his way in. The wind had picked up again overnight. There was bound to be drifts of snow that would challenge his intentions. Ted, who was turning out to be a great asset, living right next door, had removed the batteries from both pickup trucks. He had them stored in the mud room just inside the back door of the rental house. Danny re-installed the battery in the old truck and turned the key. There were a few seconds of straining and groaning as the crank shaft turned, making its way through the thickened oil. But after a slow count of five, the starter got the crankshaft turning faster and the ignition fired. With no more difficulty than that, the old truck was running and ready to go. Danny drove it outside the barn, stopped, stepped to the ground, and closed the barn doors.

Confirming that the scoop shovel he kept there for situations he was likely to face on the drifted roads was in the truck box, Danny honked the horn as a farewell to Syl and headed for town. Glancing both ways to assure himself that there were no oncoming vehicles, he hit the grader-created snow hump that he had kicked his way through the night before, with enough speed to provide momentum. With a thump and a bounce or two, the truck hopped through the barrier and onto Sugartown Road. He had to brake hard and crank the wheels to the right to prevent the truck from travelling across the road and into the snowy embankment on the other side.

There weren't many vehicles on the road, and driving conditions were beyond difficult. The plows were out and working, but they faced a herculean task. There was no power on anywhere in the small city. Danny could only imagine the hardships occurring behind the closed doors of the many businesses and homes he passed.

After being forced to find a creative route to avoid impassible roads, he finally pushed his way onto the driveway of the Mabry home. Syl's mother was watching from the big living room window. At first glance Danny almost laughed. Almost, but not really, knowing that his in-laws very survival depended on using every device at their disposal to hold in the last of their body heat. Mrs. Mabry appeared to be bundled in all her heavy clothing, and around it all she had wrapped a blanket.

At the first sight of the pickup forcing its way through the snow and into their driveway she disappeared. Within seconds the front door opened and Syl's parents made their way to the truck. They were burdened down with one small suitcase and three cardboard boxes of food they had scavenged from the fridge and cupboards. Syl's mother was carrying the suitcase. Wes Mabry rested the boxes on the snow-covered landing and locked the door. Before Danny could set the parking brake and get out to help, he wasn't needed. The suitcase and boxes were swung into the pickup box and the passenger-side door was pulled open. Mrs. Mabry was speaking through numbed lips even as she stepped into the truck.

"Danny, I've not seen a more welcome sight in my entire life. Thank you. Thank you for coming in. We thought to go to the ranch yesterday and light the wood stove, but Wes didn't figure we could make it with the car. I'm so thankful you have this truck. You seem to be able to go almost anywhere with it. Oh, my, I am so cold. And the heat in this cab almost makes me want to cry in relief. Again, thank you."

Danny had never heard so many words tumble from one person in so short a time. She was still saying the last thank you when Wes slammed the door, like a period being added to the end of his wife's last sentence.

Danny stepped on the clutch and found reverse gear. In a matter of seconds, he was reversing the route he had taken in. He could find nothing to say until he thought about the security of the home and the fact the plumbing would all be frozen, creating no end of damage and repairs after the space was heated again.

"Did you remember to drain the plumbing?"

"I did that yesterday. Drained the hot water tank. Removed the water feed from the meter after shutting off the main. Opened all the taps in the house. The lines should be drained, at least to where they won't break. That's all I could do. And I struggled to do even that much. I'm not very mechanical, Danny. I can only hope I got it right. What water didn't go down the floor drain spread over the concrete. The basement floor will be covered in ice, but we'll face that issue later.

"The pilot light is still burning on the furnace, so we know the gas is not interrupted. When the power returns the furnace will come on by itself. There was nothing we could do about the jars of food and all the canning done last summer. Most of them have already frozen and broken. There will be a few hours of cleanup to face but again, we'll get to that another time."

Danny again tried to think of something to say. He finally settled for, "I'm guessing that will be a common situation in a thousand or more homes. The grocery stores are going to have a mess to clean up too. They offer hundreds of products in glass jars."

Neither parent bothered to answer. They were both alternating between blowing on their hands and holding them down towards the heater that Danny had on full blast.

After driving past several cars that were running in their driveways, with people sitting inside, Wes commented, "We did that yesterday. Foolishly, I had only a half tank of gas. By evening I had to shut it down, but it helped us throughout the day. All up and down our street the neighbors were doing the same. Today, only one or two. I'm guessing there will be a run on fuel purchases as soon as it's available."

The return trip to the ranch took a half hour, with all three passengers in the truck falling into silence. There didn't seem to be much to say, beyond a repeat of the obvious.

A sharp turn off Sugartown Road, a bump and scrape through the plowed snow pile, a few seconds of driving down the lane, and the truck came to a stop behind the cabin. Wes and Danny opened their doors almost in unison. Danny quickly walked around the rear of the truck and picked up two of the cardboard boxes. When Wes made a motion to grab the other one Danny said, "Perhaps you should help Mrs. Mabry. It's slippery underfoot here."

Syl had the door open with her arms held out to her mother. In a matter of seconds, the weary couple was inside, and the boxes and suitcase pushed onto the entryway floor. Danny then returned to the truck. He wanted it sheltered in the barn. It was cold in there but at least it was out of the wind.

When Danny returned to the cabin Syl was attempting to unwrap the blanket from her mother's shoulders.

"No, dear. I'll keep this on until I'm warmed up."

"Mother, you know that's foolish. All that wrapping is trapping the cold against your body. Now let me pull this all off, the coats and sweaters too."

Like a reversal of positions, the daughter helped the mother, who was acting a bit irrationally, against all her nursing knowledge and training. Finally, the heavy wraps were removed and then the boots. Wes was following suit with his own heavy coats. Soon the two were on chairs as close as they could safely sit to the wood stove. Syl completed her ministration by placing a hot cup of tea near to her mother's hand, and coffee within easy reach of her father's hand. She then turned to the stove.

"I have a big pot of oatmeal cooking here. Danny and I both enjoy it and I well remember how you used to take to it on cold mornings. You drink those hot drinks and then go wash up or whatever you have to do. We'll be eating breakfast in a few minutes."

Syl's mother was staring at the floor. She hadn't spoken for several minutes. The impact of the past couple of days was clearly heavy on her mind. What she was thinking about could not be known until, out of the blue, as if the mention of washing up had put painful memories into her mind, she blurted out, "I peed in the snow in the back yard."

The other three were stunned into silence. Finally, Syl said, "I didn't really need to know that, Mother."

She was nearly drowned out by Danny's laughter. Wes, obviously feeling that enough had been said, remained silent, but reached over and massaged his wife's shoulder to comfort her.

A half hour after arriving at the cabin Syl's parents had taken their breakfasts and were feeling reasonably warm. With Syl's encouragement they had retreated to the bedroom, after being assured that the bedding had been changed that morning and that they would not be a nuisance to Danny and Syl. With everyone knowing that the little cabin provided for no other options, the bed would be given to the parents while Danny and Syl would make do on the couch.

Simply lying on top of the covers, with a loose blanket pulled over them, Wes and Mrs. Mabry were asleep within seconds, the first real sleep either one had enjoyed for three days.

Chapter 3

Danny and Syl sat quietly through the morning, not wishing to awaken the sleeping parents. Neither had anything important to do. Danny paused in the reading of a new book purchased in Hawaii and thought of his writing but pushed the thought aside. Finally, he picked up the phone and called Ted. Moving as far as possible from the bedroom door, he spoke quietly, asking about the welfare of the family of renters. Comforted by the assurances of their wellbeing, he kept the receiver in his hand while he pressed the disconnect with his finger after saying, "Call if there's anything you need."

Ted returned the same offer of assistance and closed off the call.

Danny sat there working through a new thought. After a few seconds he set the phone back into its cradle and reached into a drawer for the phone book. When Syl asked what he was thinking about he answered, "There's an elderly lady just down the road. Lives alone in a big rambling old farmhouse. Mrs. Kingsbury. You haven't met her yet. Power out, no heat, can't cook anything. Tough time for the elderly. I'm going to give her a call."

When no one answered the call after a half dozen rings, Danny decided to let it ring for a while. At, perhaps, fifteen rings, although he hadn't counted, it became clear there wasn't going to be an answer. He replaced the handset and looked at Syl. No words were spoken while thoughts scrambled their way through Danny's mind. Finally, knowing what her husband wanted to do, Syl said, "You had better go check it out."

Wordlessly, but appreciating Syl's insight, he stood and pulled the fleece lined coat over his sweater. His big boots, a knitted scarf and a woolen toque pulled down to cover his ears, completed his preparations. His warm driving gloves were stuffed in the pockets of the coat. With a simple nod to Syl he slipped out the door.

The driveway into the Kingsbury farm site was blocked by plowed up road snow, the same as all the others. The unbroken expanse of snow in the lane told Danny that no one had been in or out for at least two or three days, perhaps longer.

Not wanting to risk getting his truck stuck, he parked, shut off the engine to preserve the precious gasoline, and hoofed his way across the plowed barrier and down the lane. The snow on the level was about two feet deep, hopelessly deeper where it had drifted.

No one in farm country ever used the front door.

Many front doors hadn't been opened in years. In Danny's rental house, the Mulholland family, the original owners, had a big old mirror-topped hutch across the front entrance. They left the piece behind when they moved. It was still there, blocking the entrance and making the door unusable.

Danny walked past the old Kingsbury house and swung onto the four steps leading to the back landing. Here, too, there were no marks interrupting the surface of the snow. Knowing he would receive no response to a knock, he turned the knob and opened the door. Like the habit Danny himself had finally adopted, no one in farm country bothered locking their door. Danny stepped into the rear porch and stopped, looking for signs of recent activity. The wall pegs were heavy with accumulated coats, coveralls, and miscellaneous outer wear, plus two halters and a bridle, most of it probably untouched since Mr. Kingsbury had passed away years before. The shelf above was cluttered with hats and gloves of every description, and the floor was laden with a collection of boots and shoes. Nothing looked disturbed.

He took the three steps to the inner door, leading to the kitchen, and turned the knob. Stepping in, he could see almost nothing. The place was cold as the tomb and the drawn blinds blocked what little light the stormy day offered. Moving first to a close-by window, he rolled the shade up and then turned to glance around. The newly released sunlight partially lifted the gloom. There, on a big rocking chair, wrapped head to foot in blankets, sat Mrs.

Kingsbury. At first impression, Danny thought she was dead. Her face, what little Danny could see between the blanket wrappings, was grey and still, her eyes closed.

Glancing around the room to assure himself that no one else was in the dim space, he couldn't help seeing a huge old cast iron coal and wood kitchen range. Beside it sat the new electric stove that had undoubtedly served for some years. There was no sign of a traditional wood box or any other fuel for the stove. There was no doubt that Mrs. Kingsbury would have been familiar with the lighting and use of the old stove but with any possible fuel buried under the snow she would have been helpless to take advantage of its wonderful warmth.

Seeing nothing worrying in the room, he again approached slowly towards the sleeping, or dead, neighbor. Step by slow step, the floor creaking with cold at each movement of his feet, he drew closer. To his amazement, Mrs. Kingsbury cracked her eyes open. He saw no other movement, no facial expression.

He quickly covered the remainder of the distance and bent at the knees to bring his eyes into level with the old lady's face.

"Mrs. Kingsbury? Can you hear me? It's Danny. Danny Framer. I live just down the way. On the old Mulholland place. We met a couple of times. I know you must be very cold, but are you hurt?"

There was only a slight shake of the head. The movement could have easily been missed.

"We have power and heat at our place, Mrs.

43

Kingsbury. How would you like to come visit with Syl and I for a while? Would it be alright if I picked you up and carried you to my truck? We have to get you to a warm place."

Danny jumped back a bit in alarm as a small dog poked it's head out of a fold in the blanket, just below Mrs. Kingsbury's neck. The dog growled a warning and Danny laughed.

"Well, good morning there, little fella. That's a good guard dog. How about you and I work together to get the lady to where it's warm?"

With that, and no further permission from Mrs. Kingsbury, Danny fought his way under the several wrapped blankets until he was able to push his arms under the freezing woman's knees and behind her shoulders. The dog growled again but he sensed no real threat in the action. The poor beast was probably starving and was certainly cold, in spite of the blankets.

"Here we go, Mrs. Kingsbury. You hold onto the pup, and I'll get you out of here."

Carefully he crossed the cold, slippery linoleum floor and succeeded in turning the doorknob, wondering why he hadn't opened the door before picking the old lady up. Mrs. Kingsbury wasn't a large lady, but with all the clothing and blankets she was wrapped in, the bundle was close to unmanageable. He about reached the limit of his strength and agility with the struggle closing the two doors, then making his way down the stairs and through the deep snow to the road. But within minutes Danny and Mrs. Kingsbury were both in the warm truck and moving down Sugartown Road.

The two driveways were on opposite sides of the road and about one-quarter mile apart.

As he pulled to the back of the cabin, he blew the horn, hoping Syl would hear and open the door. She did, and Mrs. Kingsbury was soon positioned on the bed that Syl's parents had recently vacated, claiming a new lease on life after three hours of rest.

Danny spoke to Mrs. Kingsbury, hoping she could hear. "Mrs. Kingsbury, You're safe now. This is my wife. Her name is Syl. The other lady is her mother. They are both nurses. They know what to do to help you. Trust them and they'll take good care of you."

With that, Syl pulled back the top blanket the woman had wrapped herself in. The little dog jumped out like it was sprung from a jack-in-the-box, and landed on the bed beside his master, startling Syl and her mother, both. Syl let out a startled 'yelp' while her mother leaped back two steps, and then began to laugh.

Danny chuckled and said, "Sorry. I should have warned you."

He moved into the kitchen after, again, putting the truck in the barn, and poured himself another cup of coffee. Sitting at the table in his usual position, although both the chair and the table were new, he glanced at his father-in-law, comfortably leaned back, with eyes closed on the new, two-position love seat. Thinking he was resting, rather than sleeping Danny asked, "Are you feeling better? Thoroughly warm?"

Slowly Wes Mabry opened his eyes and raised his chin from its resting position. He was slow to answer.

"I'm fine now. We both are. Thanks to you and Syl. But I was sitting here thinking of all the suffering in our small city these past three days. In the city, and around the farm and ranch lands. Your neighbor would be dead by tomorrow morning if you hadn't thought of her. How many helpless old people are there scattered around the area in exactly the same condition, and facing the same bitter end?

"As I was considering that, I found myself praying for God's mercy to fall upon the land. And for His strength and caring to cover the stalwart men who are right this minute trying to repair broken power lines and clear away fallen branches. We can be thankful that the telephone lines were put underground years ago so at least we still have some communication.

"It's a helpless feeling to know there's not much else I can do. Don't misunderstand that. I know perfectly well that God can do all things, but in this physical world he has gifted men and women with capabilities and skills and placed them where they can do the work that needs doing. But not all of us are gifted that way.

"Take just the two of us. Clearly you could have excelled in higher education, but, I believe, with the guidance of God, you chose a different path. A path that involves the physical. And you are putting those gifts to good use. I, on the other hand can't tell a left-hand hammer from a right-hand hammer. And right now, with the storm abating somewhat, it's the men with physical skills that we're depending on. No teachers or administrators needed today, no presidents or prime ministers, although I like to believe we are of value in different circumstances.

"Anyway, I found it a comfort to pray for those who are suffering."

Both men paused and looked around when they heard the water being turned on in the bathtub. Pushing his questions aside, Danny nodded in understanding and agreement with what Wes had said moments before, but if he had any words to add they were stopped by Syl's voice from the bedroom.

"Fellas, I need you to turn your backs to this side of the cabin. We need to get Mrs. Kingsbury into a warm tub now. She's not as chilled as Maria was, way back when, but she's cold enough to cause concern. You just look the other way and leave it to Mom and me. And it would help if you could distract this dog. Maybe get him something to eat and a drink."

Syl had little patience with dogs in the house, but her mother was adamantly more so. When the little animal tried to follow them into the bathroom, he made the mistake of getting under her foot. With a small yelp the dog came skittering across the floor, boosted, both men guessed, by coming into contact with the side of Mrs. Mabry's shoe. While she wouldn't kick the little dog, it was no stretch of the imagination to picture a sweeping thrust of Mrs. Mabry's foot, propelling the troublesome animal out of the way. Danny grabbed the little guy and pulled him onto his lap. The dog growled at him but soon settled down. Danny held him until he heard the bathroom door close, then set him on the floor and went to the fridge. He had remembered a small bowl of oatmeal left over from their breakfasts. He warmed it a bit in the microwave, dumped it into a plastic tub that he wouldn't mind throwing away after the dog was finished with it, and poured just a bit of milk into the dish. They didn't have enough milk on hand to spare much for the dog. He didn't have to call the mutt. The pooch had been watching his every move.

With the dog problem dealt with, for the moment at least, and the bathroom door closed, Wes returned to his position on the love seat.

Danny picked up his book and found where he had left off.

Within a couple of minutes, Syl came from the bedroom with an armload of clothing. She dumped the whole lot, piece by piece, into their new automatic washer, without trying to sort out colors or fabrics, and reached for the soap. This being the first wash in the new machine, Syl was a few minutes reading operating directions. With that done, she adjusted the dials and turned the machine on, standing by while it filled with water for the very first time. Danny asked over the sound of the water running, "Problems?"

Without turning around Syl said, "You don't want to know."

With that little bit of enlightenment, neither Danny nor Wes pursued the matter.

When Mrs. Kingsbury was bathed, dressed, and feeling warm again, Syl helped her to the table. She was sitting eating her first meal in several days, dressed in Syl's clothing while the dryer worked on her own recently washed outfit. She had spoken very little, seemingly traumatized by everything that happened. Laying her fork on the edge of her plate she looked at Danny. She spoke slowly and carefully, clearly fighting back emotions that were about to open her eyes to tears.

"Young man, I have thanked the two ladies for their care, and I have thanked God, over and over for such neighbors. It's time I said the same to you. I have to assume that God put it into your mind to come to my house. And I am eternally thankful that He did. Thank you so much. I owe my life to you and these good ladies."

Danny, a bit embarrassed by the whole event, tried to downplay his role in the matter.

"You are very welcome, Mrs. Kingsbury. I'm glad you're warmed up and feeling better."

Mrs. Kingsbury didn't prolong the time but changed the subject with, "I wonder if I may make a phone call? My family will be worrying. I'm sure they called but I didn't hear the phone and would have been unable to answer if I did hear it."

Syl simply slid the phone towards her and said, "You make all the calls you wish."

The act of dialing the number was painfully slow to watch as the elderly woman struggled with arthritic fingers still a bit numb from the cold. But finally, she held the receiver to her ear and, after the call was picked up on the other end of the line, spoke to her daughter. When the two had said what had to be said, Mrs. Kingsbury held the receiver out to Danny.

"My daughter up in Red Deer wishes to speak with you, Mr. Framer. Her name is Gloria."

Again, the thanks were effusive and genuine. Gloria finished with, "May mother stay with you for another day, or until the roads clear up enough to travel? I'll be down to get her just as soon as possible."

With that assurance and an exchange of phone numbers, the call was ended.

Chapter 4

With the help of his ever-present jumper cables and a bit of patience, Danny got the new tractor started and moved out of its storage spot in the barn. The tractor and its front-end loader were woefully undersized for the task of snow removal, but it bested a scoop shovel by a long way. With nothing else to do until the crises was over, with the return of the power in the city and district, at least tackling the driveway overwhelmed with the white stuff would get Danny out of the house. Even facing the bitter cold on a tractor with no cab protecting the driver was a welcome prospect compared to twiddling his thumbs in his little cabin that now housed five people and a dog.

He had no sooner pushed snow a few feet away from the barn door when a family, sitting on two horses, turned into his yard. Startled by the sight, he stepped off the machine and walked towards the cabin. His visitors appeared to be a family of five, the father sitting the saddle aboard a big black, with one child holding on behind. The mother followed on a smaller animal, sitting bareback with two children seated, one before her and what Danny judged to be a young boy behind, gripping his mother's coat.

Clearly, even from a distance, Danny could see the family was in serious distress. He wasn't surprised at that. Thousands of people would be in similar distress. What surprised him was that they were horseback. And in his yard.

He stood beside the cabin while they made their slow way down the driveway. When the father pulled abreast of Danny he simply said, struggling between emotions and seriously cold cheeks and lips, "Neighbor, we need help. The kids are starving and freezing. Saw the reflection of your yard light last night. We're a bit higher than you and the light was the only thing visible in the night sky. I had to figure you had power from somewhere.

"I've been arguing against my pride all morning. Finally knew I had to come a-begging. Truck's out of gas. Driveway's blocked solid anyway. Too far to walk for the kids. Just have the horses. Please, friend, can you help the kids? Got a baby here, under my coat. Been crying and fussing for the most of two days. Please, sir!"

By the time this short speech was sputtered through freezing lips, Wes was standing beside Danny. Without waiting for Danny's response, Wes went to the woman and kids. Holding up his arms to the child at the back he said, "Here, let go of the coat, I'll lift you down."

The child was wrapped so thoroughly Wes couldn't be sure if it was a boy or girl. It didn't matter anyway. The child pushed his scarf-wrapped face more firmly into his mother's coat. The troubled eyes were focused on this strange man.

The mother turned a bit and said, "Go ahead, Teddy. Let the man lift you down."

As Wes lifted the boy down, Syl was there to lift the little girl from her mother's embrace, and then rush into the cabin, urging the boy to walk ahead of her. Wes then helped the mother, who was so cold she was unable to lift her leg off the horse. Trusting Wes, or perhaps, not even caring anymore, she held onto the horse's neck and simply allowed herself to slide sideways, knowing either the man would catch her, or she would fall into the snow. Either choice would be an improvement on where she had been sitting for the past hour. Wes did catch her but was unable to hold her weight. The most he could do was ease her fall into the deep snow. Wes and Syl together got her to her feet and headed towards the cabin.

While that was happening, Danny lifted another young child down from the big black. Syl was there to guide the child inside. Danny then turned to help the father. Not knowing what condition the man was in, he asked, "Do you want to pass me the baby or can you dismount one handed?"

Wordlessly, the fella opened his coat and gently lifted out the cold and hungry baby. The child's whimpering had been muffled by the big coat up until that time. Danny gripped the baby carefully and turned towards the cabin. Mrs. Mabry, having rushed outside without taking time for coat or boots stood there.

She said, "Give me the child."

The father stumbled on half-frozen legs and feet as he landed on the frozen driveway, after dismounting. Danny was just going to help the man to the cabin when the back door of the big house opened, and Ted rushed out. With no preamble he said, "The cabin is too small for that bunch. Bring them to the house." He was reaching for the father's arm as he said it.

With glazing-over eyes the father allowed Ted to turn him towards the big house. Danny rushed to the porch and turned the mother in the direction of the house, as well. Then Wes and Danny went into the cabin and picked up the children, with Wes picking up one and Danny taking the other two. As quickly as conditions allowed, they carried them to where Christie was holding the back door open. Syl's mother, still with no winter clothing on, carried the baby to the house. With the family safely inside, Christie closed the door. Syl rushed out of the cabin and said, as she passed Danny, "I'll go see what needs to be done."

Danny watched her rush away and then said to Wes, "Go inside and see what the coffee situation is. I'll be in shortly. After I house these horses."

On his way back from the barn Danny shut off the tractor. The snow would wait for another time. He and Wes sat drinking coffee in silence while Mrs. Kingsbury slept in the other room, and the two nurses were caring for the desperate family's needs, next door. Helplessly, they looked at each other, until Wes said, "As I was saying earlier, we each have skills for the moment of need. Those folks don't need either of us. They have what they need with Ted and Christie and with our two women."

Danny could think of no response, so he remained quiet. A few moments later, the thought entered his mind that Wes had referred to Syl, his daughter, as Danny's woman. So early in the marriage, Danny was still sorting out all the ramifications of the whole matter. And to have his father-in-law so firmly release his daughter into the new relationship was an assurance of acceptance to the new groom. 'She is my woman. I am her man. A two way surrender. In love, for life'. Private thoughts, after the public ceremony, only a few weeks before.

Chapter 5

Having done all he could do for his new visitors, Danny went back to clearing snow from the driveway and yard, hoping the ever-present wind didn't return it all before the next morning. If a chinook would follow this storm there would at least be enough melting and softening of the top layer of snow to form a wind-defying crust after it froze back up. Ranchers hated crusted snow, but it would suit Danny just fine.

Life was ever that way, it seemed. The grain farmer prayed for rain to feed his crop while the neighbor next door needed two weeks of dry, warm weather to get his hay cut and baled.

Syl and her mother managed to put an evening meal together after scouring the cupboards to see what was on hand. The original plan, of course, was for Danny and Syl to get the shopping done upon their return from their honeymoon. But with that not being possible, the pickings were going to be pretty skimpy in a day or two.

Mrs. Kingsbury woke and joined them for dinner. Wes said grace, and as they were passing the bowls around the table Syl glanced up at the wall clock. Laughing, she said to no one in particular, "Just to think, it's only twenty-two hours since we landed on the return trip from Hawaii. It seems like we've been home for a month. What a busy day and what a lot of problems for one day."

Mrs. Mabry said, "Perhaps Danny will work all this into a story someday."

Danny answered, "Only if I change genres and write a horror story."

Evening comes early at that latitude in the winter months. Before full dark overtook the land Danny had a couple of things to do. Immediately after the meal he put his warm clothing back on and went to the barn. He drove the old truck up beside the faithfully running generator and fueled it up with diesel from the bulk tank mounted on the back of the truck. He had bolted the unit into the truck box during the haying season a couple of years before. He carried diesel fuel for the two tractors and now, the generator. It had saved both time and money with the tractors and was now essential for the generator.

With that done and the truck and tractor back in the barn, he walked to the big house. Too cold to wait for the door to open he simply turned the knob, stuck his head into the room and hollered, "Anyone home?"

Christie hollered back, "Just me. Everyone else went to the beach for a swim and an ice cream cone."

Danny stepped in and closed the door. Ted joined his wife in the kitchen. Following close behind was the fella that had led his family for shelter on horseback.

Danny grinned at him and asked, "Y'all feeling like life just might be worth living again?"

The man stepped forward with his hand held out. He spoke quietly but firmly, "I'm told your name is Danny. I'm Graham Wills. And truly, between you and these good folks, I and my family literally owe you our lives. You know full well that I'll never be able to repay you, but anything, just anything at all. You ask. If I've got the means, it's yours. And I hope our friendship to top it off."

Danny responded, "I've known for a couple of years that I needed to get around and meet the neighbors. Sorry it took a near disaster to finally meet you, Graham. As to payment, I'll settle for the friendship and the knowledge that you made it through. I trust the kids and your wife are well."

Graham turned back towards the inner room, where all the kids were gathered around a woman sitting on the floor reading a children's book out loud. The kids appeared to be wholly engrossed in the tale.

Graham, said, "Bonny, come meet Danny."

Danny quickly said, "That's alright, Bonny. Don't break up the reading party. It's good to meet you both and to see the kids looking alright. That was a cold ride you made today. Anyway, I've got to get back to the cabin. I just went out to do a couple of things. Went to feed your horses too, Graham, but they were already cared for."

"Hay and water. That and a bit of TLC. Found the stack of bales inside the barn and the hydrant outside working just like summertime. That's all a horse wants or needs. Thanks for housing them."

It was a long night for Danny and Syl. Wes and Mrs. Mabry were given the bed. Mrs. Kingsbury, not quite petite, by fashion dress standards, but not a big woman either, fitted herself onto the love seat. Danny and Syl made a pallet on the floor, using an opened sleeping bag as a mattress and two woolen blankets over top to ward off whatever drafts might creep into the old cabin, in spite of the remodel. Danny though of hauling the bunk bed mattresses up from the crew quarters in the barn but Syl assured him the power would be on by morning and they could take her parents home and reclaim their own bed. With some doubt about the matter, Danny agreed to make the best of it.

Everyone was up before the sun fully rose over the eastern horizon. No one had much to say, fighting through the dregs of a night of broken sleep, and a bit of worry over what the day might bring. Danny, making room for the women preparing more oatmeal for breakfast, and finding a retreat to the barn to be a release of whatever tensions the crowded cabin thrust upon him, was surprised to find Graham already caring for the horses.

"Good morning, Graham. I take it you might be in the habit of rising early."

"All I've ever done, Danny. Farm. Oilfields. A short hitch in the army. There's no sleeping in on any of it."

Danny grinned and responded, "Missed the army part, myself. But the other two are plenty familiar."

The two men visited for only another minute, then, to escape the continuing cold, headed back towards the houses. As he was passing the generator, mounted at the base of the power pole, Danny noticed a lit light bulb glowing on the roof of the generator shelter. The electrician had told him it would be there to indicate when the public power supply was on and dependable. Danny stopped and said, his chin pointing towards the light, "Well, look at that, Graham. That bulb tells us the power is back on. That means I can shut off this generator. It also means it is probably back on at your place too."

Danny kicked away enough snow so that he could open the door to the generator shed. He knelt to peer inside. Remembering the sequence for transferring the load from the generator and back onto the public supply, he opened one switch and then closed another. Before shutting off the engine he backed out of the shed and looked towards the cabin. Wes was standing there with a big smile on his face.

"Is the power on?" Danny yelled.

"Sure is. And we just got a call from a neighbor. It's on in town too."

Danny turned the knob that controlled the engine. When the indicator pointed at 'stop' the engine wound down and came to rest. The silence was as welcome as the generator's power output had been.

Closing the shed door, Danny stood erect, smiling at Graham.

"This thing will need some servicing, but that can wait for a bit. Let's get the truck out and I'll run you up to your place. I'm thinking Bonny and the kids should stay here until you get the furnace working."

With that agreed on, Danny drove the truck out of the barn while Graham went to tell Bonny what was happening.

Before leaving, Danny walked to the cabin and said, "I'm just going to run Graham up to his place and I'll be right back. Then, if you wish, Wes, I'll take you to town. When you're sure the house is ready, I'll bring Syl's mother in."

Not waiting for an answer, or stopping to sit to breakfast, Danny pulled the door closed behind him. Within ten minutes, after winding his way around and past the many snowdrifts, he and Graham were sitting at the entrance to the Wills farm, looking at the hopelessly blocked driveway.

"You've got some walking to do, ol' buddy."

"Ain't that a fact. Well, the walking doesn't much worry me. But that's a lot of shoveling to get a vehicle out."

"Get the house warmed up and the water running. First things, first, and all that."

Graham nodded agreement with Danny, opened the door and said, "I don't see anyone else waiting here with a shovel, so I guess I've got it to do. Thanks again."

Danny drove back to the cabin, where Wes and his wife were waiting, anxious to get home. Danny stepped into the house and noticed his mother-in-law reaching for her coat.

"Are you going in or are you going to wait for a report from Wes?"

"I'm going in. One of the reasons is that Mrs. Kingsbury will be coming to town with us. We can't all fit into the truck so if you don't mind making another trip you and Syl will have your cabin back, all to yourselves."

Syl thought an explanation was in order, "Although she knows she's welcome here, Mrs. Kingsbury will be much more comfortable at the house, with a room and bed of her own. And if the roads are clear for driving, I expect her daughter will be coming tomorrow."

"Whatever suits everyone the best is fine with me. But I'm burning up fuel keeping that truck warm for you so let's shake a leg and get this done."

In just over two hours, Danny was back at the cabin, having taken two trips to deliver everyone safely to town and, after waiting in a lineup, fortunate enough to top up the truck's gas tank at the Crossroads Café and Service Station.

Wondering if there was yet more human cargo to deliver, he stopped beside the big house and knocked on the door. When he was inside, he asked Ted if Bonny had heard from Graham.

"Yes, and the furnace is on and warming the house. He's not sure about the water yet but they can melt snow for drinking if need be. Bonny and the kids are anxious to get back. Can you make one more trip?"

"That I can do. You get the kids ready, Bonny,

and I'll go to the cabin to see Syl for a minute."

Danny turned the truck around and pointed it back out the driveway before Syl slid behind the wheel. Bonny, not quite understanding what the plan was, ushered the kids in, sitting one on top of the other, and then squeezed in herself, with the baby snuggled tightly against her breast. Danny waved after telling Syl, once again to drive slowly, and headed to the barn. He had put a two gallon can of gasoline, kept ready for the ATV, in the box of the pickup with instructions to leave it at the mouth of the driveway. When Graham broke out of the drifted-in driveway the fuel would be there for him to get his own pickup started and running.

Syl waited at the mouth of the driveway while Danny completed a cold half hour ride, returning Graham's two horses to him. He then climbed into the pickup, rubbing his freezing hands together and unwrapping one of the scarves that was wound around his face.

"Home, my dear. And the sooner the better."

Chapter 6

After a good night's sleep, and another breakfast of oatmeal, this time without milk, and with the cabin again housing just the two of them, Danny went back to clearing his own driveway. Syl was busy in the house, washing bedding, clearing up dishes and, generally getting the cabin back into shape. It had to be done that day because she was back on hospital duty at six the next morning.

Danny had been fighting with his own thoughts as he pushed the last of the troublesome snow. There was just no way he had the heart to do what his mind was suggesting to him. Finally, he came up with a mental compromise.

Leaving the tractor running while he went into the cabin to warm up and have another coffee, he told Syl what he was planning. She listened patiently before saying, with a smile, "Why, my dear, I knew yesterday that you were going to do that. What took you so long to come on side? And, like I said, a magnet to the needy and desperate."

With a deep exhalation of breath and with mysterious thoughts running through his head, he said, "That's a bit discouraging, you know. I've only just learned to spell your name correctly and here you've got me all figured out, down to what I'm going to do in the future. I ain't come anywhere near to figuring you out yet."

"Danny boy, when you figure me out you can write another book, giving instructions to husbands all over the world. It will be a guaranteed best seller."

Danny couldn't think of a reasonable response, and rather risk saying anything that he'd regret later, he simply stood, picked up the pot and refilled his coffee mug. He sipped for a while in silence before shaking his head, as if dislodging an unwelcome thought, and mumbled. "Dang. Don't that just beat all."

This time it was Syl, who had no idea what he was referring to, who figured out it was her turn to remain quiet.

Danny recruited Ted to drive the pickup, waiting long enough for Danny to drive the tractor to Graham's snow blocked driveway. Syl was to phone Graham telling him to walk out to the public road when he saw Danny approaching. It was clear that Graham would need to clear his driveway at least enough to get to town for groceries, but Danny had no heart for doing it for him. The compromise he had worked out in his mind was to loan the tractor to Graham and let him fight off the cold while he did the work for himself. Danny felt he had suffered enough doing his own driveway. He found himself satisfied with the plan.

Tractors are not noted for speed. The two and a half mile drive to the Wills farm gate was a test of endurance and determination, taking even more time than the slow walk with the horses had taken. At least with the horses he had been able to kick them into a trot a couple of times.

Danny was thoroughly chilled by the time the unit covered the distance in top gear. Both Graham and Ted had their timing figured out. The three men met at the drive entrance. Danny stiffly stepped to the road and said, "I've fueled it up. It's small for the job and there's no way you can clear this whole mess out, but you should be able to break a trail through. Dress warmly my friend, that's a cold, bitter job, in spite of the winter sun. Whatever message that sun seems to be sending remember this, it's all a lie."

With no more to say, and with Danny needing to get into the warmth of the truck cab, the men parted. Ted soon had the pickup turned around and headed back home.

Danny sat with yet another cup of coffee. Syl was fussing around the kitchen cabinets, creating a shopping list for when the grocery stores would again be open. Danny, only half in jest said, "Do you remember when the pilot said, just before landing back home, that if we wanted to sleep in the lounge chairs at the terminal, the plane was returning to Hawaii the next morning?"

Feeding into the half-jest, Syl said, "Alright, but then we would have missed all this fun."

"Right. I forgot for just a moment how much fun we've been having."

His momentary spell of self-pity was broken by the ringing of the phone. Danny answered and listened as a female voice said, "Mr. Framer, this is Gloria Weld, Mrs. Kingsbury's daughter. I'm in town. At your in-law's house, actually. Mom phoned and gave me the address. She's looking and acting great, by the way, thanks to all of the help she received, and especially you, Mr. Framer, for thinking about her when the power was out. I am planning on driving out to the farm right away. There are a few things that Mom wants, and I'd like to look the place over. See what the damage is after the storm. I'd like to meet you and your wife. Would it be convenient to drop in for just a few minutes?"

With assurances given, Gloria said she would be there in about a half hour. Danny decided to use the time to make a couple of calls. The first was to the boarding stable, where he was assured that their three horses were fine and had not suffered during the power outage.

"We hauled a lot of water one bucket at a time from the old hand pump, but all is well now."

The next call was to his friend, Box who was jokingly smug when he bragged that their power had not been interrupted. Danny responded, again jokingly, that he was sorry he called. After a brief update on the situation with the ranch and Box's on-going romance with Maria, he phoned his mother, knowing his father would be at work. Their conversation lasted longer than he had planned for, with Mrs. Framer saying how thankful she was that things were getting back to normal for he and Syl and then going on to bring Danny up to date on the wider family matters, as if he had been away for months, rather than just the three-week honeymoon in Hawaii.

When Gloria arrived, the introductions and welcomes were kept brief, with Gloria saying, "I don't want to be too late getting Mom home. She's never been a good traveler and to drive in the dark on snowy roads in freezing temperatures would be a cause for great alarm to her. But I wanted to meet you two and thank you again. Then, Mom wants her purse and a few items of clothing. And I want to check the place over.

"I'm wondering, Mr. Framer, if you would be good enough to come to the house with me. You say you shut off the water pump and I thank you for that. But I'd like to see how you did it. And then, I'd, well, I'd just feel better if someone was with me. That's a big old creaking house. After the freeze up, who knows what else will creak and where my imagination might take me?"

"I'll be glad to come over if you'll call me Danny."

"Alright, Danny, let's do it now so I can gather up Mom and get back on the road."

Gloria had some trouble when the drifted snow in the driveway rose well above her winter boots, but soon they were at the back door of the big house. Danny opened the door and went in first. Stepping into the big kitchen, Gloria said, "Look at that big old wood stove. My, how Mom loved that old stove. I couldn't begin to calculate the meals mother and grandmother prepared on that thing. It would be in the thousands, for sure. The first thing Mom said when I talked to her today was that if the wood box had been full like it always was before Dad died, she'd have been fine. And that's the truth too."

Danny responded with, "I have a friend. Name of Box. His automatic response to things like that is, 'circumstances. Just the circumstances'."

Gloria nodded and said, "Yes. Circumstances. Mom shouldn't have been here alone for at least these last five years. She was barely able to get around. Driving the old pickup to town for a bit of shopping tired her for days. There's a nice newer car in the garage but she preferred the pickup, saying she didn't want to wear out the new car. Can you imagine? And now, to think she could manage a wood pile is out of the question."

Staying a respectful few step behind, Danny followed Gloria around the old house she had been raised in. She said nothing until the tour was finished and her arms were loaded down with clothing picked from her mother's closet. She had the sought-after purse hanging from her wrist. Arriving back in the kitchen, and glancing around before stepping towards the door, she said, "This is really three houses, built at different times by different people, each new section built onto the other. My great grandfather had a shack here in the very early years. At that time, it was common for folks to stop in just to say hello. Great grandfather knew John Ware, Pat Burns, George Lane, George Emerson, and oh, so many other true pioneers. Great grandfather wasn't really a part of that group. He and my great grandmother came along about a half a generation later.

"The shack was pulled down when my grandfather built the first home for himself and my grandmother. That was just before the first world war. That first stage was what is now this kitchen, which was the entire house at the time. It was built onto as my father and his siblings arrived. That, of course, is the center section of this ground floor. When my father was ready to marry, the last part, what is now the seldom used sitting room, and most of the second floor were added.

"Grandmother and grandfather lived with us until they passed away. Mother shared her home and her kitchen until not too many years ago. Back then, it was my mother who insisted that running water and interior plumbing be added. Grandfather grumped around about the foolishness of all that, but mother stood her ground. And growing up, I was glad of that, being a bit selfish, I suppose."

Danny had nothing to say about the Kingsbury family history, but he did add, "Well, the furnace is working and it's warm in the house. You won't know about frozen and broken water lines until someone checks it out. That's too big a job for today. But come and I'll show you where I shut off the pump."

Stepping onto the outside porch, Danny pointed at his nearly filled-in tracks through the deep snow angling across the yard towards the pump house. "I'm not sure you'd be wise to do it today, but if you were to follow my tracks through that snow to the pump house, you'll find an old electrical box on the wall. I simply pulled the switch lever down. To turn it back on you just reverse that. Do you want to go see it?"

"I'll take you word for it. Let's get out of here."

The next day he locked up the house with a hasp and padlock, at Gloria's request.

Three days later, Syl had completed her first go around of day shifts, now enjoying days off with three nights looming ahead. Graham had returned the tractor, with thanks. When some stores were re-opened Danny stood in line to shop, while Syl was at work. The newspaper was full of hardship stories, which Danny completely ignored. Only later was he told that the story of his rescue of Mrs. Kingsbury was among the group of published tales.

Danny had risen with Syl, in the darkness of early morning to drive her to the hospital for the shift that began at six a.m. Both Danny and Syl were familiar with early mornings, but with the winter's cold and the almost complete darkness at five a.m., as they were driving to the hospital for the start of the day shift, the winter darkness took on an almost unreal aspect. Danny's main concern was that Syl not be on the winter roads by herself. Plus, he had, from the first time he had become aware of the shift start times, been concerned about Syl having to make her way across a darkened parking lot. Riverside was a pleasant, small city with very little crime but still, having a couple of dozen nurses walking through the dark to their vehicles could become a temptation to someone with less than pure intent. Caution was called for, in Danny's opinion.

After delivering Syl as close to the door as possible, he found himself waiting in his warm truck, sitting where he could oversee most of the parking lot, until the nurses were either in the building or in their cars, heading home. He took private satisfaction from this bit of staff oversight.

While Syl rested from the long hours worked, Danny had his manuscript laid out on the table and the ever-present coffee pot steaming on the wood stove. And Christmas, which Syl would work through, on night shift, was just around the corner. Winter had barely begun.

Chapter 7

Syl was sleeping, working herself out of her 'zombie mode' as she called it, after the three twelve-hour day shifts. When the phone rang Danny grabbed it as quickly as possible to quiet the noise. It was Syl's father on the other end of the line.

"There is something we need to discuss, Danny. Would it be convenient to drive out now?"

With the assurance that the timing was good and with the advice that Syl was sleeping, Wes promised to be quiet. A half hour later, Wes, and Syl's mother stepped onto the porch. Danny welcomed them in and waited while they took off their winter coats.

When they were seated around the table, Wes laid a large brown envelope before them.

"This is for you, Danny. The publisher has obviously taken me for your agent, although I have assured them that is not true. But no real harm done. It just means this mail is a day longer getting into your hands."

With that, Wes removed a two-page document and set it on the table, facing Danny.

"There's your signed contract, son. I took the liberty of reading it over. You'll see when you read it that the couple of changes you requested were included. You assign all the publishing rights, worldwide and in any language. This is for books only. Movie or TV rights remain in your hands. It's all pretty standard stuff."

Wes waited for Danny to comment or ask questions. When that didn't happen, he pulled a check out of the envelope and, with a big smile, laid that before his son-in-law."

Danny studied the numbers without touching the document. Blandly, almost in shock, he said, "That's a lot of zeros."

"Indeed, it is, Danny. And if the book is as successful as both I and the company hope it will be, the next check could well have an additional zero on it."

Danny still had not touched the check, almost as if he were frightened of it, or in such awe that touching it would be somehow irreverent or profane. He leaned back in his chair and studied this man who had not only raised a beautiful young lady who had become his wife but had also opened doors and paved the way for the beginnings of his publishing success. He could think of no appropriate words.

The spell over Danny was broken by a small noise from the bedroom. He rose and stepped to the bedroom door, just cracking it open enough to say, "Your folks are here."

Syl, half asleep, had nothing to say but she did

push the covers aside and swing her feet to the floor. Danny backed away and closed the door. He went to the wood stove and put another kettle of water on to heat for tea. Mrs. Mabry had made the first pot for herself, but Syl would want some too. It would be ready when she appeared.

Syl dressed, washed her hands and face, and pulled a comb through her hair. She was soon seated at the table with the others. Her mother said, "The good news is that nursing is very satisfying when things go as planned, and you are well paid. The bad news is that the shifts don't get any easier as time passes."

Syl, still fighting the temptation to return to her bed, simply nodded.

Danny pushed the contract and the check towards Syl and waited while she looked them over. Still not in a talking mood, she simply wrapped her hand over the top of his and quietly said, "I'm so happy for you. Well done."

Wes, remembering that he had said nothing similar added, "And we too would add our congratulations, Danny."

The following silence was broken by Wes saying, "Danny, this story that is being published is clearly beyond the first work of most new writers. Now, I understand it is actually your second work, but the same truth still holds. You say you have no particular education that helped you but judging from the experience of thousands of writers who have gone before, you are either the next Dickens or Hemmingway or you have something else that would more completely explain your short writing history."

The question was not really stated out loud but still, it was clearly wrapped up in Wes's statement. With no reason to keep his writing history secret, Danny said, "Well, perhaps Dickens if it came down to looking for inspiration. But I'm not a fan of Hemmingway so I hope it's not that."

He hesitated before saying, "The winter evenings and days off are long and boring in a construction camp. Each man has to find his own way through. Some men go to town to party as often as possible. Some gamble, playing poker evening after evening, in the bunkhouse. Both groups too often go home close to broke after their northern tour, completely losing track of the high pay that drew them north in the first place.

"I'm not a drinker or a gambler so I turned to reading. I took a more serious approach to the stories than I had just a couple of years earlier when I read only for entertainment, or escape. After I read through every book on the shelves in the rec room, I began seeing how a story is put together. Almost as a joke on myself, I decided to give it a whirl. I have the habit of observing things. Curious, I suppose. I had packed away a number of incidents on the construction site. Storing them in memory, that is. That, together with what I had learned about the system behind it all, the system that justified the spending of such enormous sums of money, I seemed to see a story that almost wrote itself. Then there was the intrigue of those who opposed the petroleum industry and the various governing bodies, all hoping to get their sticky fingers into the same money pot, or at the least, to influence the industry itself.

"My handwriting is not good, nor fast, but rummaging around in a storage room I discovered an old Underwood typewriter. The kind where you have to push the keys hard, driving the strikers down far enough to leave an impression on the paper. There is nothing quiet about those old machines. Nevertheless, I dragged it into my room and set it up with great intentions. It would be no faster than handwriting, but it might turn out a document that would be easier to read."

Danny paused while he took another sip of coffee.

"Well, after I picked up a package of paper on my next freight run to town, and a new ink ribbon, I closed the door to my room and started. I had no idea where the keys were or what all the levers and buttons on the typewriter did, but I started in. Having no concept of how to type, it was a slow start. And even with my room door closed there was no hiding the clack, clack, of the old machine.

"What I accomplished first, was I gained a lot of attention from the other men. And a lot of teasing. As one of the youngest of the crew the men loved to tease me anyway, so that was no big change. Some fellas wanted to know if I was writing to my mommy. Others suggested that I had a sweetheart, or several sweethearts, judging by the typing racket, evening after evening. I knew if I fessed up to what I was really doing the teasing would only get worse.

"One day, perhaps a month after my first tenuous beginning, when the kitchen and dining hall quieted down for the night, I took the pages I had written and found a cup of coffee. Alone in the dining room, I reread what I had written on the first thirty pages. As I was absorbed in that, one of the cooks brought his own coffee over and pulled up a chair across the table. It was the end of his shift, and he was clearly tired. He said nothing for a while but finally asked what I was writing. Obviously, he had also heard me hammering away on the old Underwood.

"I knew this man's name, but nothing at all about him. I suppose, thinking about it, I gave a foolish answer to his question, something to ward him off and prevent further enquiry. But he persisted. Simply holding out his hand, without words, he asked to read the document. Reluctantly, and embarrassed at my own efforts, I pushed the pages across the space between us. Silently, he picked them up and began reading. Just as silently, I drank coffee and tried not to look at him, fearing to see a scowl of disapproval on his face."

Danny stopped long enough to take a drink of his now lukewarm coffee. He stood and walked to the sink, pouring out the half cup that was left. With the comment, "I'm no fan of cold coffee," he refilled the mug and took his seat. For several seconds he said no more. Syl, finally coming fully awake, said, "Danny, my love, have you forgotten that you were telling us a story?"

Danny didn't answer but he did resume the telling.

"The cook, Aaron Walsh was his name, he said nothing at all, nor did he look my way, until he finished all thirty pages. Then he stood, placed the pages back on the table, touched my shoulder in some kind of a signal I couldn't make out, and said, "Keep at it," and walked out. I had no idea what to make of all that, but I imagined I heard a bit of a catch in his voice as he said it."

Wes said, "I imagine the signal you sensed was the message that your first writing effort was a good beginning and was worth pursuing."

Danny allowed Wes's comment to pass, saying only, "Almost the exact same scene was repeated about a week later. Only this time Aaron didn't ask to read the new pages. He simply sat there; his hands wrapped around his coffee mug, staring at me. He stared so long I got really uncomfortable. But finally, he spoke. 'Did some writing myself. Long time ago. Pretty good at it. Took two years of college by correspondence. Two stories published. Made a bit of money.'

"The time gap after those simple, but telling statements were a story in themselves. It was as if he wanted to say more but, at the same time, wished he had never said anything. But since he had opened his story to me, I said, 'You might just as well tell me the rest. I'm not going to let you alone until you do.'

"I'm pretty much sure each one of us could fill in the rest of his story without his or my help. Life was hard after taking over his parents' farm. Little, if any time truly free time. No extra money.

"Wife left him. Somehow, the city lights had

made their farm life appear dull by comparison. Took the kids. Three girls. After a year he received notice that his divorce was final. His wife remarried. Moved away. Kept the kids from him. In another year she was again divorced. She left for another new start in some other area. Of course, she took the girls. He had no idea where they went. Aaron no longer even knew his family, or they him. He filled the lonely hours with the bottle. Lost the family farm to the bank. Or at least, most of it. His brother saved a piece for himself. Missed a publisher's promotional tour. Didn't write anymore. Finally lost his publishing contract. Gave it all up. Recognized the bottle was destroying him so he signed on as cook's helper at a dry camp. No booze allowed. Ever. Went cold turkey and survived that. When I met him, he was five years in the north. That was at his second camp. Stayed sober through three different camps, rising to full cook.

"The long and the short of it is that he took me under his wing, so to speak, and walked me through the really rough spots in my writing. And there were a lot of rough spots to walk through, some where I almost lost the storyline. Corrected me where I went chasing rabbit trails. Great help Aaron was. I have much to thank him for."

Syl, understanding that the story was finished asked, "Do you know where Aaron is now? Have you ever kept track of him?"

"It's strange that. Neither of us made any effort to contact the other. But a year or so ago I got a call from my old company manager. They were starting a big new project and were wondering if I was ready to come back to camp. Of course, the answer to that was simple but we chatted for a minute anyway. Among other things, I asked him if Aaron was still on the payroll. Apparently, he left shortly after I did. Only stayed a few months in the third camp. The company thought they had lost track of him. But they were short of cooks. Searching the old records, the accounting department came up with an address. They had kept it on file for tax purposes. The fella I was talking with said he had found a phone number somewhere and finally tracked Aaron down. He didn't want to return north either. Turns out he was back on the farm. His brother's farm this time, hoping his brother would get over his anger from the loss of the family holdings. Just a bit northeast of Red Deer. I should have called him right away, but I didn't. I plan to correct that oversight now that I have this contract in front of me. I'd love to send him a printed book but that will be a while coming."

Wes said, "Be sure to call him. And ask what has become of those two books he had published before. Let me know."

Syl stood and stretched, saying, "It's time I got some grub on the stove. Are you two staying for dinner?"

Both of her parents stood. Her mother replied, "No, dear. Our dinner is in the oven. We'd best get home."

Chapter 8

Danny spent the remainder of the afternoon writing, while Syl, after lunch, lay back down for a bit of extra rest. She silently admitted that she was indulging herself but that didn't make her change her mind. After lying there for a while, strangely, the thought flitted through her mind, 'It won't be this easy when we have a family.' That thought caused her eyes to pop back open, asking herself, 'where in the world did that come from'? She tried to settle down again after smiling at the thought of children but was unable to rest. She stretched, swung out of bed, and headed for the shower.

Danny waited until late evening before dialing the number he had been given for Aaron Walsh. Instead of connecting with Aaron, his brother Adam answered. At the request to speak with Aaron, the answer was, "Aaron is not here. Who am I talking with please?"

"My name is Danny Framer. I worked in the

construction camp with Aaron some years ago. I was hoping to reconnect with him."

"Well, Danny, this is Adam, Aaron's brother. Some of the family would like to reconnect with him but so far, that hasn't happened. For myself, I'm hoping to have nothing more to do with him. He caused a lot of trouble for me and mine. And no, I don't know where is. Have no idea at all. Don't really care."

"I'm not sure I know how to read that, Adam. Do I take it he's back in some remote camp? Did he mention anything such as that?"

"No, not as far as I know. Got up one morning and he was gone. Ain't seen nor heard from him since. But he did say he'd had enough of camps. Just takes off sometimes, and he might not report back in for weeks or months. He finds cooking jobs here and there and just stays to himself. There's little welcome for him here on the farm. As I said, others of the family feel differently."

After just a moment of silence while Danny struggled with his next question he said, "I'm not sure how to ask this gently, Adam so I'll just right out ask. Has he fallen off the wagon?"

"No, Danny. That's one thing I'm pretty sure about. He has talked a few times about his lost and wasted years. He holds considerable bitterness towards himself, along with a good dose of embarrassment. I don't think he'd fall again. He just seems to be a bit lost and aimless."

"Adam. If you would write down my name and number perhaps you could ask him to call me when you next hear from him."

Danny ended the call and set the receiver back in the cradle, while leaning back in his chair, and staring out the window. Syl emerged from the bedroom, showered and dressed for what remained of the day.

"Alright, Mr. Framer. I know that look. You're deep in thought, while also troubled. Who are you planning to rescue now? And are you going to wait until the need presents itself or are you planning to go in search of it?"

"No such thing, my love. I'm just sitting here working on my story. I don't know where you get such fanciful thoughts." He covered all this with his trademark lopsided grin.

"Sure, sure. Anyway, what do you want for dinner?"

A phone call that evening from Gloria Weld, Mrs. Kingsbury's daughter, left Danny and Syl with much to talk about.

They hadn't spoken to Gloria since she had come to get a few things for her mother from the old house. She had thanked both Danny and Syl profusely at that time, for rescuing her mother during the big storm.

"Good evening, Danny. This is Gloria. Mother wanted me to call you. She has made a decision. The family wanted her to make this decision years ago, after father died. But it took that dreadful storm to push her into it. And that leads me to thanking you again. Mother was quite insistent that you be made to understand, again, that she, quite literally, owes her life to your thoughtfulness. So, thank you."

"I have been fully thanked before, Gloria, but I appreciate your mother's words anyway. Of course, the ladies, my wife and my mother-in-law were really the ones that pulled her through once we got her into a warm place. And I'm happy to hear she is doing well."

Gloria said, "The decision mother made, Danny, and the reason I am calling, is that she has decided the farm must be sold. She can't go back there and no one in the family wishes to farm. There is one half section of land, two quarters, plus the buildings, all old but also all usable. We haven't valued it yet, but mother wanted to be sure you had the first chance to purchase it if you were interested."

The line fell to a prolonged silence. Clearly, neither Danny nor Gloria knew where to take the conversation. Danny finally said, "That's a whole new thought, Gloria. I'll have to stew on that for a while. I have never once thought of purchasing more land. Can I have a few days to run that through my mind?"

"Of course. We need that time anyway to value the property and sort out what to do with the furniture and things in the house and other buildings. How would it be if we talk next week around this time?"

"That would be fine. That gives Syl and I time to think too. But perhaps you can tell me what has been done with the land in recent years. I see some hay coming off in season, but I've paid no attention at all to what else was growing there or, really, on any other neighbor's land either. I've had enough to think about on my own place."

"The land is entirely in hay. In his later years my father found that he didn't have the stamina to grow crops, so he seeded it all down to grass. It has been rented out since father died, to Mr. Clarence Bradshaw. He left it in hay, although Mother gave him the right to grow whatever he wished. He owns the northern half of the section. He lives on another quarter across the road from that half. You could probably talk to him and see what plans he may have. He is no longer young so I doubt if he would be thinking to purchase if given that opportunity. But feel free to talk with him. We're keeping no secret about mother wishing to sell."

When the call ended, Danny and Syl, who had heard enough from Danny's end of the conversation to figure out what was going on, sat looking at each other. Syl was the first to speak.

"I can't say that I'm surprised she would want to sell. I can't imagine her returning to that big old house."

Danny answered, "Well, of course, you are correct on that. But do we want to own more land? It's a brand-new thought for me."

Syl surprised Danny by not dismissing the idea immediately. "Why don't you go over and speak with the man who rents it. There might be some insights there. And as you said before, when you phoned from Hawaii about the power plant, you had a good year with both cattle and hay. It might be a good time to make a wise investment."

Danny had never heard Syl talk like that before.

Her business aggressiveness caught him by surprise. After a brief staring match, with Danny finally giving in, they agreed that a visit with Mr. Bradshaw would be an appropriate first move.

With that idea laid down, Danny put a bit more wood in the stove, to hold overnight. Syl straightened up a couple of things on the cupboard before they shut off the light and called it a day.

Chapter 9

Still having no clear plan or any solid thought on the offer from Mrs. Kingsbury, Danny drove the old truck out of the barn and headed to where he hoped to locate Clarence Bradshaw. It turned out to be a simple task, as the Bradshaw home was the only one on the two-mile road. He pulled as close to the house as possible and hurried to the door. The wind was whipping around every available corner, carrying snow and small, broken off chunks of ice with it, making the day miserable.

Danny had been seen approaching. Before he could knock, the door opened and an elderly, cheerful-looking lady said, "Come in here, young man. You'll freeze half to death out there."

Danny thanked her and entered. As Mrs. Bradshaw started to close the door, the wind grabbed it and pulled it out of her hands. It closed with a window rattling slam, startling Danny, and the grey-haired lady, both.

Danny lifted his hat off and said, "I assume you are Mrs. Bradshaw. I'm Danny Framer. I live over on Sugartown Road, across from the Kingsbury place."

He was about to say more in explanation of his visit, but the woman turned towards the hallway on the other side of the kitchen and hollered, "Clarence, we have company."

She then went to the big wood stove and fussed with the coffee pot. It surprised Danny to again see a wood stove in use. It appeared that the old timers were having a difficult time leaving them behind.

Danny stood silently while he listened to a newspaper being folded and laid aside. Then, with a bit of a groan, someone stood and shuffled across the floor in the other room. The scuffing of the steps said that the walker was wearing loose fitting bedroom slippers.

Danny wasn't sure what he had been expecting, but it probably wasn't the aging, wizened man that appeared in the doorway. He had taken only a few steps into the room when Mrs. Bradshaw said, "Clarence, this is Mr. Framer. He's the one that rescued Edith last week."

Clarence Bradshaw approached Danny with his left hand gripping his wide suspenders and his right hand extended. He was shorter than both Danny and his own wife, slight but wiry of build. Danny could see his tough interior under the exterior tiredness. The old man's movements were slowed from age but not from weakness. The ruddy complexion appeared to be permanent, as if years of summer suns and winter winds had settled under his skin. Danny made the immediate judgement that this man could work beside younger men and hold his own, as long as he could hold to his own speed.

"Mr. Framer. We have been neighbors for far too long without meeting. It is a pleasure to finally say hello to you. And to thank you for what you did for Edith. We wondered about her but could barely care for ourselves during that terrible storm. And the power outage. We couldn't have gotten the truck started. The roads were blocked anyway, so the most we could do was call. My Annie phoned over a couple of times but received no answer. That caused us some worry, you can be sure of that. But, again, there was nothing at all that we could do. Oh, Annie phoned both the county folks and the police, but neither could do anything. They said there were hundreds of people locked in just like Edith."

Mrs. Bradshaw entered the conversation, speaking to her husband. "Mr. Framer is also the one who came to the rescue of Graham and Bonnie and the children. They rode their horses right past our driveway. They could have come here. The house was always warm. But I'm happy they made is safely to your home Mr. Framer."

Clarence Bradshaw wasn't to be moved from his talk of Mrs. Kingsbury.

"I offered last fall to lay in a supply of stove wood for her but she's a stubborn old coot. Said she guessed she could still bring in a few sticks of wood. Asked me, 'what do you think, I'm too old to care for myself?'" He chuckled a bit before saying, "Stubborn. It wasn't till after the rescue that we learned she had no wood she could lay hands to. Stubborn old coot."

Mrs. Bradshaw said, "Clarence," with an accusatory voice. Clarence ignored her, carrying on with his own thoughts.

"Everyone in the district has heard about how you came to the rescue. Thank you, again."

Clarence held a firm grip on Danny's hand during this entire conversation. When he finally allowed Danny's hand to go free, he stepped toward the table and gestured for Danny to join him. Annie Bradshaw said, "I just made the coffee. We were about to have some when you came to the door. Please sit down."

Clarence was all set to return to the subject of the storm but Danny, trying to look forward, hoping to put the storm behind him, and wishing to get on with the purpose of the visit, said, "I heard from Mrs. Kingsbury's daughter, Gloria, last evening. Mrs. Kingsbury is fine. But Gloria says she has decided to sell her place. She has offered it to me, but I am pretty undecided right now. To help me decide, I asked about who had been working the land. She, of course, gave me your name and the direction to your home.

"I really have to confess that I have not been a good neighbor. I don't know if you folks will understand what I mean by this, but I'm not country by birth. In the city we're more apt to mind our own affairs and leave others with their own matters. It's quite common to not know the names of people living just a few doors away. And then, I tend to be a private person anyway, content in my own world.

I'm going to have to work on that. That's all by way of an apology for not getting to know you folks before several years went past.

"I met and talked with Mrs. Kingsbury a couple of times, but I couldn't say I really knew her. And I never once wondered about the land. I probably should have known who was working the land, but I didn't. Gloria suggested I drive over and meet you so we could talk about needs, and the future. So here I am."

Clarence chuckled as he said, "About time the old fool sold out and moved to where the living is easier."

Annie Bradshaw quickly answered, "Clarence, that's no way to talk about Edith. She's been a great friend and neighbor for a lot of years."

Clarence smiled at his wife and nodded, as if she should understand his meaning.

"Of course, she has. But that's exactly what I'm saying. She's been a good friend and neighbor for far too many years. Should have been comfortably settled in her grave long ago. Her and us too, far as that goes. Half the countryside should be in our graves, kind of clean house, is what I'm talking about. Give the country a fresh start. Let the younger people enjoy all the hard work and short rations."

He closed out that thought with a choking laugh.

Mrs. Bradshaw came with the coffee. As she was pouring for Danny, with one hand on her husband's shoulder, for balance, she said, "Don't listen to the old fool. He just talks to be doing something. Bored most of the time. Never know what might come out of his mouth next. Be glad when spring comes, and he can get out and go visiting. Waste some neighbor's time, give me a few moments of peace."

Danny, startled at first, came to see that it was all said in good jest. Just two old people enjoying a few minutes with a newly befriended neighbor. He hardly knew how to proceed, but the silence around the table was a sure indication that the Bradshaws thought it was his turn. The subject at hand was still the potential purchase of the Kingsbury land. It seemed obvious to Danny that the Bradshaws would have an interest in the matter since they had been earning a part of their yearly income from the half section.

"I'm not sure how to move forward here, Mr. and Mrs. Bradshaw."

"Well," interjected Clarence, "you could start by calling us Clarence and Annie. I appreciate your respect of age, but neighbors don't pay much attention to that. We're just folks, like all the other old neighbors."

Danny smiled and nodded before saying, "Alright, first names it is. And, of course, I am Danny. My wife is Syl, short for Sylvia. But the question still lies before us. I'm not at all sure that I want to purchase more land. I've got a fair good thing going now. But Gloria put the matter on the table with that phone call. I suppose I have to address it. And that means that we have to talk. If you had plans to purchase the property, if that opportunity should arise, I would simply back off, recognizing your prior right, regardless of what Mrs. Kingsbury now says. If, on the other hand, you have no such plans, I would have to do more research, including asking you some questions about the hay yield, and possible problems with the condition of the grass. With the whole area buried in deep snow, I'd only be guessing about the land and what it can grow.

"Understand, I am not a farmer. I thrust myself into the cattle and hay business on a whim, a few years ago. I happened to see the land-for-rent sign as Mr. Mulholland was nailing it to a post. I stopped, as I say, on a whim. I had been in construction camps up north for some years and was searching for something different to do. I sort of hit it off with the Mulhollands, and things moved ahead almost faster than I could really think it through. At first, I rented. Then, when the Mulhollands wanted to move to the coast, I purchased the section.

"Mr. Mulholland was a great teacher and a big help to me. I'm sure I would have failed miserably if he hadn't taken me under his knowledgeable wing. So, now, do I wish to expand? I'm not sure. The first question in figuring that out is to find out what your position is."

Clarence and Annie looked at each other for an uncomfortable length of time, leaving Danny fidgeting inside, if not visibly. Clearly, the two older farmers were talking without speaking. Danny idly wondered if he and Syl would ever grow to the point where that unspoken communication was possible. As he was nursing that thought, Clarence cleared his throat.

"The old girl has solved a problem for us, young man."

Again, Clarence chuckled, leaving Danny adrift, searching for his meaning.

"I'm old, Danny. I won't tell you how old, but old. I'm old. My wife is old. This house is old. My machinery is old. My farming ideas are old. I'm stuck in my own ways of doing things and those ways, too, are old. My kids are old, for that matter. Our last horse got old and died several years ago. I'm too old to ride, anyhow. Why even our dog is old."

Clarence seemed to be smiling inwardly as he glanced out the window, planning out his next sentence.

"We've talked for hours, Annie and I, wondering how to get out of the hay business and, if we solved that matter, how would we tell Edith that we're no longer able to farm her land. Can't hardly farm our own, for that matter. Can't hardly hire help anymore either, what with the oil companies offering more wages than are good for a young fella to have in his pocket, all at one time. But if she was to sell, that answers all the questions at once. We would probably sell too. At least the matching half to hers. We would keep this home quarter we live on. We do pretty well with the one quarter of oats. Grade to pony oats most years. I could keep doing that until my old combine up and quits. Perhaps you want to purchase our half, along with the other half."

Danny could hardly breathe. All he originally wanted was a break from the routine and remoteness of camp life. A spur of the moment decision had put him into the cattle business, and then the hay business. How big did he really want his farming and ranching enterprise to get?

The whole question, like his own life, was becoming complicated. Day by day he was beginning to think of himself as a writer. That was no easy transition. And considering that his first book wasn't even on the market yet, it sounded almost arrogant. Prideful in the extreme. He couldn't image publicly describing himself as a writer, an author. But secretly, he held the thought. Of course, the calf and hay businesses kept him busy for only a few months of the year, less than half really. There was nothing stopping him from working the land for half of the year and writing the other half of the year.

These thoughts flashed through his mind, all mixed up with other thoughts. Financing. The use of his limited capital. His deep-down lack of farming and ranching knowledge, along with his lack of self-confidence which he worked hard to hide. His true long-term desires, which were not completely known or fixed on yet. The temptation to strike out, striving for bigness whether he knew what he was doing or not.

Questions. So many questions.

The human mind is truly beyond comprehension. That thought came, pushing the other thoughts aside. Probably less than two or three seconds passed while all this was going on inside his head. Finally, he lifted his eyes to the waiting couple.

"Wow, you have really thrown down the gauntlet before me. I'll certainly think about all that and discuss it with Syl, who has a more level head than I do. I tend towards the dramatic, the expressive.

At heart, I'm probably a dreamer. Syl is practical in all her ways."

When there was no response from Clarence, Danny continued.

"Gloria says that Mrs. Mulholland hasn't decided on a price yet. But if I'm hearing correctly, between the lines, so to speak, I'm guessing you've thought about that."

He let the statement rest right there.

"We have indeed. We've talked with old Blaze Neasham, who's been around these parts since it was still Blackfoot country, it seems. He's the auctioneer in town. Knows the value of a sack of potatoes, a prize milk cow or a piece of land."

Clarence reached to the small side table beside Annie's rocking chair and lifted a pad of paper and a pen over to the space before him. Cautiously, slowly, as if writing his last will and testament as he took his dying breath, he put down a number, along with the short explanation that the number was for the half section only.

His penmanship was beautiful, just short of calligraphy, emblematic of the era when learning the basics, in the one room schoolhouses, was still seen as primary. When that was completed, he turned the page towards Annie, although there was no real need for that. She was perfectly able to read it as he wrote. Finally, he turned the page around and pushed it across the table to Danny. Danny studied it silently, although he had also read the number as Clarence wrote it down.

The three people glanced at each other, their

eyes holding for just a moment before moving on to the next person. Danny's mind was whirring like an electric adding machine. Nothing was said. Danny hadn't touched the paper.

Finally, gathering his thoughts and getting to the meat of the matter, Danny forthrightly asked three questions, wrapped into a single enquiry, so there could be no misunderstanding.

"Folks, I have three questions. First, is the land fenced adequately for grazing cattle? Second, in a year with an average hay yield, could the hay sales income justify this purchase price. Third, is there no one in your family that wants the land or who would complicate a sale?"

Annie spoke first, leaving Clarence with his mouth open and words pressing for escape.

"Danny, those are excellent questions. Clarence can answer to the fencing. But since I do the accounts for this lazy old man, I can tell you that the answer to the second question is yes. The smaller mortgage a person held the easier it would be, of course, but yes, in an average year the net cash income is adequate. It would be better, and safer if, after a better than average year, some funds were set aside to cover off the drop in income in a poor year.

"As to the family, like so many people on the land, that might have been our biggest disappointment in life. We raised five children. Three boys and two girls. All matured into adults we can be proud of, but none of them wanted to farm. It was the same for Edith. Her kids ran off to the city as soon as they were out of school. I've often wondered if it is possible that we worked them too hard when they were young. They missed out on so much. When their friends from school were playing hockey or taking dancing lessons, our kids were milking cows or driving a tractor. When the church kids were going to summer camp, ours were building haystacks, back when we built them with horse and wagon and pitch forks. There's a true skill to building a stack, but none of that matters anymore. And that's not even starting on the cold outhouse, heating bath water on the wood stove, frosted over bedroom windows...

"Oh, it goes on and on."

There was a silent pause, almost as if Mrs. Bradshaw could see it all again in memory.

"In any case, Danny, no one in our family is going to contest our decision to sell out."

Clarence was looking at the tabletop and kneading his crooked, arthritic, work hardened fingers through each other, like a puzzle he was trying to solve, or perhaps visualizing his youngsters building those haystacks. He finally answered the fencing question.

"You could run cattle in there alright. All four quarters are separately fenced. No cross fences. Oh, there's always a sagging post or a loose wire. That's to be expected. But I would say the fences are good. Of course, they're old. Not as old as Annie here, but old."

Annie came back with, "And I'm not as old as you, you old coot."

Clarence reached out and took his wife's hand

before saying, "You're right again. And Edith's barn is even older than that."

Danny left a few minutes later with the agreement that they would hold the meeting secret for at least a week or two while he sorted out the many issues surrounding both the Bradshaw and Kingsbury land options. The Bradshaws agreed that it would be alright to share the auctioneer's estimation of the land value with Gloria. The two half section parcels would be about equal in value, although something would have to be added for the Kingsbury buildings.

Chapter 10

Danny called Gloria Weld with a report on his meeting with Clarence and Annie Bradshaw. Her first response was, "Was he his old irascible self?"

Danny laughed as he answered, "I would say that's a fair definition."

Gloria said, "Well then, I'm guessing he's doing just fine."

To the price laid on the land by the auctioneer, Gloria hesitated before saying, "That's perhaps a bit higher than we have discussed here, and with the family. But we could easily be out of touch."

"You would have to allow for the buildings too, though, Gloria."

"Yes, I suppose. But all the buildings are old and have been unused and unmaintained for years. There's machinery too. Why Mom refused to sell it after Dad died has always been a mystery to me. Even Dad's old pickup truck is there in the garage, along with Mom's newer car, which she hasn't driven much and will never drive again. Machinery ages quickly, to be replaced by constantly newer designs. I don't think there'll be much value left in any of it. Mom will want her car, but the rest can stay there.

"I don't know, Danny. I'll have to have another talk with Mother about the value. I'll bring up the value of the buildings and machinery, but I doubt that will change anything too much. But the real question today is, are you showing interest in the purchase with all this research?"

"I'll have to be honest with you, Gloria. Financially, it's a stretch. Especially if I move on the Bradshaw land at the same time. I wouldn't be comfortable mortgaging the home place and I don't have enough cash for a purchase without sacrificing my cattle business."

"Could you make it work if Mom held the mortgage with a reasonable cash deposit and a ten-year payout at current interest rates?"

There was a long pause while the phone line stayed silent. Things seemed to be moving more quickly than Danny had been prepared for. He would have to be careful about what he said.

Finally, Danny answered, "I hadn't thought of that. I thought only of the bank, and I don't like, or trust banks. I'll have to think hard on that and discuss it with Syl. If you will give some thought to the final price, including the buildings and whatever machinery is there, Syl and I will put our heads together on this end."

"I'll get back to you on the price, Danny. But I can tell you right now, I don't see much value in those old buildings. Perhaps a bit in the house."

"That's up to you, Gloria. But while you're thinking on that may I have permission to look through the buildings and the machinery?"

"Of course. And I won't be long in getting the price nailed down."

Christmas was almost upon the land. At first Danny and Syl tried to convince themselves that the three weeks in Hawaii was gift enough for their first Christmas together. But as the days numbered themselves off and the time closed in on the season, Danny had a change of heart. While Syl was working a day shift he went into town and purchased a beautiful new saddle for Syl. To accompany this, he located and bought a nice piece of jewelry. He then found something for his mother and then his father. Syl had already picked out something for her parents.

That evening, concerned that Syl might feel badly on Christmas morning if she received his gifts while holding true to their plan herself, he fessed up to what he had done. Syl laughed and said, "You're just fishing for a gift. Why, Danny Framer, you surprise me. I thought you were made of sterner stuff than that. It kind of brings you down to earth. You know, down here where the rest of us live. You big dope! Did you really think I wouldn't find something for you? Silly man. How could I let Christmas go past without finding a special gift for my brand-new husband?"

That Syl's decision might have caught Danny flat

footed without anything to give, did not become a part of the brief conversation.

Christmas Eve Day was cold and blustery. Danny was staying close to the fire while Syl slept. She had worked the first night of a set of graveyard shifts that would last through the Christmas holidays and had been sleeping only a couple of hours when Danny heard the vehicle stop, after pulling close to the cabin door. He watched through the small kitchen window to see who was coming. The sign on the side of the van said, "Uptown Florists." The driver came quickly out of the truck and slid the side door open. He lifted out a large paper covered package, which Danny assumed was flowers, and held it, tucked securely under one arm while he quickly closed the van door. With hurried steps the driver was soon on the porch. Danny swung the door open and waved the man in, indicating with a finger across his lips that he was requesting silence. He had already told the shop, when they called for delivery instructions and directions, that his wife was sleeping off a night shift. He couldn't be sure that the message had found its way to the delivery man.

"Mighty cold day for tropical flowers." The driver whispered. "But these should be alright. It's warm in the van."

Danny studied the oversized package before whispering, "I didn't order flowers. Who are these from?"

"Don't know, fella. Might be a card inside. All I know is they're paid for with a nice tip for me bringing them out here on a cold day, and I've got a van full of other orders to deliver so I'll be on my way."

Danny thanked him and gently closed the door after he left.

Danny, knowing Syl would get more pleasure out of unwrapping the surprise gift than he would, left them where the driver had put them, and went back to his writing.

The flowers were still fully wrapped when Syl awoke from her sleep. She came out of the bedroom yawning and rubbing her eyes with the heel of her hand and took a seat on Danny's lap, when he slid his chair back and opened his arms. She put her arms around his neck and nestled into his shoulder, to give her a minute or two to wake up, a habit they had developed shortly after their marriage. She sat there oblivious of her surrounding for, perhaps one minute. Finally, she noticed the wrapped parcel on the table. Without moving she said, "What's that?"

Danny, reluctant to release his hold around her waist, answered, "I don't know. Man brought it out. You'd best take a look at it."

With another yawn, followed by a slight push on Danny's chest, Syl sat upright, and then stood to her feet. With another questioning look at her husband she reached for the scarlet red tie on the top, that held the protective paper sack closed. Danny silently thought, *I'd have simply torn the paper*, but he said nothing. She glanced into the opening and looked back at Danny.

"Flowers. A giant bouquet. Did you order these?"

"Not me. You had best pull that paper off and see, perhaps there's a card inside. Maybe an old

105

boyfriend, hoping for a second chance." Syl ignored his comment.

Syl soon had the bouquet exposed. Taped to the side of the vase was a big, blue envelope. She reached for it and sat back down on Danny's lap as she tore it open. Slowly she pulled a note from the envelope and unfolded it. Glancing at the bottom of the page to see who it was from she said, "Why, it's from Mr. and Mrs. Gable. That couple we put on the horses, back in Hawaii."

Danny studied the flowers and then said, "Well, that's about the biggest bouquet I've ever seen. You'd best read the note. It isn't going to read itself."

Syl flattened the note paper out and held it so they could both read.

Danny and Syl.

How can we possibly thank you for what you did for us in Hawaii? We might be sitting on that log yet if you hadn't come along. We want to apologize for not getting in touch before you flew home. When the taxi stopped at our hotel, neither of us was able to move our legs or get out of the car. It was more than stiffness from the riding. Somehow Sonja's diabetes had taken a serious turn for the worse and my blood pressure was off the charts. We were both feeling faint and unable to care for ourselves. The taxi took us to the hospital. By the time we were released you had flown back home.

The hotel refused to provide your address, citing client confidentially as the reason. After we were back home, we finally had the presence of mind to phone the horse stable. When I explained the situation, they provided me with this address.

We owe you more than we can say. But as a tribute to your concern for our wellbeing, and your creativity, please accept this bouquet and the enclosed air tickets, and the one-week lodge accommodations, at the same location in Hawaii. Both the tickets and the lodge reservations are open dated so you can make your own reservation when it is convenient.

It might please you to know that Sonja and I are both, under doctor's supervision, entered into a one-month health camp, beginning on Jan. 2. It is impossible to explain how we allowed ourselves to get into the condition we are in. We are going to change that. And, perhaps, if it is not too late, I will take riding lessons.

Thank you again. Merry Christmas and may God bless you in all things.

Terrence and Sonja Gable

Danny and Syl read the note, studied the flowers, but had nothing to say. The gesture was beyond anything they expected or thought of.

Chapter 11

As the lights were dimmed at the end of another day of indoor rodeo, Aaron Walsh finished wiping down the big steel stove top, the activity that signaled his duties were completed, after the long, busy, tiring day.

"One more week in one more town, one more arena rodeo, BBQ, and you'll need to find a new grill-man."

"What you mean by that? Ain't anywhere near the end of the season yet."

"Well, season or no season, I'm feeling the call of home, my friend. We finish up the next gig and I'm pointing my wheels north. That gives you the time you need to pull in another grill-man. Anyway, if I breathe in the smoke off this grill much longer as it swirls around my head and lays its smoky odor on my clothing, they won't have to embalm me when my time comes. I'll be pre-smoked and cured. Last a hundred years lying out in the open air. No, sir.

I'm hearing the call. There's only one answer."

BBQ Barnes guffawed as he thought up an answer, "Why shucks, you ain't hardly even basted yet on that grill, let alone broiled. Ain't been at 'er long enough for that. Why, I was sleeping out on the grass one hot night up to Montana, looking for a breath of cool air, don't ya know. Coyote came along, drawn by the sweet smell of brisket around me. Fix'n to take a bite off'n my leg. Gave 'er a sniff and a lick. Plum woke me up, that did. That coyote, he sat on his haunches jest a gnaw'n on my tough o'l hide, hop'n to get a chunk tore off, with me watching his every move. Weren't no time at all after he got his first whiff and lick of my smoked and seasoned ol' black hide, he tips his head to the night sky. Just like he was native born to the south, he outs with a lonesome howl. Near sent chills down my spine, that did. Well, sir, after the second howl he's ask'n for a Lone Star beer in a deep Texas drawl. That's basted and broiled both, my man."

As he always did when BBQ went into one of his tall tales, Aaron listened, smiled and moved on.

"You're a good man and a great cook, BBQ, and I've enjoyed my time with you. But all good things have to end. My time with you is ending and my absence from home is ending about a week later, or as soon as I manage to drive through about ten states, most of them deep in snow, and cross the border. I'm homesick, my good man, even though there's no one there anymore except one brother who I ain't done any favors for in some time. Don't even know if he'll hang out the welcome sign or if he's ever left a lantern burning off the end of the porch. But I'm heading north anyhow."

The barbeque rig had been backed into the arena, separated from the passageway that allowed for the movement of the horses and cattle, by only a temporary chain link fence. When questioned about his chosen location for the concession stand, BBQ Barnes, who had been following the circuit for years, laughed and said, "What y'all got to understand is, folks love a bit of horse dust along with their BBQ. Enjoy watching the animals too, as the cowboys bring them in or out. Kind of drags them into the action. Adds awe-then-tis-ity to the occasion, don't ya know!"

BBQ Barnes, a big jovial black man who had made his living cooking and entertaining for many years, had a couple of big steel plates that fit over the gas jets in his homemade grill and broiler rig. Along with that set-up he also had a wood and charcoal fired rotisserie for broiling brisket. It was a mark of inventive genius that he had managed to build the unit and have it approved for indoor use, subject to adequate ventilation.

Barnes, a combination cook and entertainer, made a specialty of barbeque brisket, like so many outdoor cooks were doing. But he didn't stop there. The grill had turned out thousands of creatively mixed and cooked hamburgers, along with wieners for the kids. An endless supply of homemade, deep browned baked beans and sourdough biscuits were the specialty of the house, all created and overseen by Mrs. Barnes and her helpers.

The highlight of his year was the Calgary Stampede, but during the winter season he travelled the southern and indoor rodeo circuit, taking a few fill-in jobs as opportunity allowed, between rodeos.

Business was good. BBQ knew how to lift folks out of the stands and bring them in with their wallets in their hands, like the Pied Piper of smoky foods. If the sounds of his booming voice singing old country, announced by the banging of the big hamburger flipper, along with a few gospel songs didn't do it, the smell of slow broiled brisket was sure to. His contract stipulated that the grill had to be vented to the outside, and it was. But BBQ wasn't above closing the damper from time to time, to allow a whiff of broiled brisket and fried onions to waft its way into the spectator stands. All by accident, he would have you understand.

Aaron clanged the metal scraper on the steel top, the way BBQ was fond of doing, knowing the clang of metal on metal, along with his loud, singsong voice extolling his gift of the "best brisket between here and just about anywhere else" was like a magnet to hungry rodeo watchers, and a few who weren't hungry, but who would still lay out the coins for a sample of his offerings.

After the last clang, Aaron put the scraper down and announced, "That's it. Good night, all you charming people. I'd love to stay and help you sweep up and straighten out the chairs and such, but my union contract forbids that. So, goodnight, don't be late in the morning."

All through the next rodeo stop, Aaron and BBQ

Barnes exchanged thoughts and offers, criticisms and platitudes, and anything else BBQ thought might cause Aaron to change his mind. But in the end, the two men shook hands with warm feelings, and the next morning, true to his promise, Aaron was on his way home.

The camper van had been purchased with convenience and frugality in mind. As he headed north, and home, Aaron was able to sleep and eat and, in the few evening hours left to him, after driving enough miles for the day, find a rest area parking spot. He would then sit back and relax on the big swivel easy chair in the back, and write, in longhand, on his new novel.

It required some effort to stop himself from sinking into remorse over his drinking years and the loss of his original publishing contract. Working on a new story provided enough incentive to let the other concerns of his life slip out the window, although, feeling the industry wasn't big on second chances, he had no real hopes of ever returning to a serious writing career.

In no particular rush and knowing that each additional day marked off on the calendar would take him closer to the warming month of April and the last of the long winter, with the snow turning to runoff water and the land baring itself again, ready for another summer, he pushed north at a modest pace. Three weeks after bidding farewell to BBQ Barnes and his workers, Aaron drove into the farmyard. It wasn't the old home place. Aaron had lost that to the bank after his wife left him, taking his three precious daughters with her. Aaron disguised the hurts of her going, by slowly, over the months, spending more and more time inside a bottle. He had never, before that time, been a drinker, but he found the change fairly easy to take on, once started. And once started, the path forward was totally predictable. The only bright spot on the whole ugly mess was that his brother, Adam, had seen it coming. He managed to peel one half section out of the family inheritance and hold it for Francie and himself. But Adam had never truly forgiven Aaron for losing the home place.

Adam, in the corral, working with a new horse, stopped what he was doing at the sound of tires on gravel, and looked over the top rail. He didn't recognize the vehicle and had little interest. He was not in the habit of welcoming strangers. With the loss of the family farm some years before, his life had taken a bitter turn. Since then, the relationship with his wife and grown family had suffered to the point that he found it easier to spend his time in the barn or yard, or, in season, out on the half section of land he had managed to save from the bank. He was blind to the fact that the coldness in the family relationships was the result of his own bitterness, which he found ways to express far too often.

Aaron looked at the corral first, before casting his eyes towards the house. He thought he had seen some movement. A second look confirmed it. A man, he assumed it would be Adam, was looking over the rail, watching the approaching vehicle. Adam may have remained hidden if he hadn't been wearing a crushed and filthy Stetson. But the pressed felt rose well above the corral rail, giving away his presence. Aaron let out a breath and thought, *Might just as well step right into it.*

He pulled the van to a stop, reached for his own Stetson and stepped out onto the muddy yard. Strolling slowly, to give Adam time to consider his arrival, he made his way across the yard.

Aaron's greeting was brief, and different from what Adam had expected.

"Howdy, Adam. Got lonesome for family. Been gone too long."

"Some might say that. Others might say it's not long enough."

The brothers stood their ground, about three or four arm lengths' apart, with the corral rails between them, each wondering what came next. Finally, Aaron said, "I'll just go to the house and say a quick hello to Francie and then get on my way, if that would suit you best, Adam. Don't mean to be a problem."

"Problem is about all you've ever been."

"I've owned up to that, Adam, and I'll own up to it again if that lets you rest easier. But that's been some time ago now. Thought you might have found a bit of forgiveness in your heart."

Nothing was said by either man for a count of five, before Aaron again said, "Well, I'll be on my way. You can say hello to Francie for me. Sorry to intrude."

Aaron was about halfway back to his van when Adam hollered, "Well, dang, man. It's goes against everything I think is good for me and mine but come to the house. We can at least have a coffee. Anyway, I have one bit of news for you."

When Aaron turned back to the house, Francie, standing on the back porch stoop, shielding her eyes from the afternoon sun, spoke out.

"Aaron? Is that really you? Why, sure enough, I believe it is. Aaron, you get yourself over here. I've been saving up a hug for years, just for this moment. I'll not wait another minute."

Aaron stood awkwardly, with his hands hanging slack at his sides while Francie gave him a long, tight hug.

"Aaron. Oh, Aaron. Where at you all been? It's been years. It ain't right, you running off like that."

Aaron could hear Adam's big rubber boots slopping through the mud. Speaking so only Francie could hear he said, "I was hoping Adam might have mellowed a bit. Since I see that's not happened, I'll just say a quick hello and get out of your hair."

"You'll do no such a thing. You'll kick off those muddy boots and come into the house."

In spite of all of Adam's bitterness, Francie still held sway in the house. It was her last sanctuary for family and sanity. Both men automatically, as if they understood the situation, kicked off their boots, hung up their heavy coats and lifted their hats off. No one wore a hat inside Francie's house.

With coffee poured for the three of them and a slice of fresh baked cake sitting before each man, no one spoke for a long, compressed minute. Francie finally reached across the table and held onto the top of Aaron's hand.

"Aaron, you're looking good. Healthy. Strong. I do believe you've been taking care of yourself. But we haven't seen or heard from you for years. Where have you been and what have you been doing?"

"Well, Francie, I've been about everywhere a man ever sat a horse. I signed on with a fella that cooks and runs a concession on the rodeo circuit. Winter times, he works the arena circuit. I run the grill for him while he cuts and serves brisket. It's not like working in a food outlet with a big menu but it paid well. And since I have no other connections, it didn't really matter where I hung my hat. Bought that travel van siting out there a few years ago. Travel in it. Sleep in it. Cook my own food in it.

"And to answer two other questions I know Adam has stored up, no I am not drinking and no I am not re-married. No booze since my time up north in the camps and no woman since Cookie run off.

"One other thing and then I'll get on my way. Again, I apologize for the past, Adam. All of it. We were all hurt, and I take the blame on myself. Always have done. You already know that when Cookie left, I fell apart. I may have gotten through that by itself, but when she took the girls and wouldn't let me even see them, it was too much. I was too weak.

"But, Adam, I have been saving my money since I went to the camps. All those years I've been saving. Never spent a cent that didn't need spending. I don't know how you're making out with the half section, plus what you had before, but if there's something

116

I could help with, I could spare a few dollars. I owe you that much, at least."

"You owe me half my life, never mind a half section. But your money won't make it better or any easier. Now, before you leave you need to know. We got a phone call, oh, quite a few weeks ago now, from Clara. Or someone claiming to be Clara. Called me Uncle Adam and asked about her Aunt Francie, so it might have really been her. She asked for you. When I told her we had no idea where you were she asked if there was anyone who might know. I told her we had received another call a while back. Someone named Danny Framer. Said he worked with you and that you had helped him with some writing. He left a number to reach him. I gave Clara that number and I haven't heard from anyone since. I invited her and her sisters to come for a visit, but she made no commitment. That's all I have for you."

While Adam was talking, Francie was jotting down the number Danny had left. With a boiling cauldron of competing thoughts inside his head, Aaron pocketed the slip of paper and stood, reaching for his hat. He shrugged into his coat and, leaving his cup of coffee and the cake untouched, he turned to Adam.

"Adam, I've done what I know to do. You think you've suffered, and you have. But so have I. And I can't imagine what kind of a life Cookie has put together for those girls. She was never stable, even as a teenager. You know that. And then she disappeared. She wouldn't even accept child support from me. Wouldn't supply an address. I haven't seen my girls in all those long years. You might think on that, Adam, and imagine losing your kids.

"I'm leaving now Brother. I won't be back to trouble you. If God is as merciful as I believe him to be, perhaps he will keep you from making any mistakes that are too big to fix. Goodbye, Francie."

Neither Adam nor Francie moved or spoke as the door closed behind the departing Aaron. They sat in silence at the kitchen table until they heard the motor start, and then the wheels were crunching through the wet gravel of the driveway. Adam's lips were sealed shut in stubborn bitterness. Francie was cradling her face in her hands, trying to hold back the sobs.

Chapter 12

Aaron, filled with sadness, remorse and disappointment, and wishing to get as far from his home country as possible, but also knowing he had to call Danny, drove to town and found a phone booth. He dialed and waited through three rings before a voice came on the line.

"I'm hoping to speak with Danny Framer. Is he there please?"

"This is Danny. Who's calling?"

"Danny. Think back a few years. Construction camp cook. Washed up writer."

Aaron had more to say but Danny, in his excitement, almost shouted out, "Aaron? Is this Aaron?"

"That would be me, old friend. It's good to hear your voice. I just came from the farm. Adam said you had called and left this number, so here I am. He also said he had given my daughter Clara this number. Did she ever call you, Danny?"

"She did. Aaron, where are you? You need to get

yourself down here. There is so much we need to talk about."

"You give me directions, Danny, and I'll point my wheels towards you."

With that done, Danny returned to his writing. But his mind was a scattering of thoughts and possibilities. Aaron. Aaron had called. Aaron was on his way. He would be several hours, but he was on his way. It was difficult to imagine. So much had happened. There were so many possibilities. So much for the two men to discuss.

Danny seemed, some days, to have so many half-completed tasks that he hardly knew which to tackle first. All of that went against every good plan he had ever made and vowed to hold to. He had always said, 'do one job and finish it. Then start another'. Or, as he at times mentally paraphrased from the writings of the apostle Paul, 'this one thing I do'. Although he took the words out of context it was still good advice, a good life lesson.

But he knew what was coming. What couldn't be denied or delayed. Even though it was a job he detested, he knew he had to set the writing aside and attend to the fencing of his cattle yard. That had to come first. He had gone back to his writing only to escape a couple of rainy days.

Even with his few years in the cattle business he understood that with the call of spring came the need to give attention to the fencing, the water system, the loading chute and whatever else made the summer grazing of calves an endurable, and profitable, undertaking. Last spring, he had found a small group of trees that had fallen across the fence. Aspen have a limited life span built into them They were apt to reach that time and fall to the ground, when it was least convenient. It took him two full days to clean up that mess. He hoped for an easier time this year.

He looked again at the typewriter and the stack of paper, but it was as if there was a lighted sign in his mind that flashed on and off, saying 'fencing. Fencing. The calves will be here in one week'. It was a difficult reminder to push aside.

With the re-write of the original piece, the one he had written in the camp, years ago, completed, and sent off to the professional typist just a few days ago, he had been free to start again. New title. Not yet decided upon. Chapter one. A ream of paper at the ready. New ribbon in the typewriter. Ideas bubbling up in his mind, demanding release, each scrambling over the other in their push to the front, wanting to come into the light first. He was ready to continue what was started, to type 'Chapter Two', and continue the thoughts already on the page.

How was he to put on work clothes and saddle a horse to ride fence? In the rain. Still, that's what he had to do.

Later, after hours of riding and attending to the needs of the ranch, and thinking of Aaron, he turned back towards the barn, soaked, saddle sore after a winter with little riding, and with more than just a few barbwire scratches. Thinking of the days ahead, Danny could easily sink into a melancholy or even something worse. The thought of having to chase calves through the bush adjoining his property if they escaped their pasture, had kept him at the fencing task. But now the time on his big pocket watch told him he had to pick Syl up from work. In fact, he was dangerously close to being late.

He had begun driving her to and from work right after they were married. The thought of a woman alone walking through the darkness at six a.m., where the inadequate parking lot lights failed to properly illuminate the way, haunted him. She had never been left alone since that time.

Cantering back to the barn, he soon had his horse stabled and fed. Again, he looked at his watch. Showering and changing clothes would have to wait. He stepped to the old pickup and headed to town. He could just be on time if no one had done anything stupid on the road, blocking traffic.

An hour after leaving the farm he was back, this time with Syl sitting on the passenger's side and both of them too tired for long conversation. Danny dropped Syl off at the cabin with his eyes on the van parked beside the barn.

"I'll be in right soon, my weary wife. I have dinner in the oven, ready to turn on, but I'll look to that when I see who that is in the van. I expect it's Aaron."

He had told Syl about the earlier phone call on the drive home.

Syl watched out the window as Danny parked the truck and got out. A tall man wearing a white Stetson stepped out of the van. The two men studied each other for a few seconds before they closed the space between them and shook hands. The age difference that had, back at the construction camp, separated man from boy, seemed to have melted away with the passing of the years. Now it was just two old friends greeting after being too long apart. Obviously, neither was the hugging type. It was a long handshake as the two men studied each other, both seemingly unaware of the rain.

Danny freed himself long enough to open the barn door, back the truck in and re-close the door. Then, he and Aaron made their way to the cabin. Syl had put the coffee on the wood stove after stirring up the fire and adding a couple of sticks of poplar. With much laughter and the kicking of mud off their boots, the two men stepped onto the porch. Danny would be removing his boots. Syl could only hope Aaron would follow suit. When the two men came through the door, Danny seemed to have found a way to put the day's tiredness behind him.

With a big smile he said, "Syl, I want you to meet Aaron. Aaron, this is Syl, my wife of not even a half year yet. She's just off a twelve-hour shift at the hospital but perhaps she'll listen to your lies while I get out of these wet clothes. And I see she's already put a fresh pot on so if you can be patient that will soon be ready."

As Danny quietly made his way to the bathroom for a shower Aaron lifted his hat off and hung it on a peg beside the door. He ran his hands through his hair and said, "Pleased to meet you, Syl. Danny always needed a bit of looking after so I expect you've got your hands full. I'm happy for the two of you. And I have so many questions, but most of them can wait."

"Welcome, Aaron. I've heard much about you. The writing, of course…"

She was about to continue but the questioning look on Aaron's face stopped her.

"Of course, you couldn't have known. Sorry about that Aaron."

She reached to a shelf behind the kitchen table and lifted down a hard cover, library edition book. She passed it to Aaron, saying, "Danny credits you with the fact that this is published and on the market."

Aaron took the book and studied it, reading the title, and then slowly wiping his hand across the dust cover. Tenderly he turned the volume over, studied the back cover, and then opened it to the title page. When he read, *'dedicated with great respect to my friend and mentor Aaron Walsh,* he became so choked up he couldn't say anything for a moment. He read the short statement again, wiping his hand gently across the page as he had done with the cover.

Slowly, he sank onto a kitchen chair, as if his legs no longer had strength. He then ran his finger over the name at the bottom. Danny Framer. So quietly, Syl almost missed the words, Aaron whispered, "He did it. He really did it."

He seemed to be frozen in time, perhaps back in the late-night hours in the camp kitchen, drinking coffee and talking writing, unable to move, unable to speak. Looking at him, Syl started to understand Danny's respect and carrying for this man who had nurtured and encouraged Danny's writing gift. She saw, in his eyes and his manner, a caring and a joy at Danny's success. She saw no envy, no jealously. Perhaps a bit of remorse, knowing he had thrown away his own career.

Chapter 13

When Danny and Syl were finally showered and dressed for dinner, sitting with Aaron, each of them with a cup of steaming coffee on the table before them, Danny said, "Aaron, you'll want to know about the girls."

Aaron said nothing but his eyes never left Danny's face.

"Thanks to your brother, Clara did call here. They were in Calgary. Had just arrived and checked into a motel. She immediately confirmed that her two sisters were with her and that they were fine. Just a bit weary from the travel. They had driven in from the coast with Clara doing all the driving. The road conditions were questionable with snow and slush along the way. Of course, Clara asked about you right away. She was some disappointed when I told her I hadn't heard from you in years.

"I invited the girls to come for a visit, at least. They drove down the next day, just in time for another of our infamous winter wind and snow-storms. Rather than send them off looking for a motel in the storm, we invited them to stay for a day or two. You can see that we don't have much room here, but they were perfectly happy with a couple of bunk bed mattresses hauled in from the crew quarters and pushed together on the floor.

"They're good kids Aaron. I know nothing at all about their mother or where they were raised, but they're good kids."

Aaron was silent as he soaked this all in. He finally put his thoughts together and asked, "As happy as I am to know they're here and that we might have another chance at family, I'm wondering why they came. Did Clara say anything about that?"

Most of what they knew would be told by Syl, but Danny addressed the question.

"The simple answer is that they came to find work, at least for Clara, and to find a new life somewhere out here. We both sensed there were undercurrents. Issues with the lives they were leading. But they were very careful with their words. They will probably have more to say to you. We didn't expect to hear their whole life story. After all, Syl and I are complete strangers to them."

"I'm a complete stranger too."

Neither Danny nor Syl had an answer for that short statement.

After some further thought Aaron said, "Becky and Abigail should still be in school. So should Clara, as far as that goes. Maybe college or university. I don't see how Clara can make enough money to support her sisters. Where are they living now? You say they sat out a storm here with you. Where did they go then? I'm hoping they're still in town."

Syl took over the telling from that point.

"My folks took them in for a couple of weeks while they looked into jobs, school, apartments, etc. I'm happy to say they fell in love with the girls. Both of my parents are pretty good judges of folks. You can take it as a positive thing that they hit it off so well.

"Clara found a job. She's working down at the seed and feed store. They found a small apartment here in town and the two younger ones are in school."

Aaron could have easily asked the questions of his girls, once he had the chance. But from the bit of information he had, it would seem they were pushing at life and circumstances, moving themselves forward.

Aaron said, "Clara is not really old enough to take legal responsibility for her sisters. I'm surprised the younger ones got into school or that they weren't hassled by the child welfare people."

Syl didn't tell Aaron that her father was the school administration manager and that he had spoken up for the girls. All she said was, "Well, it all worked out alright."

One final question seemed to satisfy Aaron for the moment.

"It seems the job of a beginning clerk in a feed store must pay more than I imagined it would. I wonder if their mother gave them some money that's been helping them through."

Then the light seemed to come on in Aaron's mind. He cast his eyes between Danny and Syl and back again.

"You're helping them, aren't you?"

Danny fidgeted with his coffee cup while he studied the tabletop. Syl was less intimidated.

"Aaron, here's how it is. Danny has had good years on the farm. I'm working full time, and nurses are paid reasonably well. I bank all my earnings, have been since I was living at home before we were married. Although we obviously don't know the future, we consider ourselves blessed. Danny, especially, had some valuable assistance as he was getting established on the farm. And my folks helped me all along the way. And, of course, you were a great help to him with the writing. We are honored, in turn, to be able to share our blessings. And as Danny said when the subject was being discussed, "There is no one I would sooner help than Aaron or his girls.""

Aaron said no more on that subject. He looked at his watch and said, "I wonder if it's too late this evening to call the girls."

Syl simply smiled and pushed the phone across the table. With her other hand she laid a slip of paper beside the phone.

"Here's the number. You go ahead. Danny and I have to slip over to see Ted and Christie, in the rental house, for a few minutes. You take your time."

As they rushed through the persistent drizzle, Danny said, "Good plan. Aaron needs some privacy."

Chapter 14

When Danny and Syl returned to the cabin Aaron was gone. They didn't hear from him again for several days.

During that time, Danny was putting the finishing touches on the fencing and corrals in what was now the much looked-forward-to true harbinger of spring, the arrival of the recently weaned calves. He had re-worked all the gates, oiling the hinges on the metal gates and tightening the wire on the couple of remaining barb wire units. The rental scale was in place. All he needed now was to confirm the delivery time, and button up the final agreement with the couple of people he had hired.

Maria had again jumped at the chance to ride Danny's Toby horse, directing the animals into the squeeze chute while Danny weighed, and ear tagged them. Syl, who had arranged for days off would make careful notes on the tag numbers and weights, as Danny hollered out the information.

But he needed one additional rider, someone to stand by and do whatever came to hand. He had thought of Aaron, but the man had not returned yet, or contacted them.

With no other name in mind Danny drove to the Wills farm to talk with Graham. The two men had spoken only once since the desperate family had arrived at the D-F ranch, seeking help during the storm and power failure.

Graham saw Danny coming and quickly walked up from the barn to greet him.

"Good morning, neighbor. It's good to see you. Have you got time for coffee and a visit? I know Bonny would like to say hello too."

"Some other time, Graham. But please pass on my greeting to her. Right now, I've only got a few minutes. I've come to see if I can hire you for three or four days. My calves are arriving day after to-morrow and I'm short one rider. I've got the horse and saddle, and the job isn't too difficult, if all goes well. Actually, if I could be sure all would go well, I don't need another person, but you know how things have a way of drifting sideways. We'll supply lunch and wages if you can cut loose for that time."

"You know what, Danny? This entire farm operation of ours has me doing the bulk of my work from the seat of a tractor. And it's at least another week, perhaps longer, before I can get on the fields. I'd love a few days of riding. I'll ride that lazy gelding of mine down. It will be good to work him a bit. They get so spoiled just hanging around the barn, they're of little use. Some riding will do him nothing but good.

"Lunch sounds fine, but no wages expected or accepted. I'd take it as a few days off. Kind of an adventure. You let me know exactly when you need me, and I'll be there."

The two men talked a bit more about what was needed as they strolled back towards Danny's pickup, and then, very briefly, about Danny having purchased the Kingsbury and Bradshaw lands. Graham's raised eyebrows said, silently, something like, 'that's a sizable chunk of investment for a beginning rancher or farmer'.

Understanding full well that he owed no explanation to anyone, Danny still felt that a short explanation might be in order. Mostly to convince the neighbors that the sale price was fair and that he hadn't somehow taken advantage of two elderly owners. Speaking to Graham might be one way to get that message out.

That both families had agreed to reasonable terms was no one else's business.

With a chuckle Danny said, "I've never met the auctioneer in town, but both families used his advice to set their sale prices. He sounds like a bit of a character. I'd like to meet him some day. Now, all I need is about ten or twelve good years in a row to make the numbers work."

In truth, he could make the numbers work in far less time with good weather and good markets, neither of which were guaranteed.

Graham laughed and shook his head at the mention of the auctioneer. "Old Blaze Neasham. Been around here for years. Yes, he's a character all right. Good man though. Knowledgeable. If he set the price, there's little chance of it being wrong. Just seems to know. Talks to people all day long. I guess he picks up enough along the way to keep on top of things. I hope that all works out for you."

As he was climbing into his truck, Danny smiled and waved at Bonny and one of the pre-school children who were standing on the back porch.

The day before the calves were to arrive, Aaron showed back up. Syl had completed her day shifts and was now off work until after the calves were dealt with. She confirmed with Aaron that he was free to stay for dinner before determining to put a special welcome meal in front of the man. That Aaron himself was a professional cook intimidated her for just a few minutes before she put the thought behind her.

As Danny fussed around, doing work that really had already been done once, in preparation for the calves, the two men talked. Aaron sat on the corral railing and offered humorous suggestions while Danny checked and double checked the fences, railings, gates, and the scale. When he was going over the squeeze chute, he hollered up at Aaron, "How be you come and stick your head in here so I can see if it really works. I'd hate to have a last-minute repair on my hands with a truck load of calves waiting."

"Naw. I can see from here that you've got it all under control. Otherwise, I'd be happy to help. Of course, you already know that."

"And you know that sarcasm does not become you, as some wise man once said."

The two friends laughed and moved on to another topic. Later, over a well-prepared dinner, which Aaron repeatedly complimented Syl on, the talk naturally turned to Aaron's girls and what he had been doing the past couple of days. It took only a moment to realize that Aaron was prepared to talk it through, and that the evening could stretch out for some time.

"I don't know how it turned out the way it did, but somehow the girls seem to have their heads turned in the right direction. They're young women to be proud of. I see a bit of unsteadiness with Abby, the youngest but I'm hoping it's mostly a growing phase and that being settled down here will allow it to pass.

"I didn't ask, and they didn't offer much information on their mother. I do know that Cookie has been married at least twice since our divorce. And the girls were unanimous about being weary of constant moves. I have no idea how Cookie made a living or if they were supported by the men she was with. She has no real education. We went to school together from first grade until she dropped out after grade ten. She lived at home, on her parent's farm, while I completed high school. We were married young, right after I was out of school. My parents tried to talk me out of it, but I wouldn't listen. The folks were both struggling with some health issues that turned out to be more serious than we first thought. Adam and I worked the farm. We were young and made some mistakes. It was a struggle but somehow, we held it together. For a few years, at least.

"Cookie was always a bit unstable. I don't mean in a mental or emotional way. It was just that she was never really happy. Always wanted more. Wanted different. Wanted some new adventure. It used to be said of people like that, that they were forever looking over the pasture gate. She sometimes seemed to be driven by those desires. You might ask why I married her, knowing all that. Well, the simple answer is that I loved her. All my life growing up on farms about ten miles apart, the families knowing each other well, going to school. Occasionally going to church, as often as either of us went, which wasn't often. I loved her the whole time.

"You could logically ask what attracted me to her. Why did I love her? There is no clear answer to that. Oh, she was beautiful and full of fun but that's not enough to hold a marriage together. No, there was more than that. But I truly don't know what it was. You find an answer to the love question, Danny, and put it in a book, and you'll burn up the presses trying to keep ahead of sales. I loved her. That's all. Still do, I suppose, in some strange way."

Aaron seemed to want to tell his story. Neither Danny nor Syl interrupted. After a moment of quiet, when Aaron appeared to be reminiscing silently, he continued.

"Certainly, I have not been attracted to another woman since she left. Which is strange in itself, I suppose. But she somehow managed to care for the girls and, as I said already, they're good girls. Why Cookie held them away from me I can't answer. Anyway, that's water under the bridge. I'm trying to look forward. Plan a future. It's too soon to talk to the girls about that yet, but we'll get there. There are a lot of years to make up. I'll not do that in a couple of evenings of visiting."

There was some more talk of Aaron's situation but finally he said, "Now, Danny, tell me how you got into this ranching and farming business. You, a city boy and a skilled writer, which I need to hear all about, by the way, I would have never once suspected that ranching was in your future."

Danny told the story in brief, ending with the simple statement, "After that big storm, our elderly neighbor couldn't return to her place. None of the younger members of either the Kingsbury or Bradshaw families wanted to farm They both offered their land to us. And here we are."

"Why do I think you've shortened that story somewhat?"

Syl laughed and said, "That's my Danny, Aaron. Expressive in his writing but talks only reluctantly when he is the center of the discussion. There is indeed a bigger story but I'm not sure you're going to hear it all this evening."

Danny walked around with the coffee pot again before saying anything more. Syl turned down the offer of a second piece of apple pie, but both of the men dug in again.

Danny grinned at Aaron and said, "None of that land story matters, my friend. What matters is that the D-F ranch has the land. One full section. Plus, this home section, of course. What else matters is that you need to settle down and create a new life for yourself. And I have that all figured out for you. I'll explain if you wish and then you can simply nod in agreement and thank me for my thoughtfulness and creativity."

"Wow. How often in life does a man get an offer like that? Of course, you may be thinking that I didn't do all that well on my initial life's plan and you'd be correct on that. So let fly. What's in my future?"

"Simply put, my farmer friend, you need to go back into farming. Or ranching if that title sits better on your mind and matches your boots better. You need to purchase the buildings across the road, on the Kingsbury place. I've put the wheels into motion to cut off twenty acres to go with the home and buildings.

"We had a contractor in this winter. The interior of the house is all remodeled and fixed up. Painted throughout. New flooring where it was needed. All new plumbing where the frozen lines had burst. We did all that with the idea of putting it on the market this spring. It's a great old home. you'll love it. You and the girls can have a good life there.

"You'll have enough land for horses or chickens, or whatever. You'll work for the D-F during the season, taking over the entire farming operation, which right now is cutting and baling hay. I'll deal with the cattle. We'll be a great combination.

"During the winter you write. You're going to be published again, I have no doubt of that.

"In short, your traveling days, and the girls' unstable days are over. Now look amazed at my wisdom and thank me. There is no need to bow in gratitude, but if you feel you must..."

Chapter 15

The coming and going of the calves wasn't quite 'old hat' to Danny and his crew, but it did get easier, and ran more smoothly each spring and fall. As usual, Sol, the cattle broker had delivered well on the purchase. The five hundred fifteen animals that now wandered the pastureland of the D-F ranch were a quality bunch showing the welcome potential for profits if... there always seemed to be an 'if' in the equation. Danny had been aware from the start that the numbers of calves he was purchasing pushed the land to its grass growing limit. After the drought of the previous spring, he was tempted to cut back but he figured he could spread some animals to the Kingsbury land if the situations became difficult again.

Danny and Aaron were working over the fertilizer spreader Danny had inherited in the purchase of the Kingsbury place. At first, they thought it might be beyond repair but a day and a half of scraping rust and forcing a few bolts loose, so parts could be removed and repaired, and the unit was about ready again to do its job.

Danny glanced up at the sound of tires on the gravel driveway. He didn't recognize the unit approaching. Pulling his pickup to a stop a comfortable distance from the two working men, the driver slowly, almost reluctantly, it appeared, opened the door. Even more slowly, he stepped to the ground. From a distance, it seemed the stranger might rather get back in his truck and put the D-F behind him.

But as the man came a bit closer, Danny recognized him, in spite of the fact that the visitor's head was tilted to the ground with his hat brim covering most of the top of his face. Only when he was close enough to speak comfortably did the man look up. Danny was amazed to look into the eyes of Bo Scanlon. Bo had been one of the K-bar riders who had turned rustler the previous summer. After his arrest and court hearing he had been sentenced to six months in prison. He was released in five, but Danny had heard nothing about that.

"You're surprised to see me, Danny. Mark me down as being even more surprised to be here."

"Well, Bo, I'll say that I am surprised, and that's a fact. I didn't know you were out. I'd heard that Trevor sold out and moved somewhere, him and his family, all of them. Kind of thought you might do the same."

"I couldn't, and I can't, Danny. Reasons why don't matter right this minute."

After a short pause, with neither man knowing

how to proceed, and as if Aaron were not there, Bo finally said, "I've come for two reasons, Danny. The first is to apologize personally, to a friend I treated shabbily. I have no valid excuse for what I did. And I'm not denying my actions. I could say we had been facing some serious financial troubles brought on by the doings of others, and that would be the truth. But that's not reason enough. Never in my life would I have believed I could become a thief. A cattle rustler. But there it is. The facts are the facts. I've paid my time and am now free. Except I'm not really free.

"Everywhere I go, folks who have known me for years turn their eyes away when they see me. My wife and kids have stuck with me but there's no joy in the home, only shame. And I can't find any way to make a living. Feed my family. I guess I could go to work on the rigs, but I know nothing at all about that world, and I'd be away from home for weeks or months at a time.

"Danny, I've come begging. I know you bring in a herd about this time of year. I can see your new bunch out past the barn. Cutting to the chase, Danny, I'm asking for a job. You already know I'm a good rider and a good cattleman. I'd take care of your animals for you, and I guarantee you can trust me. That other is behind me. I don't care what the wages are. Just enough to pay the power bill and buy a few groceries, would be alright."

Danny and Aaron stood in silence; Aaron seemingly having forgotten the wrench he still held in his hand.

"You may wonder, Danny, how I could even have

the nerve to ask. Well, here's how it is. If you could somehow forgive me, and learn to trust me again, that might go some distance toward showing my regret, wipe out my shame and to being accepted again into the community.

"If your answer is no, Danny, I'll understand and say no more."

Danny was truly torn. He did need a summer rider. But that Bo would drive into his yard was far beyond anything even his creative mind could conjure up. The two men stood ten feet apart staring into each other's eyes. Bo's lips finally began to quiver. Not wanting to embarrass the man more than he was already, Danny looked away. He caught Aaron's eyes, noting the questions he wanted to ask.

Danny wasn't much on preaching, although he held strong beliefs. He was more on doing and showing, than telling. But he had a good memory and his memory, both from his private reading and from the many messages he had heard in church over many years, argued that forgiveness was a part of the life of faith. Of belief. But he also recognized that trust, once broken, was almost impossible to repair.

He glanced briefly at Aaron, thinking of how it must have been with Cookie, knowing that if Cookie came back, Aaron would never trust her again. But the bond between husband and wife was tighter, and more damaging when it was broken, than the bond between rancher and rider.

Could Danny trust again?

In the space of time for several deep breaths, and an internal fight with his druthers, Danny was left perplexed and hoping he was making the right decision.

"Bo, you ask a lot. In the end, I received my animals back, although they had been sorely abused. There was little lost to the D-F. A few dollars and a lot of time. I do need a summer rider. I would normally discuss this with my wife but this once I'm going to make my own decision. Don't you make me regret it. I'll take you on. There are no living accommodations here. No meals supplied. You look after yourself on that. Brown bag a lunch or something. You can stable a horse or two for the summer. The ranch will feed them. You care for them yourself. Caring for the other ranch horses will be a part of the job. You'll be here at eight in the morning. If all is well, and there are no animals in trouble, you go home at five. You have Sunday and Monday off. You start tomorrow.

"You earn normal ranch wages, paid every two weeks. You do not talk about the D-F, me, my family or ranch business, outside or anywhere off the ranch. If anything comes to me from outside, you'll be kicking a pebble down the road. And there's no need to talk about what happens if you're pulling the wool over my eyes.

"Is that an agreement?"

Bo smiled for the first time. Just a small smile, perhaps more of wonder and relief than of joy or happiness.

"That's an agreement, Danny. I'll not make you regret it. I'll be here in the morning. I'll have to ride the horses over. I don't have a trailer. We're only about ten miles apart. I'll bring them in this afternoon. And I'll be here and ready for work in the morning. Thank you, Danny."

Bo turned to leave but Danny stopped him.

"Bo, you'll be rubbing shoulders with Aaron here. You might just as well meet now. Aaron is an old friend, recently returned from his own travels. He'll be doing the hay lands this summer and caring for the machinery. You'll see to your own jobs, but if there's a need, you'll back each other up. We don't have so many hands on the payroll that we can always do just our own jobs."

Bo glanced over and nodded his head. "Aaron."

Aaron's greeting was just as sparse, "Bo."

Chapter 16

As usual, Danny did his research, and then did it all again, before purchasing fertilizer for the hay land. Calculating the cost against the potential gains, and the dwindling funds on hand, he purchased only enough for the Kingsbury half section. His available working funds were dipping into the uncomfortable range.

Working together, Danny and Aaron got the old Kingsbury three-ton grain truck running and proved out. Transferring title from a long-dead man and getting insurance was a hassle but finally the unit was on the road. When the hay lands were dry enough to drive on without hurting the grass, Aaron drove to the feed and seed store. He and Clara grinned at the thought that father and daughter, after so many years apart, and with Aaron so long out of farming, were back almost to where it had all gone wrong, all that long time ago. Clara wrote up Aaron's order, charged it to the D-F ranch and said, "Do you know where the loading platform is, Dad, around back?"

"I think I can find it."

A young man in work clothes was standing aside, waiting his turn at the order counter. Aaron had been studying him out of the corner of his eye. When Clara passed him his sales slip he whispered, "I do believe you're gathering admirers."

Clara responded with easily-seen-through, fake exasperation, "Daaad!"

Aaron was home a couple of hours later with enough fertilizer for one quarter section. He would start spreading it in the morning. The Kingsbury barn had a wide runway with high doorways. Perfect for keeping the truck and its expensive load out of the rain.

Danny stood at the fence line watching as Aaron slowly pulled the spreader for the first time. The hopper was full, and the well lubed spreader wheel turned nicely. Satisfied that their repair job had done the trick, Danny waved Aaron on his way.

Bo was nearing completion of his first week of herding on the D-F. The only surprise of the week was when Maria drove into the yard. She was just in time to see Bo walk his afternoon horse from the barn. She stopped dead in her tracks, not believing what was right there before her eyes. Here were two old friends, face to face. Or are they now enemies? Ex friends? Well, whatever they were now, they stopped and stared at each other.

Certainly, Maria's father, since Bo had rustled K

bar stock, as well as the D-F calves, would consider Bo as the enemy, or, at the very least, the enemy of the K bar, if not personally. Bo and Maria had known each other for the many years Bo had worked on the ranch. Bo had helped teach her to ride. The feelings of hurt had run deep through everyone on the K bar when the rustling had taken place.

Maria found her voice first. She asked, "What are you doing here, Bo?"

"Working. As much as that might surprise you. I bombed on all my other work searches. In desperation, I came hat in hand to Danny. Somehow, he dug up whatever was needed of forgiveness to give me a chance at redeeming myself. I figured if one of the men I hurt would forgive me there may be a chance to live with my head held high again. Eventually. Some day.

"I intend to take full advantage of the opportunity. I'm caring for the D-F cattle for the summer. Leaves him free for other ranch matters."

It took Maria several seconds to work that through in her mind. She finally settled for, "Well, I don't believe there's a man in the whole country, other than Danny Framer, that would have done it. Mind you don't blow your one chance."

"I won't. But it seems I should be asking what you're doing here."

"No secret. The kids up in the rental house are learning to ride. I've been teaching them. I'm sure you've seen their pony in the barn or the pasture. Started last summer. They're already doing well. I thought it was time to get back at it this spring, so here I am."

Bo nodded at the answer and said, "Time I got back into the saddle too. I just rode in to have my lunch and change horses. Better go."

"Good luck, Bo."

Bo settled for a small nod and a tip of his hat.

With the slow warming of the spring days, Danny had taken to spending evenings in his big chair under the cover of the cabin porch, as he had done back in his single days. Syl was having a cup of tea in the matching chair. They both heard the vehicle coming but neither spoke, waiting to see who it was. Before long, a vehicle neither knew, a vehicle with out of province license plates, pulled to a stop. The driver looked over at them and smiled as he waved from inside the car.

Syl couldn't have been more surprised if Santa Claus had arrived wearing red shorts and a T top.

"Heavenly days, that's Cousin Phillip. You remember, from the dinner Mom put on. Likes to be called Ace. Has a head full of opinions and little else. I think I've seen about everything now."

Ace slowly got out of the car, stretching and shrugging his shoulders, as if he had been driving for hours. And perhaps he had. He smiled his way across the fifty feet to the cabin and finally said, "Greetings, Danny and Cousin Syl. I'm guessing you're surprised to see me here."

Danny left the talking to Syl. Ace was her cousin. She could deal with him.

"Phillip, I might have expected just about anyone else. Where in the world did you come from and why here?"

"Logically, of course, I've come from home. From the Big Smoke, as some call it. Long drive. I've done nearly six hundred miles today. Happy to stop. Actually, I intended to be here earlier but there was a danger of freezing rain north of the big lakes. Best to wait that out."

"Alright, that explains the mechanics of the matter. What about the reasons?"

"The reasons, my dear cousin, are both simple and yet not so simple."

"Try simple. We western folks tend that way, don't you know."

"Alright simple. Simply put, even though the snow was about a mile deep out here and the mercury was frozen to the bottom of the scale during your wedding, I liked what I saw. I liked the people I met. I've come to see it all again, when the snow is gone, and the grass has greened up."

"And what's your bigger or longer plan?"

"Well, now, we are venturing into the not so simple. I'll gladly explain all. A cup of coffee would probably assist in the telling if you could spare one. It's been a while since I've stopped."

Danny rose to his feet and wordlessly stepped into the cabin. He was only a minute returning with the brew. Phillip received it with gratitude. Nothing was said about cream or sugar.

While Danny was on his feet, he pulled a chair over and deposited it beside the visitor. Although normally standing slightly over six feet and looking reasonably fit in spite of the bit of extra weight he was carrying, he slumped, almost collapsed, when he sat, cradling the coffee mug on his lap.

"Long day," he said again. "Probably should have stopped a few hours ago, but I got a glimpse of the mountains, and it was like they were drawing me."

Danny and Syl sat silently while Phillip took three big swallows of coffee. After the first one, he closed his eyes and tasted the hot brew, swishing in his mouth just a bit, savoring it almost reverently, as if the coffee were a matter of life or death.

"Alright. The not so simple. You were born and raised eastern, Syl. I don't know your history, Danny."

He paused there as if to give Danny time to explain. When Danny remained silent, he continued.

"Anyway. Yes. Well. Eastern. The big smoke. Where we locals are convinced, right down into our tiny hearts, that we live in the very center of the universe. If the West is ever mentioned at all, and that is not often, it is with derision, or as if it was a standing joke, a burden we easterners had to bear. I confess to having been included in that belief all my life. It's kind of born into the bloodstream, like our DNA. But, in spite of my obvious arrogance during my very unfortunate outburst at dinner that evening, I left here with serious questions in my mind. When I returned to the office, I started really looking at the people I worked with. Now, don't get me wrong. They're good folks. But narrow. I had never seen that before. Never noticed it. In myself or in the others. I had simply no comparison to help my thoughts. And then, at a Christmas party with my usual cohorts, listening to the various conversations around the room, the shallowness really came home to me. Again, I must stress, these are good people. Work hard. Pay their taxes. Love their families. But they lack curiosity. There is little, if any, desire to know about the rest of the country or of the world.

"I mean, when you already live in the center of it all, why bother? And the saddest part, the one I had the most difficulty with, was the truth that I was exactly like the others. I was deeply uncomfortable with that truth."

Pausing, Phillip gave time for any response while he swallowed more coffee and, again, there was only silence.

"You warned me, Syl, about both the men and the women I would meet at the wedding. You warned me to keep my opinions to myself. To keep my mouth shut. You couldn't know it, but I was very much paying attention. Whereas, back home we, for the most part, rely on the group for strength and for assurance, propping each other up in our self-delusions, I seemed to sense that the younger set at the wedding, especially during that impromptu dance, could and did, stand alone, needing no external strength.

"I finally saw, Danny, that you are that kind of man, and I was happy for Syl when that light came on for me. I have no doubt at all that Syl can depend on you and your strength to carry you through the tough times that come to all of us.

149

"And then, what can I say about Box and Maria? A lovely couple. Box, a happy, jovial man, hiding an internal strength beneath his foolish talk, if I see it correctly. Taking charge but not seeming to or making a big deal out of it. Maria, lovely and modest at the same time. I looked at the cowboys and their wives or girlfriends and the three or four nurses that were there, and I saw strength and health and freshness. I danced with one of the local nurses, a girl born and raised in the west. She exuded a natural self-confidence.

"I remembered all that when I was with my friends at that Christmas party. And I found myself wanting what you have. Or at least some of it."

Again, Phillip paused and again, neither Danny nor Syl chose to fill the verbal vacuum.

"If you'll have me, I want to spend at least the summer with you Danny, working on the ranch. I don't need wages. Financial management is one thing I have nailed down pretty well, so my funding is more than adequate. I won't be a financial drag on the ranch and, I hope, not a physical drag either. I wish to learn to ride. I want to learn about cattle. I want to drive a tractor and stack hay. I may stay or I may return east in the fall. That's yet to be decided. But at least for the summer I'll do whatever job you assign to me and do it gladly, as long as I'm learning at the same time."

With that short speech Phillip was truly finished. It was time for Danny or Syl to speak. It took a while.

When Danny had sorted some things out in his head, he said, "Just a few miles back, on the edge of town, you passed a motel and restaurant. The restaurant is great. The motel not so much. But it will do for one night. You go get yourself some sleep and come back in the morning. Not too early. I'll be with the cattle until mid-morning and Syl is on day shift, so she won't be here."

Phillip groaned and stood. Stretching his back, he again said, "Should have stopped hours ago. Thanks for listening. I'll do as you say. Good night."

Danny and Syl sat silently while they watched Phillip turn the car and head back down the driveway. They then looked at each other and broke out into laughter.

Danny said, "Aaron, Bo, now Phillip. Who's next?"

"Do you remember what I called you a while ago?"

"Let's see. I believe it was handsome. No wait, it was smart. No that might not be right either. Was it wise? I give up. You had better remind me."

"Well, I agree you are all those things and more, but I believe I said you were a magnet to the needy and desperate.

"And while you're running through names, you forgot Maria. And what about Ted and Christie. You forgot Mrs. Kingsbury and the Gables, in Hawaii. And then how could we forget Graham and Bonny Wills, arriving during the storm, horseback, with suffering children? And as you've already said, there's Aaron and the girls, and Bo. And now here's Phillip. And Box fits in there somewhere. No, my loving and practical husband, you are very definitely a magnet to the needy and desperate."

Chapter 17

Three days later, Phillip was settled in, using the basement room at Syl's parents' house. Syl had some questions about that, but she kept them to herself.

Syl was enjoying a day off while Danny was across the road, working with Aaron on the fertilizing project. The spreader had given a bit of trouble, but it was working again. Danny was there only to observe and be ready with a box of tools if he was needed.

Grinning ear to ear, Phillip slowly rode Danny's Toby horse up to the porch. Without saying anything to discourage her eastern cousin, Syl noted that his feet were jammed fully into the stirrups, and he was gripping the horn with one hand. He was sitting off center, putting more weight on the right side of the horse, than the left. Bo had been assigned the questionable task of getting Phillip mounted and pointed in the right direction. He was riding, making slow headway, but he wasn't allowed anywhere near the cattle yet.

Danny and Syl were both surprised and pleased that Phillip had been as good as his word. In just the short few days, he had listened without argument to Bo, and he had not balked when Bo put a shovel in his hand and pointed at the horse stalls and then the wheelbarrow. The teaching was Bo's job, unless Danny stepped in. Syl would leave it to Bo to correct Phillip's use of the saddle.

Aaron completed the deal with Danny, to cut twenty acres of land containing the home and outbuilds from the Kingsbury place. The subdivision wasn't approved or finalized yet, but it had been started. The motherless family moved in on the hope that the county would not be long in approving the subdivision. After making so many moves during their growing years, the girls were loving the fact that they had a long-term home, and that it was large enough that each could have a bedroom. All in all, Aaron's life had taken a positive turn. Whether he stayed with the D-F ranch or ventured out into another direction would be decided when the time was right.

There had been mention of opening a breakfast café in town but that was for the future. In any case, Aaron hadn't really convinced anyone about his seriousness on the matter.

After the calves had been on the grass for a few weeks, Danny rode out with Bo to look the situation over.

"We need rain, Danny. There's only been a sprinkle since that heavier downpour that melted the last of the snow. The grass sprung up fast but hasn't grown much since. This close-up quarter is grazing down too quickly. And we're barely into spring. At the rate the grass is growing we'll be in trouble, come August. This early heat's hard on the animals too."

Danny had come to the same conclusion. And it was, indeed, hot. Almost unbearably hot for June. He considered the options for a few seconds and then said, "How would it be if we take advantage of that bottom bush quarter for a week or so. Give this quarter a complete rest. Get the animals some shade, as well. That back quarter is pretty well watered. It may hold for a while, although most of it is bush."

With that agreed on, Danny jogged back to the barn, tied off his horse to the corral railing and saddled Syl's Boots, using her old saddle. Her new saddle was more or less on display. She had used it only twice, returning it to the cabin and cleaning it thoroughly after each use.

Danny drove the pickup across the road to the farm to see if Aaron could spare Phillip. With that agreed upon, Danny and Phillip were soon re-mounted and headed out to the pasture. When they joined up with Bo, Danny said, "Phillip, we're going to move these animals. Bo is going to give you instructions. I'll say just one thing before I leave you with Bo, and that is, 'don't get these animals riled up. Calm is what we want'. Perhaps Bo can explain to you how the horse is smarter than you, for the working of cattle anyway. Now, I'm going ahead to open gates. You listen carefully to Bo."

Giving no opportunity for questions, Danny rode away.

Later that evening, Phillip, who had finally found the ranch men calling him Ace, was ready to drive home. He stopped briefly at the cabin porch. Danny and Syl were at their regular evening stand, coffee and teacups in hand. He was smiling from ear to ear, although clearly hurting from all the riding. He grinned at Danny before asking, "Well, boss, we got those calves moved alright. Is it time now for me to purchase spurs and a six-gun?"

Syl laughed and said, "I'd say it was time, Phillip. Don't buy any bullets yet thought. You're not quite ready for that."

"Dang. I somehow knew there would be a catch. Anyway, I've worked my way into the second week on the D-F. Thought I'd tell you that I'm enjoying it, and again, that I appreciate the learning experience. And I'm reasonably certain my body will heal. Eventually."

With a wave he eased himself back into his car and was gone.

Syl looked at Danny and said, "I don't know anymore. You figure it out."

Danny responded, "I'm not much on figuring out, my dear."

"Sure, you're not."

Chapter 18

June turned into July and still there was no rain. The fertilized Kingsbury quarter section had shot up quickly and was still growing, although only slightly better than the unfertilized quarter. The northern half of the section, the Bradshaw land, had started reasonably well too but was showing little recent growth. The quarter on the original D-F was better than the Bradshaw but not nearly as good as the Kingsbury land. Danny and Aaron, driving slowly around the fence lines to assess the situation were both silent and contemplative. Danny finally said, "Kind of makes me wish I had put out the money to fertilize the whole lot, but I wasn't sure at the time. And it was a sizable investment with no personal experience to back it up."

As the pickup continued to roll along the edge of the field, with dust rising from the wheels, Danny asked, "What's the latest we can get rain and still hope for a hay crop?"

"Well, my friend, where our family farmed is a wetter country than this, so I'm only guessing. We seldom lacked for rain, although there were a few troublesome years. We were more apt to get rain when we were trying to bale or combine. But to throw a tentative answer your way, I'd suggest we may have a maximum of, perhaps, two weeks, before a decision has to be made. Let's say the third week of July. And forget a second cut. That's just not going to happen."

Danny nodded and said, "I'm going to have some unhappy customers. There are cattlemen depending on this hay. And I'm depending on some profit from it."

As Danny drove, with his eyes and mind on the grass, Aaron studied him. He had a question. But how far would their camp friendship take him into Danny's private affairs? It was true they had become good camp friends in the north, but many men did. That in no way meant that most would remain lasting friends after they returned to their own homes or took on different construction projects, scattering across the land, anywhere that would make them a living.

The men had come from all over the country. When they returned home after their hitch, they would live hundreds, or perhaps, thousands of miles apart. Some would forget right away, as they became occupied with family or on the next work project. Some would write or phone a time or two before the calls became less frequent and were finally forgotten.

But Danny and Aaron had the writing in common. Would that make a difference? Danny had published a book, largely with Aaron's guidance. Danny's thanks indicated that he had not forgotten. Now they were working together. Perhaps just one question would stand the test. He promised himself he would not push the matter.

"Can I ask you a personal question, Danny?"

Danny took his eyes off the grass long enough to glance across the cab of the truck and grinned at Aaron.

"Ask away. If I open the door and shove you out, you'll know I don't want to answer it."

"Long walk back. But I'll take a chance. Those hay customers. The ones that were going to write checks to cover expenses and show some profits for the D-F. If you don't get those checks, are you in serious trouble? We've never talked about how you financed all of this, so I don't know what your debt load is. Big investment though. Can you survive a bad summer? Then, to complicate matters, with a poor hay crop there will be cattlemen who are dumping their yearlings into the feeder market at cut prices. Then who knows what might happen to the slaughter market a few months from now? It's all related, and out of the rancher's control. Like a chain with someone else holding the links together. Are you fix'n to get into trouble?"

Danny pursed his lips and slowly considered his answer. He could picture his father facing the same situation. Calm, cool, deliberate. Perhaps even evasive. Applying some of his teaching from his growing years, Danny said, "No, I won't be in serious trouble. Losing an entire year of productions will set the long-term plans back some, but it won't break the D-F. Outside of the cost of this section of land, I don't carry much debt and what debt I have, has an offsetting fund set aside to keep the vultures at bay. I'm in no danger of losing land or cattle, if that's your question."

What Danny wouldn't discuss and didn't want even mentioned was that the offsetting fund was a combination of his book royalty advance payment and Syl's personal savings. Neither was to be touched except in the most dire circumstances. Thinking on this, and then back to Aaron's question he said, "The bigger problem to me is how to respond wisely to the situation on the ground."

"How would you approach making that decision, Danny?"

Again, Danny answered slowly. Finally, he said, "Well, when I purchased the original cattle and rented the land, I researched the history of cattle prices. I didn't even know how to go about that. I had to have Mr. Mulholland walk me through the terms, short form words used in publishing the prices, and all of that.

"I went through the same process again when I purchased the Mulholland land. The difference was that I had a couple of years' experiences with both hay and cattle by that time. But I still asked questions and sought advice. When I bought this land, I went through it all yet again, for the potential in hay as well as in land uses. I have no interest in crop farming, but I had to consider that too. My final enquiry was to Mr. Kane, longtime owner of the K bar, and a very successful rancher. He and I got off to a rough start, but we managed to sort that out. You will recall Syl telling you the Maria story. It's Maria's father I'm talking about."

"What finally convinced me on this land is that Kane said, 'If you decide not to purchase that section, please let me know. I'd like it for myself. I'm always looking for hay land.' That's a pretty strong recommendation. So, I went with it."

Aaron responded, "And now?"

"Now we'll wait and see. And pray for the best. I can push any big decisions off for a while. A couple of weeks, anyway. We could maybe take off what grass is here and then run the cattle over here for late summer graze. Lots to think about. I'd probably talk with Kane again if push comes to shove this summer."

Chapter 19

It was another hot summer Saturday afternoon. Syl was on a day off. Aaron and Ace were both taking the day off, as well. Aaron to be with his girls and Ace, so he had said, to rest and hope for his aching body to begin the recovery process. Danny spent the morning riding with Bo, looking the calves over one by one, or as close to that as possible. He then left Bo to ride fence line while he, himself, checked, once again, on the grass situation, on both the pasture and the home place hay quarter. There would be hay but, clearly, not nearly a normal crop. The question rattling around in the back of Danny's mind was, 'do I keep it for myself or sell it off to my usual customer? I may need it but so does he.'

Only one pasture quarter had been grazed yet. That and the bush quarter. Together with the untouched third quarter, they could carry the stock for quite a while. With Danny satisfying himself on all of that, he rode to the cabin. He put Toby on a long tether, allowing him to graze on the yard grass.

Syl and the two youngest of Aaron's daughters, Becky and Abby, were holding plates of cold cuts, cheese and a slice of bread, on their laps on the cabin porch. Syl waved at Danny as he approached on foot. Becky scooted out of Danny's chair with an impish grin on her face.

"Caught you," said Danny. "I turn my back for just a short while and here you are, keeping my wife from her work, eating up all my food and sitting on my chair. I don't know what this younger generation is coming to." Becky grinned and stuck her tongue out at him.

Syl asked, "You hungry?"

"A bit. But you sit and keep an eye on these girls. There's no telling what mischief they're going to think up next. I need to have a good wash. Then I'll see what might be left in the cupboard. Can I get something else for you?"

"No, I'm fine. I may have a cup of tea later but for now I'm fine."

It wasn't long before Danny returned with a plate similar to what the girls were enjoying. He took his seat and glanced from one girl to another. "What's up, girls?"

Abby responded, "We brought Dad's two old books over. He finally dug them out of one of those boxes his friend brought down from the farm. He said you were going to show them to someone."

Momentarily Danny reflected on Aaron's original assessment, thinking he may have seen a bit of unsteadiness, as he termed it, in Abby. Whatever

Aaron saw was not in evidence to Danny. Perhaps Aaron feared he saw a bit of the girls' mother making itself known. The girl was certainly pretty enough to draw attention, both the welcome, as well as the unwelcome kind. Whatever Aaron though he saw was none of Danny's business, and he would never ask. Aaron's family was Aaron's to deal with.

Hopefully, with a family and a home, plus a father who obviously cared, and who was gaining in steadiness himself, as the days went by, was having a good influence on the young lady.

Syl stood, picked the books from a stack of papers on a small table and passed them to Danny.

Danny set his fork on the side of the plate and looked at one cover and then the other, wiping his hand over each, in turn, as if he was reading braille, or his fingers could sense something from the ink.

"I'd love to read these, and I will as opportunity rises, but your dad wants them, Syl, so I'll take them to church tomorrow and drop them off at the house after."

"Actually, it's all arranged. The girls, all three of them, are coming to church with us. They say their dad hasn't exactly promised yet, but he'll likely join them. Then we're all going for lunch. We'll meet my folks at the restaurant. You can give dad the books then. Or, if Aaron decides to join the girls, he can pass the books over himself."

Danny had no quick comment, so he turned back to the finger food and potato salad he had plated up for himself. He had a question but wasn't sure he should delve into the topic. The last thing he wanted, after Aaron and his girls had made a start at family again, was to bring up difficult subjects or get into the middle of a family question. He ate another cracker with cheese as he thought. Finally, trying to be as casual as possible he said, "It will be great to have you girls join us at church. I know nothing at all about your family. Did your mother take you to church?"

For once Abby was quiet, leaving Becky to answer the question.

"Mom only went a few times with us, but she always insisted that we go, whether she was with us or not. We didn't always want to go, but we went anyway. Mostly. And then we seemed to be forever moving and changing towns. That meant finding a new church. In some of the small towns there was no choice. But mostly we found a place to attend that wasn't too bad."

Becky's and Danny's eyes were locked together as she talked. When she was done, he simply nodded his thanks and asked no more.

The porch was silent for only a moment. Becky, at seventeen, was learning to hold her thoughts to herself. The talk of church seemed to have put her into a quiet mood. But Abby, at fourteen was still a chatterbox. A dramatic change in subject matter appeared to have no effect on her at all.

"Will you teach me to ride, Danny?"

Only half teasing Danny answered, "No. Girls shouldn't be wasting their time on such frivolities. There's work to be done. Houses to clean, clothes to wash, potatoes to peel, socks to mend, homework to do..."

He was interrupted immediately with gales of laughter from both girls. Syl just smiled.

Abby said, "Danny, that's all such a bore. Anyway, Syl rides and Maria rides. She's teaching the kids next door. If dad buys a horse, will you teach me?"

"Well, young lady, I'll tell you what. You talk to Syl. Maybe she'll let you try her Boots horse. That might be better than pushing your dad for a horse when you don't even know if you'll really enjoy it or not. Then, if you do all right on Boots, perhaps either Syl or Maria will give you some lessons. I really can't promise to find the time to do it. There's not many spare minutes around here in the summertime."

That seemed to satisfy Abby and she turned to Syl, ready with the next obvious question. Danny stood, said a general 'thank you' for the lunch and turned to the tasks he had assigned to himself for the afternoon.

The next morning Danny got out the .32 convertible. It had only been on the road a couple of times since the wedding. But how could he not get it out on such a beautiful Sunday morning? He and Syl would enjoy the ride to church in the collector car. On the graveled, Sugartown Road they kept it covered. But once they arrived on the blacktop they pulled over and dropped the top down. As they were parking in the church yard, Clara drove up. Her father was sitting on the passenger side of the front seat, with the two younger girls in the back. Their arrivals were timed such that they all walked across the sunbaked asphalt parking lot together. Danny withheld any mention of Aaron's presence. He left Aaron's books in the car. He would return them later so Aaron could give them to Wes himself, at lunch.

After greeting a few folks in the foyer, they took their seats and quietly waited for the service to begin. Danny and Aaron were several feet apart, but during the singing, Aaron's tenor voice could be heard. It was a quiet, but pleasantly confident voice, as if he was familiar with the songs.

After the service, gathering again in the foyer, the two youngest girls were huddled with two others, a guy and a girl, about their own age. They knew them from school, although they had only been in school a few weeks before the summer break, the kids seemed to be friends. Clara, no longer in school, had not met them so she hung out with Syl. Knowing her parents' church would be out at about the same time, Syl was anxious to get to the chosen restaurant. She eased away from the people she had been talking with and moved towards the group of kids. Aaron and Danny walked outside, waiting just in front of the open doors. They had both taken on the habit of allowing Syl to deal with the girls.

As Syl was approaching the kids, a startlingly beautiful woman approached from the other direction. Syl said, "Come on, girls, we need to go."

As the girls reluctantly started saying their goodbyes, the other woman said, "We have to go too, guys." She then stepped towards Syl and said, "Good morning, Syl. I've missed you the past couple of weeks. I was away for a while and then I assume it was shift work for you."

"Right you are, Belle. I'm still having trouble putting families together here. Are these two your children?"

She smiled as she said, "Yes. These two belong to me. Some days I would gladly sell them or adopt them out but today I'm still claiming them. I don't know these other girls?"

Belle stepped forward and offered to shake hands with the three girls, beginning with Clara, who had walked over with Syl.

"Good morning, ladies. I'm Belle Farley. I see you know my two children. You must have met in school."

With that confirmed she shook hands with the two younger Walsh girls and asked for their names.

Syl said, "These girls are neighbors and friends. Their father and my husband skipped out, leaving me to break up the little party here."

Belle glanced towards the door but didn't see Danny. "It looks as if they've moved off on their own. I must let you go. We wouldn't want the new bride keeping her husband from his lunch." Her smile said it was meant in jest.

"Well, I'm not sure how long the new bride label lasts but I must be pushing the limit. A few of us are going out for lunch, Belle. We'd love to have you join us. We're meeting my folks over at the Westside Cantina. The kids can visit, and it would be good to get to know you a bit better."

When one of the kids said, "Please, Mom?" Belle responded, "The invitation sounds tempting. Are you sure we won't just be in the way?"

"I'm sure. Come on, I'll introduce you to the girls' father and my parents."

Abby thought she could help by saying, "You won't be in the way, Mrs. Farley. Danny always does whatever Syl says. And my Dad is pretty laid back too."

The two women laughed while Syl said, "Thank you, Abby. It really isn't quite that way but never mind."

The group moved to the doors and looked for the men. They were halfway across the parking lot looking at a .55 Chev a church member had rebuilt and polished up. It was parked next to the .32. Studying them briefly made Syl think about the heritage convertible they so rarely had time to take out of the garage. She was glad Danny had thought of it that morning.

Danny glanced up and saw the ladies and kids heading their way. He said something to Aaron and they both stepped away from the re-built car and waited. When they were close enough Syl said, "Belle, this is Aaron Walsh, the girls' father. Aaron is a newcomer to the area. He's running the farm for Danny until he gets settled in. Aaron, this is Belle Farley. These are her children. They're join-ing us for lunch."

Danny smiled and said, "Hi, Belle. I haven't talked with you since you were away. How is your mother? I understand you were needed to help her get through a serious illness."

"That's true, Danny. She's fine again, but it was

awkward with the kids in school. I had to leave them with friends. But all is well again. And it's good to meet you, Aaron. You have a lovely family."

Aaron, after long years alone, was no longer comfortable with meeting women. The thought that there would be a Mr. Farley showing up, lifted much of the pressure from him. Still, he couldn't help acknowledging, silently and privately, that she was a beautiful and graceful woman. *The kind of woman that I...Well, never mind.*

"Pleased to meet you, Belle."

In the restaurant, joined by Syl's parents, the kids took a table a bit apart while the adults, including Clara, had a large corner booth, within speaking distance of the kids. After the introductions, as if he could wait no longer, Wes Mabry said, "All right, Aaron, I've waited as long as I intend to wait. Where are these books of yours?"

Aaron, his confidence in his writing, and ability to follow through on new commitments, shattered by years of trauma, most admittedly, brought on by himself, hesitantly lifted the books off the seat beside himself and passed them across to Wes. Danny's assurance of Wes's integrity and knowledge had been enough to encourage Aaron to dig out a copy of each book and bring them along.

Belle, sitting two spaces over, with Clara between Aaron and herself said, "You're a writer, Aaron? That's wonderful."

Aaron was attempting to think up an answer without having to go into his somewhat sordid past when Steve, Belle's son, said, "A writer. Hey, that's neat. All Mom ever does is read, read, read. The house is full of books."

"That's enough out of you, Steve." Belle smiled as she said it but there was no doubt Steve took her meaning.

Wes held the books, one at a time, and ran his fingers across the somewhat wrinkled dust cover. Syl watched silently, wondering what it was about books that made men run their hands across them when they first came into their possession. She had seen both Danny and Aaron do the same thing as her father was now doing. She had no answer, and she didn't enquire.

Wes read the name of the publisher on the second page. He glanced up at Aaron and said, "Sand Pebbles Publishing, Los Angeles. I'm not sure I've heard of them. Did they do a good job for you at the start?"

"They did. Originally the sales were good. The rest is totally my fault."

"Well, none of that matters now. It only matters that you have a full release from the old contract. I'd like to take these and read them. Would that be alright with you?"

"Of course, that's why I dug them out and brought them in."

Wes nodded and asked, "And do you still have the original typed manuscripts?"

"I do. They don't look like much anymore, after being stored in a cardboard box for years, but I have them."

Aaron was looking sober and uncomfortable. It seemed that only Danny noticed. In an attempt to ease the situation, he said, "I suspect, Aaron, that Clara, and perhaps the younger girls too, would like to read them if you have other copies."

"I managed to save a few. I could dig them out."

Clara was saying nothing, but she never took her eyes off her father. Danny's attempt to bring her into the adult conversation wasn't altogether successful.

While he was struggling for another way to change the subject, to ease Aaron's plight, Belle's fourteen-year-old, Olivia, broke into the silence.

"Mom, Syl is going to teach Becky and Abby how to ride. If she'll give us lessons too, would you drive us out to their place? Please, Mom?"

Syl looked somewhat surprised and said, "That's not completely decided on, young lady. We have some things to consider first."

Syl and Belle looked at each other. Belle was clearly thinking of possible problems where horses were concerned. She had heard of the outrageous costs of horses, tack and lessons, to say nothing of stabling. Syl was thinking that she was reluctant to get any more involved in another's family situation. Being friends with Aaron's girls was a blessing but she wasn't sure how far she wanted it to go. And to add two more kids was a bit of a daunting prospect.

Syl finally said, "We'll have to see how it goes, girls. You have to remember that I still have a job that keeps me pretty busy, and our horses are really working horses. If they're needed on the ranch, that's their first responsibility. But I promise to keep it in mind. Is that alright?"

Olivia answered, "I guess. Thanks."

Abby leaned into Olivia's ear and said, just loud enough for the adults to hear, "She'll do it."

Those around the table laughed. All except Aaron. After so many years apart, he was reluctant to discipline his girls or even correct them too severely. Hopefully the time would come when he would have more confidence. And perhaps more influence in their daily happenings.

Their dinners had come during all that discussion. Wes said grace and they all dug in. The two tables fell to near silence as the food was consumed. Following the dinner there was a bit more chit chat but Danny finally said, "Folks, you're going to have to excuse us. Syl goes to work in about three hours. If we get home, she can have a bit of rest before that time. And our rider is off today so I have to check on the stock. Don't rush away on our account. I can see the server coming with more coffee. Thank you all. We've enjoyed our time together."

He and Syl slid out of the booth and headed towards the desk at the front door. The manager saw them coming and rose from the stool she had been sitting on. Danny quietly asked, "Do you have the tab for our tables ready?"

"I do. Will you be covering just your own or the whole thing?"

"Let me have the whole bill, just this once."

Outside, as they were closing the car doors and automatically reaching for non-existent seat belts that weren't a part of the automotive world in 1932, Syl said, "I was hoping you would do that."

"I can't see any reason that I shouldn't pick up the

tab. I mean, after all, we're in the middle of a drought with terribly hot temperatures, which are hard on the animals, and the grass isn't growing, so I won't have a hay crop to sell. The price of cattle continues to drop at every level, and we have no idea how low it will go. Plus, I made a major investment in land that isn't going to show much of a crop."

Syl started to laugh. "Why, my dear, I do believe you are starting to whine."

Danny flashed a crooked grin at his wife. "No, not really. Just stating the obvious truth. We're in no real trouble financially, at this point. I'm just not sure it's the time to be treating too many other people too often."

Syl nodded agreement before saying, "It's not like it's going to be repeated every Sunday afternoon. Plus, Aaron was distinctly uncomfortable with the newness of it all. I didn't think it would be good to confront him with splitting up the tab. And, you may not know it because Belle rarely says anything. We chatted privately just the once and she mentioned how tight their budget is since her husband died. I'm pretty sure going out for lunch is a major treat for her and the kids."

Syl didn't have to ask Danny to keep that secret. She had long known that Danny's mind was the place rumors and gossip went to die. There was no chance at all of him repeating anything they talked about.

Chapter 20

It was the first week in an unusually hot July when the phone rang very early in the morning. Danny had just picked Syl up from Graveyard shift and she was in bed, asleep. It was still shy of 7 a.m. Danny grabbed the receiver on the first ring. A quiet hello got the response, "Good morning, Danny. I know it's early, but I needed to talk to you before you got out the door for work."

"Is this Sol?"

"It is, indeed, your friendly cattle broker."

"Hang on, Sol. Syl's asleep after working all night. I'll drag this phone cord outside where we can talk."

In just a few seconds Danny was situated on his chair with the phone to his ear.

"What's up, Sol?"

"Got a proposal for you, Danny. I understand the situation and all of that but hear me out, please. I have a steady client from out east, in the badlands area. If you haven't been down that way this summer, you can't believe the heat and drought. Well, anyway. This fella, good man, good rancher, good stock. But desperate. His pastures are burning up except for a bit along the river. He'll have grass in that one spot for a while. That will hold his breeding cows, hopefully until the rains come. Normally he summers his calves, about six hundred in all, and markets them off to the feedlot guys in the fall. But he can't wait. If he holds them any longer his grass will be gone, and he'll end up having to sell off breeding cows later on. That's not a winning option. The calves are too small for the feed lot. Even with the serious drop in prices, he's looking for other options.

"You told me about that other section of hay land you were buying and I'm wondering if you're going to get any hay off and if there might be some grazing on that piece that would take these animals into fall."

As was totally predictable, the line was silent for an uncomfortably long time while Danny sorted out his thoughts. He finally said, "You must have put an offer together before you called, Sol. Why don't you lay it out for me? I've paper and pen right here. I've got to tell you though. Things are real tight with our hay and graze situation, and the summer still holds some unknowns."

"I understand. And you're right again, Danny. My man has indeed put an offer together. Here it is."

Sol laid out the offer while Danny took notes. The essence of the offer was to have Danny graze out the calves and split the profits with the rancher at the end of the season. Without even thinking deeply Danny could see problems. How do you value the pasturing and care of calves through a summer of drought and falling beef prices? And that was only the most obvious question. Following that were who bears the losses and the veterinary costs? Without adding to that list of possible questions and problems, Danny was already thinking up a different proposition.

Sol finished with, "The rancher has his own cattle liner so the delivery to your land is a part of the deal. With this deal the rancher is taking most of the risk and you would be sharing in one half of the profits. What do you say?"

"Well, Sol, right off you know I'm going to say I don't make deals without thinking carefully and talking with Syl. She'll be awake in a few hours. I'll get back to you by the end of the business day or you can call me this evening if you're not at your phone."

"Fair enough, my friend. One final thing I don't think I mentioned. These are horned animals. They aren't as gentle as a yard animal but they're not wild either. They're used to being around folks and being handled, time to time."

The line went dead, and Danny sat thinking. The possibilities were truly attractive if there was any kind of a decent market in the fall. Even with a level or slightly down market he would still benefit from the weight gain. And grazing that section could be a good use of the grass. He might take off a bit of hay first. He would do the numbers and calculate the costs of cutting and baling. If those costs didn't outweigh the value of the crop, it might pay to hay off even the small amount of grass available.

But as in everything else in this life there were risks. He couldn't decide if he wanted those risks or not. He needed to bounce the idea past Syl, but she needed her sleep, and he had no intention of waking her. He could, however, talk to Aaron. He scribbled out a note for Syl, closed and locked the door, leaving the phone outside so the ringing wouldn't wake her, and drove over to see Aaron.

To get privacy away from the girls, the two men wandered out to the long unused corral. There, leaning on the grayed, weathered, poplar rails, the two men talked cattle, pricing, and potential. Something unexplainable created a comfortable feeling when leaning on the corral, as if it were a natural and important part, an aura almost, of being in the cattle business.

Danny outlined Sol's offer. Then he outlined the offer he intended to use in reply, assuming that Syl didn't shoot it full of holes.

Aaron listened carefully, saying nothing. When Danny was finished, Aaron asked, "You know and trust this broker?"

"I do. He's done what he said he would do in the past. I have no reason to doubt him now."

Aaron, soaking this in, hesitated before saying, "I'm sure we can both see the potential positives as well as the obvious negatives. You could make a nice profit if the grass holds, and if the markets rise a bit, or at least if they don't plummet further. And a big part of the summer is already scratched off the calendar, so the grass would only have to hold for a couple of months.

"But there's negatives too, Danny, which I'm pretty sure you've already identified. Which ones stand out in your mind?"

Danny was silent as he considered his response. Finally, he said, "Well, with Sol's offer, I would really be in a partnership. I'm not altogether comfortable with having a partner. Especially one I've never met and don't know anything about. As grateful as this unknown rancher would be now, with the solution to his graze problem at hand, things might look different to him if we get a couple of rains, and then an easy fall. If the market shows positive, he may get anxious in the early fall and demand that I sell, while we still have grass, and time before freeze-up.

"But I kind of like being able to do my own research, and discuss things with trusted people, such as we are doing now, before making my decision. That sometimes takes a day or two and I'm not much on rushing things. Plus, I've never found reassessing and changing plans to be very helpful. As I said before, a change of conditions on the ground would be an invitation for this rancher to want to reassess our deal."

Again, there was silence. Aaron broke it this time.

"Let's back up a bit. What would have to be done to hold the animals on this land for a few months? What about water? Would we have to build a corral? How much fixing will the fencing need?"

Danny more or less pointed off to the northwest, towards the corner quarter, and said, "Old home site tucked into that top corner. Bradshaw says there's a good well there. Immersible pump abandoned, but usable, down the pipe. If the water table hasn't dropped too far with the drought there should be water. Have to hook it up, of course, put in a cattle tank. Heat it if we kept the cattle past freeze-up. Might want a corral. Need a loading chute. Some fence repairs. It's all just work. Not much capital expense involved. We work every day at something. Might just as well be something that could show a profit."

Aaron started to laugh. He finally said, "That's what you might call a sparse analysis. If you write like that your style would be called spare too, or simple or, oh I don't know, something that said, 'here, in this story, there are no extra words'."

"You want I should include the beautiful warm morning, the fluttering leaves, maybe add in a chirping bird, which I haven't heard for a while now?"

Both men laughed again. The action seemed to take the edge off the seriousness of the discussion.

Aaron got right to the nub of the question. "I'm feeling that you have two problems rubbing together here. One is that you don't want to be in partnership with this rancher, and the other is that you run shy of holding debt. Do I have that anywhere near correct?"

"Sparse, as you said, but pretty accurate."

"If you could rid yourself of the partner by taking on some debt, would you do that?"

"That brings me to my counter proposal to the

deal, as I outlined a few minutes ago. If I had some confidence that rain could come our way in the next couple of weeks, the answer would be probably. After I discussed it with Syl".

Aaron nodded his understanding and added, "Fair enough, and well thought out. But if you're leaning towards turning the deal down, talk to me before you call the broker."

Danny looked at Aaron, trying to see the purpose behind that request but finally gave it up. Instead, he changed the subject.

"Aaron, what I'd like to do now, is to go and get that new hay mower conditioner out of the barn and drag it over here. The small tractor is enough for that. I think we need to get this fertilized quarter laid down and baled as quickly as possible. The hay quarter on the home place too. Maybe do the home place first, now that I think on it. Won't take much more than a day to cut it. Then get it over here. We'll bale 'er up and then look at the other three quarters after that."

I'm on it, boss. Give me a ride over to the barn. I hate to be driving that big van of mine if I don't have to."

On the drive back to the barn Danny had an idea. As Ted was still only working part time, he went directly to the rental house after dropping Aaron off. Ted was taking the morning sun on the back porch, so no door knocking was necessary.

"Morn'n, Danny."

"Morning, Ted. Got a proposition for you. Have you seen that old pickup I dragged over from across the road?"

"I've seen it."

"Think you can get it running and drivable?"

"If it will run, I can get it running. Won't take long. Of course, miracles take a bit longer."

"I think the keys are hanging from the ignition. See what you can do. Have Aaron drag it over to the garage if you want."

"Will do."

Danny, preoccupied with a cattle purchase, simply waved and walked to the cabin.

Syl, in pajamas and bathrobe, was just leaving the bathroom. It was typical for her to awake around noon, eat a small bit of lunch and return to bed. Danny gave her a hug and asked, "What can I get you for lunch?"

As she nibbled, which was about all she did at noon, he told her about the call from Sol.

She half listened before saying, "Danny, my loving husband, you do what you believe to be best. Our total net worth is solid. The bank would finance you, or you could purchase the calves from the rancher, with a decent down payment now, and guaranteed full payment when they're sold."

Danny looked at her as he let that sink in. Yes, he would technically be in debt to the rancher, but it wouldn't show on any institution's books and there would be no interest and no payments. He smiled and said, "You're a marvel. Thinking of solutions when you're half asleep and I have them right before my eyes and missed them. Now back to bed with you."

Danny phoned Sol, made a firm offer, stipulated the purchase price, the deposit amount and the timing for the final payout. He closed with, "Best I can do, Sol."

Sol, usually a fast thinker and faster talker, hesitated. Finally, he said, "He'll take it."

Chapter 21

The next three days were a frantic rush of building and preparing for the delivery of cattle. The water well man and the electrician had the pump running, with a portable power plant in service. A hastily erected, but strong enclosure protected the well head and generator from wandering cattle, with room inside for the ATV. A large, round, galvanized drinking trough was brought out from town. A bit of digging, a bit of fill in one low spot, and the unit was installed level and ready to be filled. Aaron and Ace, who it turned out were both better with hammer and saw than Danny was, put a loading chute together. Bo left the care of his calves for a few hours each day to ride fence line on all four of the northern quarters, although only one quarter would be used immediately. He used the ATV for the job, with a small trailer attached, holding a roll of barb wire, staples, heavy gloves, some tools and a couple of new posts. There would be no scaling of these animals when they arrived, and no vet on site, as the rancher guaranteed they were all vaccinated.

The men had no sooner cleaned up their mess after the building effort, and heaved a sigh of relief, when the first load arrived. Three days later, the quarter section was brimming with six hundred twenty-two yearlings. They didn't appear to have suffered in the drought. At least no more than it would take a few days of good graze to overcome. Danny, Aaron and Bo all estimated, by looks, that the animals would come up to the weight the selling rancher had quoted.

Aaron kept the ATV for his own use, herding cattle, and Ace was put on the tractor, after some instructions, to mow and condition hay. As previously agreed, Graham Wills was brought onto the payroll, and one week later the hay was baled and in stacks on the home ranch. Danny was unsure what hay to sell and what to keep. He kept it all until he could read into the future, explaining to the rancher that normally purchased from him that he would be first in line, if any feed came for sale. The new animals were settling in. Ted had the old pickup running. It would be for use on ranch property, insured but not licensed, mostly driven by Aaron.

Danny felt like he could use a week's sleep. The other men probably felt the same, but Danny didn't dare ask, in case they all wanted time off together.

Surprisingly, when the weekend came, everyone but Bo, with little discussion beforehand, arrived at church. Syl heard later that Ace had accompanied her parents to their church. What his beliefs or background was she had no clear idea. Church attendance was an accepted practice and tradition among most of the family but for some, it was little more than a tradition. She didn't know where Ace fit within that range of beliefs. With Danny on cattle duty at both properties on Sunday, he had no time to hang around after service or go out for lunch.

Late Sunday afternoon, as he rode into the barn yard to stall his horse, getting ready to drive the pickup across to the other cattle, he saw two vehicles sitting beside the cabin. Somewhat exasperated at another interruption, he determined that no matter who it was, he would leave them in Syl's care. His second look identified Clara's car and one other that he didn't recognize. He drove the old pickup to the driveway entrance and stopped. He stepped to the ground and walked towards the porch, where he saw Aaron and his girls, as well as Belle and her two kids. Danny's thoughts were a blur, and best forgotten.

When he got closer, the younger kids all came running and shouting.

"Dad's going to help us ride a horse," shouted Abby. With that announcement the others chimed in until Danny had no idea what they were saying. And then, if there weren't already enough kids in the yard, Ted's three kids came out. The way Ted's kids were dressed it was obvious they had horses on their minds as well, but they would be using the pony purchased for them the previous summer. They didn't touch the ranch horses unless they had permission and there was an adult with them.

As Danny got closer, Aaron laughed and said, "It's not quite as bad as it looks, old friend. I agreed to just one quick ride each. And we'll use Syl's, Boots horse. The others have seen some work this week. We'll be letting them rest."

Danny found enough quiet to say, "Good to see you, Belle. Welcome to our humble place."

"Syl showed me the cabin. I think it's perfectly charming. You're very comfortable."

"Yes, well, I suppose we are. Don't seem to spend much time in it during the summer months but it's warm and comfortable during the long winter days."

Syl took Danny's hand and asked, "Is it all right with the cattle?"

"All right here. I'm just heading across the road now."

What he meant by across the road was actually a drive along Sugartown Road to the corner, one mile north, past the Bradshaw place, down the short driveway where the old farm buildings used to sit, and onto the new land. There he would park the truck outside the gate, walk in, and ease the ATV out of the well-head shelter fence and attend to the cattle. He found he didn't mind the short drive, and it saved cutting through the Kingsbury place that he had sold to Aaron, and then across a half mile of fenced grassland with gates to open and close.

As he drove, his mind was struggling with two thoughts, what else could he do to assure a profit on the new cattle, and how did Aaron and Belle end up together again?

Deciding one question was none of his business, he concentrated on the cattle and pulled the starter rope on the ATV.

When he returned from his afternoon loop through the yearlings, Clarence Bradshaw was waiting for him at the gate. He put the ATV back into its enclosure and shut off the engine, thankful for the drop in the noise level. He stretched to get the kinks out of his back as he walked to the gate.

"Afternoon, Clarence."

"Afternoon, Danny, that's sure a mess of cattle you got there. Good looking animals though. And good use of that grass. Even, as dry as it is."

Danny looked back over his shoulder and kind of waved, as if to indicate the entire section. "Couldn't figure what to do with it. Not hardly enough grass growth to justify the work and expense of haying. We could easily see there would be just a few bales. Then I got this offer to relieve the pressure on the grass on a dry land ranch, over east. The price was right so long as the market doesn't bottom out this fall."

"Won't likely. Pretty much at bottom now, what with all the animals already run through the system."

Clarence changed the subject abruptly and without preamble. "Got a request. Saw you have one of those new mower conditioners. Good machine but I don't need one anymore. Too late for me. Could've used it twenty, thirty years ago. That and a baler too. Not that many years ago we were stacking it up loose with hay rack, harnessed team and pitch forks. There's a real talent to capping off a rain-proof stack. Talent that's not of any use anymore.

But that's all past now, eh? These recent few years I've been contracting out the haying. Costs a bit but I'm not able to hold up my end of the work anymore. Best to let younger fellas get all the glory.

"What I've got this dry summer is a quarter section, or near enough, of oats that are never going to grow right or mature proper. Most years I get graded for pony oats. Make a few extra dollars from the upgrade. Of course, it's the mill in town that cleans them up and makes them ready for the upscale horse market. But not all oats are worth the trouble or expense. Mine usually turn out to be worth it. But not this year.

"If you'll bring that mower and baler back over here, I'd have you take that quarter off as green hay for me. Mow 'er down and bale 'er up. Pay you well for your time and costs. Either cash or in feed bales. What do you think? You got time to do that for me?"

Danny knew when he was backed into a corner. He smiled and said, "I'll make the time. Be over in the next couple of days."

"Thank you, son."

As he pointed the pickup back towards the D-F, Danny thought, 'good job for Ace'.

He took the costs of the job in bales of feed.

188

Chapter 22

After the kids each had a horse ride, figuring Syl had enjoyed all the noise and activity she could reasonably expect on her day off, Aaron invited the Farley family over to his place for snacks and a cold drink. Somewhat reluctantly, Belle agreed. She was as skittish around men as Aaron was around women. And she still didn't know if there was a Mrs. Walsh. Nor had she explained her circumstances to Aaron. But just a short visit with some refreshments, along with the kids, should be innocent enough.

After the refreshments were put behind them, Abby led the Farley kids all through the house while Aaron and Belle sat at the big kitchen table. Clara was off somewhere enjoying her own time and space.

When quiet descended on the upstairs portion of the old house, Aaron glanced at the hallway leading to the stairs and nervously suggested, "Well, they've either all found books to read or they're plotting a takeover."

"Let's pray it's the books."

After another nervous moment Belle said, "I find it interesting that you have two published books from some years ago but nothing newer." She left the comment hanging there. Aaron could respond with a simple nod, or an explanation, as he wished.

Aaron turned his head enough to make momentary eye contact, cleared his throat, and wondered how much to tell. He quickly decided on the short story approach rather than the entire, troublesome and embarrassing full-length novel.

"When my father took sick, he and Mother moved to town. They were young for true retirement, but Dad could no longer put in a day's work. My wife and I took over the farm, along with my brother Adam. I did some writing during my spare winter hours. I took a couple of writing courses in the two years I studied college by correspondence. I was very fortunate to get those tales published. The market is incredibly competitive. Sales did pretty well for a while.

"The girls were small. The farm life didn't offer much more than work and home. Very little excitement. Came the day it wasn't enough for Cookie, that's my wife. Ex-wife. She up and pulled out. Grabbed most of what little money we held in our bank account. Took the girls with her. Disappeared. I had no further connection until I received divorce papers a year later. I've never seen her since the day she left.

"I kind of came apart. Crawled inside a bottle for a couple of years. Strange that. I had never been a drinker. Lost the farm. Quit writing. Lost my publishing contract. And here I am."

"Well, Aaron, I can sense there's a lot more to the story than that, like how you met Danny, how you got here, what have you been doing in the intervening years, how did the girls end up back here. But thanks for sharing as much as you have. Do you intend to get back to writing?"

"I guess. I've made a bit of a start and, as you saw on Sunday, Wes is hoping to use his publishing industry contacts to work my old stories through the system again. And then, I'm half afraid Danny will take a singletree to me if I don't write some more."

"You're good friends, aren't you?"

"I guess. More than that really. But that's a long story too. Perhaps another time. What's your situation, Belle? You haven't mentioned a Mr. Farley."

Belle looked as if a good portion of past hurts had risen suddenly from the ashes of time. "No, I guess I haven't. It's no secret. You could ask anyone at church or around town. Mr. Farley, my husband, and the father of my children lost his battle with cancer. That was about five years ago. I may get over it someday."

Aaron studied his house guest with compassion. Carefully and quietly, he said, "I hurt inside just hearing that, Belle. It must have been a difficult time for you and the kids. I don't know which is worse, losing a mate forever or losing one that's still around somewhere, not really knowing when they may again show up in your life. Perhaps a person doesn't get over either situation. But we heal don't we? Slowly. Kind of."

"Well, we carry on, at least."

Belle managed a small smile as she said that.

As if orchestrated by someone, the kids reappeared at that time, preceded by laughter and teasing. Steve, at sixteen and still a bit gangly and awkward, was distinctly uncomfortable among the shouting girls. Becky wasn't altogether in tune with the two younger ones either. Aaron watched them rush into the kitchen and thought, *One boy, three girls, what could possibly go wrong?*

Aaron walked the Farley family out to their car and waved them off, after inviting a return visit. Steve and Olivia both said they'd be back. Aaron was pretty sure it was the horses that attracted them. Belle just smiled at the children and got into her car. Watching them proceed down the driveway he thought, *I hope they come back.*

Danny didn't really acknowledge the compliment when Syl said, "Danny, my love, in business I'm thinking your real strong point is looking ahead. You seem to be determined to have nothing surprise you. With that in mind I'm wondering what the plan is if cattle prices aren't favorable when snow is threatening, and we want to go to market?"

After a bit of a pause Danny responded, "Well, I'm not quite as confident in my planning abilities as you appear to be, but you have most certainly put your finger on a possible problem. Actually, we bought both herds at favorable prices, especially that second bunch.

"The prices could stay pretty low, and we could still come out without a loss, or even a bit of a profit, based on weight gain alone. But that's not why we're in business.

"I've been wondering how many we could hold over, feed out. We'd have to build some facilities for handling them and work out a good water system to fight off the cold and ice, but we could do it. Bo would stay on and maybe even Ace. I don't know about Aaron. We'd have to see on that. Everyone is looking for hay and bedding straw so I don't know where we could buy more. And the bales we have now wouldn't be enough."

"Would those bales see a portion of the herd through?"

"You're always asking just the right questions. Maybe I should study nursing and you run the ranch."

Syl laughed and leaned her head back on the seat headrest. They were almost back at the D-F. It had been a long, busy night in the emergency ward, with one sick baby, an elderly lady who had fallen down her own basement stairs and a wreck on the highway. Syl was looking forward to her bed.

"Ya, well, I don't think that would work out too well. You wouldn't like some of the messes I have to clean up and I wouldn't enjoy the messes you find yourself in. I think, perhaps, we will stick to our own places."

With Syl settled down for the day, Danny put the phone outside so it wouldn't disturb her and saddled his horse. He saddled his Toby horse and rode out to talk to Bo. The men circled the herd together while they discussed the possibilities of wintering out at least some of the cattle.

"I've no experience at all with wintering cattle, Bo. Those few weeks of calving on the K-Bar don't really count. Leaving aside the problem of finding enough feed, tell me what you can about feeding young stock through the cold."

The two men rode and talked for nearly an hour with Danny asking questions and listening carefully to Bo's answers. After lunch Danny drove to the Bradshaw half section and asked the same questions of Aaron.

Chapter 23

The days continued warm and dry. The unusual, overwhelming heat seemed to have dissipated or moved on, but there had been no rain. The grass, and even the leaves on the trees were wilting. Desperate ranchers continued throwing cattle onto the market, putting doubt into the assurance from Clarence Bradshaw that the stock had all been worked through the system. The government was promising financial relief but nothing firm had been arranged. In any case, Danny had never trusted bankers, lawyers or governments. He wasn't at all sure that he wanted the government giving him money. He was pretty well convinced the government benevolence would carry with it a comeback of some kind, sooner or later.

Aaron approached Danny and said, "My friend, I'm hoping we can spread the work out between the others for a few days. I'd like to get away for, perhaps three or four days. These girls are living within three- or four-hours' drive of grandparents they've never met. Or at least won't remember. I'd like to take them up there. I don't know how I'll be received myself, but the old folks would like to know their granddaughters. I'm sure of that."

"You go, Aaron. Go while the weather remains warm. Go tomorrow if you wish. I'll fill in for you."

Two days later, Aaron and three anxious girls drove onto a somewhat tired, run-down farmstead. Clara had done the driving with Aaron's directions. The trip had been one long series of questions. It appeared that their mother had told the girls little, if anything, about the family.

To the question of names Aaron had answered, "The family name is Chernenko. Nick and Anna Chernenko. Grandpa and Grandma to you girls."

Aaron couldn't help wondering why Cookie had held the girls away from her own parents, or at least not told them about the farm and the family. It appeared that she had never been back, if the girls had it right.

Even with this simple drive up for the visit, he had to steel himself against bitter memories that threatened to overwhelm him. The girls lack of knowledge just added another layer of questions. Now the situation faced him directly. There was no longer a choice. It was too late to turn back, even if that became his intent. The house was only a few feet away and there, wondering who was arriving, stood Nick, Aaron's ex-father-in-law and grandfather to his three girls. With no sign of recognition,

Nick, greyed and somewhat stooped, showing his age, stood his ground, not approaching the visitors. To an evident question from inside the house, he turned his head to the screened-in doorway and said something Aaron could not hear.

Clara pulled the car to a stop and looked at her father, as if asking, "What's next?"

In silent response, Aaron lifted his Stetson from the seat, opened the door, stepped out and replaced his hat. He looked up at Nick and said, "Good morning, Nick. It's Aaron."

The old man was startled as he finally recognized his long absent son-in-law. Again, he turned to the doorway and said something before slowly, carefully, making his way down the stairs. There was a serious, but not unfriendly look on his face.

Aaron stepped to meet him, as Nick came down the sidewalk. The screen door slammed against the stops and Mrs. Chernenko excitedly came out.

"Aaron?" she hollered. "Is that really you, Aaron?"

By this time Nick and Aaron were shaking, with Nick using both his work worn hands, taking a fierce grip. Nick still hadn't spoken, but his lips were working, as if the words wouldn't come out. Aaron, looking intently at him wasn't sure he could speak right at that moment either. The old man clearly was attempting to swallow a lump from his throat and there was the beginning of tears in his eyes. All put together, it was almost more than Aaron could do to control his own emotions. The girls were still hanging back, beside the car.

Anna charged down the stairs and then the

sidewalk, defying her age and the arthritis that was forming in her knees, and nearly knocked both her husband and Aaron over in her exuberance. Wordlessly, she gripped Aaron around his chest and squeezed. For a slight-built woman she was amazingly strong.

"Aaron. Aaron. Where have you been and why so long? Oh, my dear boy, how we've missed you. And who are these girls?"

Aaron knew no way to be subtle. He simply said, "Grandma and Grandma Chernenko, I want you to say hello to Clara, Becky and Abby. These are your granddaughters, all grown up."

The two seniors stood in mute wonder at what had come upon them on this sunny day. Anna was the first to speak.

"My girls? Clara? Becky? Abigail?"

As she said this she was inching towards the wide-eyed girls. Nick was not far behind. Aaron kept pace with Nick.

Anna, clearly the expressive half of the grandparent duo, put her hands out towards the girls and said, "Girls, come. *Moye givchetta*. My girls. *обійми бабусю*. Give your grandma a hug."

Shyly, almost fearfully, Clara stepped forward. She was soon wrapped in a many years-long, delayed embrace. Barely audible, Anna was saying something in her native language. Clara, of course, had no idea what was said.

That her own daughter had robbed her parents of the pleasure of grandparenting was close to the unforgivable sin in Anna's eyes. But none of that would be mentioned here today.

Clara submitted to the embrace for a few seconds, before finally giving in and returning the hug, squeezing harder than Anna was, if that was possible. Anna, ignoring the other two girls for a moment, looked up into the taller Clara's eyes and said, "My dear, beautiful Clara. How I remember you and your lovely smile. And how I've missed you. There is so much I want to know but first, these sisters of yours."

She released Clara only reluctantly and turned to the younger girls. She hugged first Becky and then Abigail, telling them, as she had with Clara, how much she had missed them and that she had never failed to pray for them, day by day. "Your grandfather and me. We prayed together every day for you. That God would care for you and, one day, bring you back to us. And here you are. All grown up and beautiful. *всі виросли і красиві.* Thank you for coming to see two old people."

Nick, never finding it easy to hug people, couldn't resist Clara's silent embrace, and finally returned it with his own equally silent welcome. The other girls initiated hugs in turn and received a welcoming squeeze.

When Aaron acknowledged that they had not eaten lunch on the trip north, Anna ushered them all into her kitchen, the very center of her universe. Within a matter of minutes, as the men sipped on a cup of coffee each, Anna had dug into her fridge and brought out a selection of prepared treats, ready for the stove and her loving care. Soon, the pungent aroma of spicy homemade cabbage rolls and frying sausage and onions filled the room. Shyly, the girls looked at one another, not recognizing the odors or the cabbage rolls. And the frying ковбаса sausage, nearly brought tears to their eyes.

Aaron, watching on, grinned and said, "You'll love it all, ladies. I still miss it after all these years. Had to learn how to put all that together myself, I missed it so. I'll make it for you at home one of these days."

He turned to Nick. "Nick, how about if you show me around the farm while the lunch is being prepared. I'd benefit from stretching my legs for a few minutes."

As they were reaching for their hats, Anna called out, "Twenty minutes. Or we eat without you."

Aaron knew she had never once eaten without her husband at table unless he was dealing with some emergency on the farm. Even then she was more likely to put the meal in the warming oven on the old wood stove and wait for him.

Walking away from the house, Aaron asked, "How has it really been with you, Nick?"

Nick, as if his thoughts had been bottled up too long, was ready to share feelings that would have remained stoically secret not many years before.

"I still had a good line of machinery, but my old body wouldn't obey my commands any longer. I had to give it up. I kept just the one small hay field, foolishly telling myself that I may buy a few head, just to have some animals to watch. I enjoy seeing a field of grazing cattle, even when there's no profit in them. But that's not going to happen either. We're old and alone, Aaron. Our own two boys didn't want to farm. We held on hoping you and...

"But that's not ever going to happen either is it?"

Aaron found the words as difficult to speak as Nick did to hear them.

"No, Nick. That's never going to happen."

The melancholy of the moment drove the men into silence for a short while. Nick finally waved his arm in the general direction of the chicken coop, the machinery shed, the barn, the granaries.

"All empty now, Aaron. We even buy our eggs in town. Sometimes I think of the work we did in those buildings and on this land and I'm sad that nothing long term or lasting came out of it. But we had a good living from the farm and a good family life. Perhaps that's enough."

"You were a good farmer, Nick. I don't ever re-member you making many mistakes, in the crops you planted or the livestock you raised."

Nick said nothing audibly, but the thought flashed through his mind, *Well, I must have made some mistakes with my beautiful daughter.*

He turned and asked, "How did you find the girls, Aaron?"

"I didn't. They found me. I've never asked them for the full story, thinking it might be best to let it lay. You can ask them about their mother at your own discretion. I've not asked, and they have cho-sen not to talk about the matter. I've bought a small acreage with all the old farm buildings, including a big house. We're close enough to town to enjoy a bit of both lifestyles. The girls seem to be settled in and enjoying the stability. I say nothing of the past, hoping they'll be satisfied with what we now have, till they're grown."

As Nick let that all soak in, the two men strolled past the barn, with Aaron taking note of a large stack of baled hay, some reasonably fresh, some showing the grey of age. He stopped in his tracks.

"Why the haystack, Nick?"

Nick made a sound that may have been a quickly released breath or may have been an admission of foolishness, like an audible grin.

"Just the whim of a foolish old man. Cattle again. Of all the things we let go of on the farm, I had the most trouble giving up on the cattle. The hay was to be ready for when that front field would again hold a small herd. Foolishness."

"Hay is selling well right now Nick. If that older stuff isn't molding it could easily be sold off."

"I've thought of it. But some days I'm just too tired to get to it. There are days I don't even leave the house. The hay is out here behind the barn where I can't see it. Out of sight out of mind, I suppose. Should be saleable though. The last time I opened an older bale the feed was still good."

"The ranch I work on may have an interest, Nick. Put a price on it and an estimate of the number of bales. I'll make a call."

Nick was noncommittal on the hay but both men knew they had best get back to the house for lunch.

As the sausage and cabbage roll laden serving plates were passed around, the girls were polite, but hesitant. Following Clara's lead, they each took one cabbage roll and a couple of slices of the pungent sausage, along with a small scoop of fried onions. They each helped themselves to some mashed potatoes. They were on solid ground there. But when the bowl of thick cream arrived from the fridge, they looked on in wonder as their grandfather spooned a heaping portion onto his perogies, another dish they had no knowledge of. The excess cream warmed and thinned as it lay on the hot perogies, running over onto the sliced sausage.

Aaron grinned at the girls as he loaded his plate. The grandparents pretended they hadn't seen the girls' hesitancy.

Becky was the first to cut off a small piece of sausage and lift it to her mouth. She took a bite, chewed once, and couldn't hold back a gasp. She wrinkled her lips and nose. Tears formed in her eyes. She looked at her father, desperate for help or advice. Aaron burst out laughing.

Finally, Anna could no longer pretend she hadn't seen. She laid her fork on the edge of her plate and said, "Your Mama, she has forgotten the old ways, maybe, ya?"

Clara, who had learned something of diplomacy and politeness, somewhere along the line, answered, "She's more into prepared and packaged foods. You might say we have a few things yet to learn if we're going to stay around farmers and ranchers."

Nick pointed at the serving plates with his fork and said, "You can't buy such as this in a package at the store."

Abby was thinking, *And it's a good thing you can't.*

It took a while, but the girls worked their way, tentative bite after tentative bite, through the meal, and surprised the adults when each took a small second helping. Aaron thought to tease them a bit but stayed silent when he reconsidered.

The girls spent most of the afternoon with their grandmother, looking at family photos, admiring examples of childish embroidery and other handi-work, and wondering at a small piece of cross stitch their mother had done as a young girl. Anna had saved it all. She had also saved a cross-stitch piece she had especially made herself, for each girl. Anna lovingly lifted them out of the old gilt decorated five-pound chocolate box she had stored them in. One by one she held them out before the girl they had been made for. With each girl's name plainly lettered into the art piece, there was no need for words or explanations.

They were told about their two uncles and aunts who lived in the city, several hours' travel away, and shown photos of their cousins.

They even learned that Ukrainian for Grand-mother was, Baba, and that it pleased Anna to hear the word directed her way. By evening, after anoth-er large meal that would not fit easily into anyone's idea of healthy eating, they were ready to settle down in the long unused upstairs bedrooms.

As Aaron visited with the old folks after the girls went to bed, he asked, "Where are the boys now?"

Nick answered, "Olek, he is teaching at the university. And Anton, he teaches too, at the trade school. They don't leave the big city very often."

Aaron knew there was a message of sadness and loneliness in the statement. The old folks were hunkered down in their worn-out farmhouse while their children, all three of them, more or less ignored them. It was a story that could be repeated thousands of times.

They stayed until mid-morning the next day. Aaron was waiting to hear back from Danny. When he finally called, confirming the purchase of the old hay, Aaron explained the payment and the hauling plan to Nick, and they were ready to leave. The loving welcome and the insistence that they come again soon, relieved Aaron of a burden of guilt he had carried for years.

Except for the photo albums and Anna's recollections of childhood memories, no mention was made of Cookie.

With much waving and a single honk on the horn, Clara, drove out of the Chernenko farmyard and onto the county road. Again, following her father's directions, she drove to Adam's farm. As on Aaron's last visit, Adam was working in the corral, this time with cattle, while Francie welcomed the visitors. There were a few awkward moments when Adam walked up to the house and saw Aaron. Aaron got the first words in.

"I know, Adam. Don't say it. We've been visiting Nick and Anna. I thought it was time they met their granddaughters. We're on our way home now. Thought it might be time the girls met their uncle and aunt too."

Francie, who had been introduced to the girls before Adam arrived, named them off to their uncle. Adam, never really a happy person, man nor boy, either one, smiled and welcomed the girls. He even went so far as to join them as they visited on the porch while Francie was putting a lunch together. But Aaron and Adam were both conscious of the tension in the air. It wasn't easy to ignore, but for the sake of the girls, both managed to be civil.

Driving away after lunch, with the question being asked about Adam's anger, Aaron had little choice but to explain a bit about his failures, and the difficulties arising from them. He kept the story short, trying not to point a finger at Cookie. But when Clara said, "It doesn't justify everything you've just told us about your past, but you must have loved Mom very much."

With those words still hanging in the air he nearly came apart. The girls didn't question his silence.

Aaron wasn't asleep, but he had his eyes closed with his head leaning on the seat headrest. They were still nearly two hours from home. When a lightning bolt flared through the car windows, followed almost immediately by a crash of thunder, he sat up so quickly he bumped his head on the top of the passenger's door window frame. When the clouds dropped a pour of rain, he leaned into the windshield, looking off to all directions. Everywhere he could see, the sky was black with storm clouds. The lightning display and the thunder were only for light and sound effects, but the torrent of rain was much more. It was life itself, pouring onto a parched land.

"It's raining," he said.

Abby, always ready to help, laughed and said, "What was your first clue, Dad?"

Aaron didn't bother with an answer.

Chapter 24

Aaron and the girls arrived back in the old farmyard in the pouring rain. The girls weren't altogether happy about getting wet, but Aaron felt like dancing in the newly forming mud.

"Is that a wonderful sight or not?"

"Ya, whatever," answered Abby, as she was running to the door.

Concerned about the cattle, Aaron rushed into the house and changed into work clothes as quickly as he could. As he was dashing through the back porch, he grabbed his old hat and a rain slicker. Within a couple of minutes, he had the unlicensed pickup running and heading towards the pasture gate. He opened the gate, drove through, and closed the gate again. He had been sorely tempted to leave the gate open, figuring the cattle were on the northwest quarter. But a lifetime of discipline had him getting even wetter than he already was as he closed and latched it.

Driving slowly across the hay land, he started seeing cattle where no cattle should be, including on the quarter section he was driving across. As questions formed in his mind, he carefully steered around a small bunch of grazing yearlings and pointed the truck to the next gate. The heavy rain prevented him seeing for any distance, but he saw hazy forms through the downpour that were probably cattle. These were in the northeast quarter. They shouldn't be there either. Getting close to the next fence line, he could see wires down. He drove through, forgetting about the gate, and headed for the main gate, beside the wellhead. There he saw Danny's truck sitting on the old driveway, outside the pasture. He thought at first that Danny would be in the cab, keeping dry, but a closer look showed him Danny, on foot, with no rain slicker, and soaked through, trying to hold a small bunch of yearlings in the corner, behind the wellhead enclosure.

With questions forming in his mind, Aaron drove as close as he felt was wise, and stopped. He stepped out and hurried to where Danny was hazing the cattle into the corner.

"What's up, boss?" he had to shout to be heard.

"Got some broken wire. A few of these steers got themselves cut up pretty bad. Took a while, and some walking, and a bit of running to catch up to them, but I finally got them up here. Don't want them to get away again. If ever I needed a horse, this might be the time.

"I had Clarence call the vet. Hopefully he's on his way. Don't know what he can do though, as wet as these animals' hides are."

"What happened?"

"When the black clouds started rolling in, I jumped in the truck and got over here. These aren't wild Texas longhorns just captured out of the brush, but they're not quite tame either. And they're young. With as little rain as we've had this summer it's probable they've never been through a thunderstorm before. I just got here when the first flash of lightning, and then the thunder, set them to running.

"You never could have believed how six hundred heads can come up at the same time and how quickly these ignorant beasts took off running in all directions. They had no idea where they were going, or why, of course, it was just panic. Fortunately, they ran mostly south and east instead of breaking out onto the road allowance or onto the neighbor's land. If they'd run the other way, they could be all over the country by now. Lead animals ran through those wires as if they didn't exist. Old wire. Rusted up some. But I thought it would hold. It did too, right up until now. But these few lead steers were the ones that broke out. Got tore up pretty bad. Could be others out there too that I didn't find."

Aaron glanced through the downpour to see how bad the wire cuts were. He could see serious gashes, with a few folds of torn hide hanging loose. Blood, quickly washed away by the rain, was running down the legs on three or four of the injured animals.

"What about the other herd?"

"Bo has them in the bush quarter. They should be alright."

"What can I do?"

"You're wet already. A little more wet goes with the big pay. You can either stay here and try to hold this bunch or you can drive over to the barn and saddle two horses, grab a couple of ropes and get back over here just as quick as you can. I want to try to get these under cover before the vet arrives. I figure to somehow drive them over to the D-F."

"I'll stay," hollered Aaron. "You go. Bring Bo if he's up at the buildings. And have Ace come over to open the gates and close them once we're through. Neither man will be needed in the bush. And we don't have to take these across the road. We can use my barn."

Wordlessly, Danny ran to Aaron's truck and drove away. It was a full half hour, or more, before he returned, riding Toby and leading Boots, running as fast as he dared on the rain-slick grass. He stopped long enough to ask one of the girls to phone the vet to tell him they would be at the old Kingsbury place.

Ace drove the truck back over. There had been no sign of Bo at the barn. Together Danny and Aaron, neither with much herding experience, either on foot or horseback, eased the crippled animals towards the old Kingsbury place. It was near enough a full mile in distance but seemed like a lot longer in time, as the reluctant calves required prodding and encouragement each step of the way.

As if they were being led, a bunch of yearlings followed across the hay meadow. Riding through the gate, Aaron nodded, pointed his thumb over his shoulder and hollered at Ace, "Don't let any others out."

The two men then pushed ahead, helping Danny direct the cut-up calves through the open barn door.

Aaron left the injured animals with Danny and Ace and rode back out. For the next hour, in the cloud dimmed afternoon, he circulated through the scattered herd without finding more than a scratch or two. Those small injuries would heal without the veterinarian's help.

When he got back to the barn, the vet was busy with needle and thread, and disinfectant. The handsome young man was commenting on the damage barb wire could inflict when Clara, who was showing all the signs of understanding the needs of working people, men or women both, influenced, her father was sure, by her experiences working in the feed store, brought out a big pot of fresh, hot coffee. Her work put her into contact with farmers and ranchers, big and small. She seemed to learn a bit more each day. The vet grinned as he looked at the welcome coffee, and then at Clara.

"If I wasn't already a married man I might come calling."

Glancing at the handsome vet and feeling a bit of the tenor of his comment, she answered, "If you weren't already a married man, I might be home when you got here."

Aaron and Danny studiously avoided looking at either of them.

The afternoon had been dull and dreary under the black storm clouds. The men were rain-soaked beyond telling. The riders were exhausted and the horses, more so. But the work was done, and the vet had headed to his next call. The calves were secured in an old stall, the opening nailed shut with some scrap wood Aaron found in the corner of the barn.

Aaron led his horse out of the rain and into the barn. As he reached for the cinch strap to begin unsaddling him, Danny looking on, said, "Wait, Aaron. I'll be taking them over to my place where I can rub them down and feed them some oats. Then they might like to spend the night inside. I'll have you and Ace juggle trucks so's we end up with one here and one at my place. Then you can call it a day. You and Ace, both."

Danny was over an hour getting the horses looked after while the other men got the two trucks sorted out and back to where they would be usable the next morning. With the horses looked after, Danny stripped off on the porch, leaving his soaked clothing in a pile on the floor, and went for a long, hot shower. He warmed up some leftovers, made a fresh pot of coffee, banked the fire in the wood stove, wrapped himself in warm clothing and a blanket, and took his coffee onto the porch. There he pulled his chair further under the roof, away from any chance of rain, took his seat and spent an hour watching the rain fall and thanking the Lord for His goodness.

Chapter 25

The rain had come at the end of the third week of July. By the next day the pastures were already looking better. Or perhaps that was just wishful thinking. Danny told the men to slack off a bit after the brutal day and evening getting the herd straightened out, plus another wet morning putting the fences together with temporary fixes, and the injured animals cared for.

A few days later, Aaron was at the farm supply store picking up a few things. A small gathering of farmers and ranchers were huddled around the coffee pot that was never allowed to drain dry. Supervising the coffee counter was one of Clara's assigned tasks. Coffee and visiting were long time features of the store.

"Good to see the rain," said one boisterous fella, "But too late for a crop. Hay or grain, either one."

That started a rundown of opinions and counter opinions among the gathering. Aaron wanted no part of the discussion. The rain looked good to him, no matter what the date was.

After two days of pouring rain, followed by one of intermittent drizzles, the skies cleared, and the sun warmed the land again. The year was too far advanced to hope the moisture would develop the neighboring farmers' stunted growth into meaningful cash crops, but the grass took on new life. With the long hours of rain, the moisture had time to soak down to root level. The refreshed pastures gave new and rising hope to Danny. And it just may have moved the purchase of the second batch of yearlings from the questionable gamble side of the ledger to the possible profit side.

Spring and summer, so far, had been a long series of busy days. There were a couple of projects that Danny had been putting off. Thinking it was time to address at least one of them, he called Ace over to the barn.

"Ace, the way you and Aaron put that loading chute together made me think that might not be the first time you had a hammer and saw in your hands."

"Danny, I fell in love with wood working in eighth grade shop class. Never got over that first love of tools and wood and their many uses. Why? Do you have something here that needs attention?"

Danny glanced around at the inside of the old building and said, "Well you might say the whole place needs attention. But I have a smaller project in mind than rebuilding the barn. Come, I'll show you."

They walked the length of the barn's center aisle.

The stalls, other than the ones near the big front doors, which were taken up for the care of the horses, were all filled with farm machinery, tucked away out of the weather, waiting their turn to be needed.

Danny and Ace stopped in front of a canvas covered object, one of two that were sitting side by side. Danny reached down and lifted one corner of the big tarpaulin, indicating with a nod of his head that Ace should grab the other corner. The two men began carefully removing the cover, folding the canvas back as they lifted. When the cover was clear of the item it was protecting, and set aside, folded over a stall partition, a beautiful fringed top surrey buggy was exposed. The men stood in silence admiring the thing.

Finally, Danny asked, "Well, what do you think?"

Ace was a moment in answering before saying, "Magnificent. Outstanding. Where did you get such a thing? It must be a century old. I've seen pictures but never dreamed..."

"Well, it's old but I doubt if it's quite that old. Here. Lift this other canvas cover."

When that canvas was removed and folded over the stall partition, beside the first cover, a dual seat, horse drawn cutter sleigh lay uncovered. The two sets of shafts were standing upright beside the cutter, leaning against the outside wall. Ace caught his breath again.

Danny explained, "When I purchased the Kingsbury place, across the road, the family took what they wanted and walked away, leaving the rest behind. These two pieces were in the barn loft, kept dry and cared for over how many years, I can't guess. I had a dickens of a time getting them down without damaging them. After a couple of false starts, I finally thought to re-rope the old hay sling and lower them down, using the strength of the small tractor to slow their descent. I knew the weight would be too much for me alone. I lowered them right into the box of the grain truck and heaved a great sigh of relief when they settled back down on the truck's floor. All it cost me was a couple hundred feet of rope, which I still have for other uses.

"I think they're both in pretty good shape, but I'm hoping to get them worked over; clean and re-grease the hubs and soak the wheels in the cattle tank to tighten the spokes into the hubs and swell the wooden rim against the iron tire. Tighten whatever else needs tightening, replace any rotting wood, scrape off any peeling paint. Well, you know the drill, I'm sure. We'll complete the job with a couple of coats of weather resistant black lacquer paint. Maybe find a small piece of carpet for the floor. See what can be done with the leather seats. Replace the ragged fringe. I don't think that old one can be salvaged. Could you find any interest in that project?"

"Interest? Why, man, I'd have flown out here from down east just for the chance to work on these beauties. I'd need some tools and a space to work."

"The ranch budget is getting pretty stressed but there's room for a few tools, as long as you spend as carefully as if it was your own money. And you can work right here. We can string a line for power. Put up enough lighting so you can see what you're doing."

"With the grass getting another lease on life after the rain, the work in the fields will ease off, you can put full time into this. If you're needed at all in the field, it should only be for a day or two. When you get to the painting stage, we'll move over to the garage. If you run some water over the concrete floor, that should control the dust.

"We can roll the buggy out now if you want to start on that. We'd have to carry the cutter, but it's not heavy. We'll leave it till later anyway."

Ace was all smiles as he said, "I'll get right on the buggy. It's summer. You never know, you might even get to take it out before fall shuts the country down."

"That's fine Ace. And I've been meaning to tell you. You're on ranch wages now. That won't match your big city income but it's how we roll out here. And, by the way, I also dragged over two larger wagons. One is a democrat, the other is a larger freight or grain wagon. They're in that other shed. We'll get these done before we address the others."

Wordlessly, the much-subdued Ace just nodded. With his eyes firmly on the task before him he didn't notice when Danny turned and walked away.

Danny said nothing, but he was thinking how much Ace, or Phillip as he was named at birth, had changed during his months in the west.

Danny drove to the cabin after a morning of re-wiring broken fences. As a reward for his work, he had several tears in the sleeves of his shirt, a scratch across his cheek where a length of wire had repelled all efforts to straighten it out, blue jeans that would never look new again, and a deep thankfulness for solid leather gloves.

Syl, Maria and Christie, from the rental house, were sitting on the cabin porch. Conversation stopped when he approached. He studied the three and knew something was up.

Maria laughed and said, "Why, Danny, you look like you just returned from the wars. Judging by looks I'm not sure if you won or lost."

Danny chose to ignore the comment. Instead, he said, "When I see that look on one of your faces, I'm suspicious. When I see all three of you trying to look innocent, all doubt is lifted. You've got something up your sleeves that's going to cost me either time and work, or money. Do I want to know what it is, or am I better off in the dark?"

Maria said, "Why, Mr. Framer, how you do go on."

Danny headed for the door, saying, "Alright, if it doesn't involve me, I'll get on with what I'm doing."

Syl said, "You wash up. Lunch is done and in the oven. We can eat in just a few minutes. We're about wrapped up here anyway and these ladies must have something more important to do, somewhere else, so here it is. We've decided the picnic last summer was such fun that we should do it again. and other than our share of the food costs, all it will cost the D-F is to give some time off to whosever is working that day."

Danny nodded, and responded, "Just so I don't have to do the planning. You ladies set it up and tell me where and when."

With that he entered the house. When he came back, Maria and Christie were gone.

Syl put her old saddle on Boots and rode out to where Bo was working. She waved him to the fence line, away from the cattle, before trying to talk.

"Bo, we're going to have a ranch picnic. We did the same last summer and it was great fun. I'd like if you and your family would plan on attending. One week from Saturday. There's a nice little park just down the road a piece, with tables and a fire pit. A couple of swings for the kids. Everyone went last year, even the two cowboys we had on the pay-roll at that time. Every horse on the ranch was put into service. The kids had a wonderful time riding. And the cowboys had fun teaching them the simple beginnings of horsemanship. The kids are all older and better riders now and there's a few trails through the bush they could explore if an adult stays with them. You could fit into that wherever you feel comfortable.

"Can we plan on you being there?"

Bo was taken aback by the invitation, and the idea that he was being invited into a social situation. With the entire community knowing about his history of rustling and the months in prison, he doubted if he or his family would ever be forgiven, and again welcomed into the society of the small city and surrounding ranching community. They had only stayed in the area because of their extended family.

"Are you sure, Syl? You know how folks will talk. Gossip can be a deadly thing. I don't want to hurt you and Danny any more than I already have."

"We're not the least bit concerned about the talk of the busybodies. You just plan on being there, you and your family. There's nothing for you to bring except a couple of camp chairs if you have any. Everything else will be supplied. It's a workday for you so you'll already be here and have a horse saddled. You can ride down from here with a couple of the kids if you felt like it. You'd make friends for life with them."

Again, Bo said, "If you're sure."

"We're sure. I'll get you the time when we're closer to the date."

Sitting at dinner a couple of days after being informed about the picnic, Danny looked at Syl and said, "That was a fun time last year. The picnic, I mean. What would you think if we simply make it a ranch picnic? Maybe do it every summer. The others could volunteer, of course, help the kids with riding or games and whatever. Have some input into the planning. But the D-F will pick up the costs and purchase the food and drinks or anything else you decide is needed."

Syl laid down her fork, placed her elbows on the tabletop and looked at her husband.

"Danny Framer. That's a marvelous idea. I have three days off coming after tomorrow. I'll make a list and do all the shopping. We'll have a good time, and everyone will know they are our welcome guests. Marvelous. And yes, we could make it an annual event."

Danny, whose mind had already turned from the picnic and reverted back to ranch issues, didn't feel any further discussion was required.

When Aaron heard about the picnic the next day, he came over to the cabin in the evening, when he knew Syl would be home after working a day shift.

"That picnic idea is great. Now, I'm embarrassed that you didn't ask me to do the cooking. But I'll overlook that slight, knowing it was simply an oversight. You still have time and opportunity to redeem yourselves."

Danny and Syl were silent for a moment and then Danny burst into laughter.

"Why, old buddy, I was afraid you'd forgotten all you ever knew about cooking and would be ashamed to admit it. We simply thought to ease you out of that kind of embarrassment. But now that you've come forward with the idea, I'm sure Syl and the other ladies will back off and let you do your best. They can always jump back in if you get yourself into trouble."

Aaron went inside and helped himself to a cup of coffee. When he came back out, he said, "Syl, I truly don't know what you see in this man."

"Some days I wonder too, but then I always seem to find some redeeming quality."

Danny took no further interest in the conversation, knowing that, in reality, the decisions were already made. Aaron and Syl would plan the menu and Aaron would do the cooking. And all of that was fine with Danny.

As if the previous conversation had never taken

place, the two men moved on to ranch matters. Syl went into the cabin to get the picnic shopping list. She returned and laid it on the wide, flat, wooden arm of Aaron's chair. Without breaking his conversation with Danny, he pulled a pencil out of his pocket and made a few notes on the list. Without comment he passed it back to Syl, who read it and nodded, with a smile.

Chapter 26

Aaron had never phoned Belle before. He was nervous, and his fingers shook just a bit as he dialed the number. He had hung around the phone hoping the kids would go to their own rooms so he could talk in private. The two youngest did exactly that, but Clara sat at the other end of the table writing a letter. Aaron didn't ask who it was to. But with the evening fast dwindling into night, he couldn't wait any longer to make the call.

"Belle, Aaron here. Do you have a few minutes?"

"Sure. And if we talk long enough there's a chance the kids may finish washing the dishes and cleaning up the kitchen, and I won't have to help."

Aaron understood that she must be close enough to the kitchen sink that the kids would have no trouble hearing her. He could imagine them rolling their eyes back in their heads as they looked at each other.

"So, it almost sounds like I should call you every evening about this time if that's the side benefit for you."

Clara didn't lift her head, but she stopped writing for a moment and strained to turn her eyes up enough to look at her father.

"Well, perhaps not every evening."

"Alright. Here's what's happening. Danny and Syl are putting on a ranch sponsored picnic. There's not a lot of time. It's for Saturday, one week from tomorrow. Syl is doing the shopping and I've offered to look after the cooking. I'd like if you would help me. Can you see yourself doing that?"

"I might. Are we being invited? I mean the kids, too."

"Yes, of course. The folks in the rental house are coming, as they did last year, as well as Ace. Bo and his family are planning on attending. Syl's parents will be there. Danny is hoping his parents will drive down too. All the ranch horses will be put into service, and the kids can take turns riding. Danny or Bo, or perhaps Maria will work with the kids to teach them a bit and keep them safe."

"Sounds like fun. What's on the menu?"

"Mostly grill work. I have years of experience with grill and broiler work. Simple burgers and brisket, or whatever can be done on a grill and broiler. In the camps up north, of course, I had a full kitchen and menu, but we don't need that for a picnic.

"I called the rental shop in town. They have a big gas fired grill with a broiler attached. I have it reserved. The grill work is no problem. I'll just need some help in prep, and much of that will be done at home, the evening before. If you and the kids wanted to come out on Friday evening, we could have an easy dinner. Pizza perhaps. Then work on the picnic prep. We could do the potato salad and the Caesar salad and cut up the finger food. Have it all prepped and in the fridge, ready for morning.

"There'll be several pounds of fine ground hamburger to make into patties. I'll start slow cooking a big pot of savory beans the day before. Beans so mouth-watering that folks have been known to come to blows over who was to get the last few scoops in the pot. Might do up some biscuits. I have to think on that.

"Then, on Saturday, perhaps you could help with the grilling and the dishing out of the of the mouth-watering, 'done to perfection', culinary treats. I'll have my hands full with the brisket and the beans. How does that all sound? And, for further enticement, as a special reward, I'd like to take you out for a private dinner soon after."

Clara looked up and grinned at him. Aaron pretended he didn't see her.

There was a short, silent pause. Aaron made an attempt to cover his poor wording and his nervousness with a small laugh.

"Now, that didn't come out just exactly the way I intended."

The phone had gone so quiet, Aaron wondered if Belle had hung up. But she finally said, "I think I can see myself helping out with the picnic. The rest we will have to see about later. I am wondering though, who is to be the recipient of this reward you talk about?"

Aaron burst out laughing. "Why me, of course. Just being around you and the kids is a reward."

Clara cast him a despairing look.

After just a short break in the conversation he said, "Fair enough. I accept your conditions. Plan on being here at the house around six on Friday evening. We'll put the kids to work too. And thanks. We'll have fun. And the food will have them coming back for more. May have to cut a short stick to beat them off."

Aaron hung up the phone and sat back in his chair, looking off to the far wall, seeing nothing at all. Clara laid down her pen, folded her arms, with her elbows on the table, rested her chin in her open hands and said, "Smooth, Father. I do believe you could give lessons on winning over the fair maiden, nineteen thirties' style. Or maybe win over the scared to death widow, as the case may be."

"Write your letter."

They grinned at each other, and Aaron stepped outside to walk the property before full dark was upon them, as he did every evening.

The day of the picnic arrived with a warm, but not hot, welcoming sun. Ace had the buggy ready for the road, although not yet painted. He had soaked the old, dried-out wooden spoked wheels in the cattle trough, tightening up the steel rims. The axles were well lubed, and the wheels turned true and freely. After the shafts were attached, Ace took the position between them, as the horse would do, and pulled the rig across the yard. Ted was watching from his back porch.

"Pulls like a dream, Ted," hollered Ace. Ted waved his coffee mug in recognition and Ace pulled the buggy back into the barn.

Danny borrowed the single harness from the stables where he had rented the cutter, way back when he was courting Syl. Thinking back on that evening, drifting through the star lit snow, bundled up in blankets in the rented cutter, daring their first real kisses, seemed like an eternity ago. But in reality, the time could still be counted off in months.

He harnessed the horse and took a couple of quick spins around the ranch yard to confirm that his Toby horse would obey, and not run off with the unfamiliar clatter of iron rimmed wheels on grass and gravel, assaulting him from behind. When the horse acted like he'd been pulling a buggy all his life, Danny felt confident enough to try the half mile on Sugartown Road that would take Syl and himself to the picnic grounds.

On the morning of the picnic, Ted backed the .32 out of the garage and lowered the top. He and Christie and their two youngest children, would drive to the picnic in the convertible. Hal, his oldest, would ride the pony.

Bo's wife drove into the ranch yard with their two teenagers. Bo had just ridden back to the barn and was moving his saddle to his other horse. Syl came from the cabin when she saw the family drive up. Understanding the tenuous nature of the situation, she hurried out to greet them. Danny was still in the yard, fiddling with the buggy, and then the horse.

Bo walked from the barn. "Syl and Danny, this is Meg, my wife, and this is Bucky and Trish."

After that simple introduction Bo walked back to the barn while Syl led the others towards the garage where she introduced them to Ted and Christie, and their kids. Syl was greatly relieved when there were smiles and friendliness from Ted and Christie, to offset the deer-in-the-headlights look on Meg's face. The kids all appeared to be indifferent to the situation, perhaps because the Cormier kids were too young to have heard, or understood the stories, and Bo's kids because they had already heard the many cruel words at school and didn't much care anymore.

Bo's wife and children were already competent riders. Danny left the handling of the horses to them while he set out, somewhat nervously, in the buggy. Ted followed with the .32. The horses brought up the rear. Somewhere, Ted had found a large, orange triangle sign that he had hung from the rear of the .32.

Maria and Ace, driving out from town separately, would go directly to the picnic grounds.

Aaron and his girls had been there since early morning, preparing and broiling the brisket, although Aaron had basted and seared it the evening before, rubbing it liberally with salts and spices. Whereas the burgers took only a few minutes on the grill, the brisket would take hours for the meat to tenderize and the juices to flow. The salads made the evening before were packed on ice in sealed chests. The large porcelain pot of baked beans was sitting over low heat in a corner of the grill. Sweet onions had been sliced on a clean cutting board on the nearby oilcloth covered picnic table. Clara, and Becky, sharing the responsibilities, had both constantly wiped onion tears from their eyes. They had quit listening after the third time their father said, "Worth it all girls. Worth it all. You'll know come bye 'n' bye."

Belle, never having seen a brisket prepared before, was watching intently, while her kids were wandering down the pathways through the bush with Abby. They would show up again when they heard the horses arrive.

All eyes turned towards the road when Clara said, "Wow. Look at that."

Danny had just turned the buggy into the campgrounds. Ted and then the horses, were close behind. The work around the grill stopped as the group pulled to a halt a little way from the cooking area. The kids came bursting out of the bush trails hollering, "Can I go for a ride?"

Danny laughed and said, "One at a time."

Aaron hollered, "Keep those nags out of my kitchen."

Danny drove the rig a bit further away from the work area. He was not comfortable enough with the horse yet to get down himself to help Syl out of the buggy, but she managed just fine on her own. Staying within the campground area, he took the kids, one at a time for a buggy ride. Bo was then kept busy arranging a fair way to spread the kids among the available horse, as the kids clamored for attention. Glancing over, Syl saw a smile on his face. The first she had seen. While he was doing that, first Ace and then Maria, arrived from town. The introductions to Bo's family were quick, and Maria was sent off immediately to help the girls with the horses. Ace spread out a camp chair and settled in.

Danny's parents arrived after an early start, and a five-hour drive. Danny and Syl dropped what they were doing and walked across to where they had parked. After sincere greetings Danny said, "Come over to the table. I'll introduce you around and if I asked with just the correct tone of voice, I'm betting Syl would get you each a cup of coffee."

As lunch time closed in on the group, the smell of cooking brisket, to be followed quickly by mountains of red chili-laced sweet onions grilling in a pool of butter, and the grilling burgers, sizzling on the hot steel top, had the adults hovering close to the picnic tables. Aaron had put a large pot of coffee over a wood fire, earlier. Belle now passed it around. The pot was soon empty. She filled it again from the hand pump that was mounted over a shallow, drilled well and put on a fresh pot.

A tub of ice cold drinks was put out for the kids along with a large plastic bowl of chips, covered with a cloth to keep unwanted bugs at bay.

Sensing that lunch was nearly ready, the kids, led by Maria, tied their horses to shrubs or branches a good distance from the eating area.

Knowing what was to come, with the horses and games, Aaron had brought a bar of soap and a couple of towels. He laid them out on a small, rough board table someone had built beside the pump. When a couple of kids said they weren't really in need of a wash, Aaron answered, "Well then, I guess you're not really in need of one of these burgers either."

The wash-up was completed in no time at all, with one kid washing while another manned the pump.

Looking on but saying nothing, Danny was amazed and yet pleased at how easily Belle and her two kids were fitting in with the group. And for the group itself, the acceptance of Bo and his family was a sign of Christian maturity.

Right before they were ready to eat, another car pulled into the picnic grounds. Syl's parents stepped out and made their way to the tables. Syl raised her voice enough to be heard by all. "Hey, people, these are my folks. Mr. and Mrs. Mabry. We'll do the introductions later. Right now, we need to deal with this food."

As BBQ Barnes had demonstrated in front of Aaron so many times, Aaron himself now banged the side of his big flipper on the steel of the grill to get everyone's attention, and, at the top of his voice said, "Ol' BBQ Barnes himself has nothing at all on this here fine repast prepared for you poor suffering folks. Suffering, I say, because you've never before tasted anything in your lives to match it."

He stopped there as he opened the broiler cover. Clouds of spicy, pungent steam, mixed with wood chip smoke and even more spices wafted over the eating area. Waving the smoke from his eyes with his hand, Aaron continued.

"You'll wonder all the rest of your days how you managed to get to the ages you're at now without you've enjoyed a taste of Aaron's and Belle's grilled delicacies and broiled brisket. Come one, come all, bring your clean hands and cleaner hearts and your hungry stomachs and line up here to the right. Just as soon as Danny, our host, says grace, we'll begin dishing up."

They paused while Danny prayed and then Aaron was half shouting again. "Mrs. Farley will be passing out the grilled wonders while ol' Aaron himself will slice up this wonderful brisket. Help yourselves to the salads and such as what's available here. Lots for everyone. And don't forget to get a big helping of these sweet onions, grilled to perfection and just waiting to bring satisfaction to palate and memory. And, if by chance, you forget to partake of this wonderful pot of beans, why, that's alright. That would leave all the more for me. C'mon now, food's ready."

"Does that include me or are y'all holding all that gift from the heavenlies for yourselves? Always kind of thought when the chips were down y'all would turn out to be just a bunch of city slickers, not attuned to our sharing country ways. It shames me to have to admit you as friends."

Everyone turned towards the shouted sounds.

Danny looked over and said, "I know that voice from somewhere. Can't quite place it right now."

There were several shouts of 'welcome', and Maria stepped to meet Box and put her arm around his waist. They walked together to the tables.

Syl said, "Welcome, Box. Some folks here you

need to meet but right now we're addressing this grill. We'll make the introductions after lunch."

At Aaron's insistence, Syl had purchased fresh hamburger rather than prepared patties. The evening before, Aaron and Belle had worked together to spice it, add finely chopped onions and just enough breadcrumbs and whipped egg to hold it together and add a bit of bulk. They then hand-formed the patties and stacked them between layers of wax paper, ready for morning and the hot grill. Strips of bacon were cut in half to make them fit in a hamburger bun better. With that, they were ready for the grilling portion of the picnic.

Under mostly Belle's directions, the girls had mixed the potato salad, using eggs and potatoes that Aaron had boiled up that afternoon.

Aaron enjoyed the work and the togetherness with Belle and her children. He hoped she felt much the same. And she hadn't come right out and said, 'no' to a two-person dinner date, so he found that encouraging.

The food was all Aaron had promised. The lunch was a huge success, and there wasn't a scrap left over. Maria and Box were soon saddled up, working side by side with Bo, as they led the kids along the bush trails which were longer, and went deeper into the parkland then any of them had known before. After riding for a while Maria turned to Box and said, "A person could get lost in here. I'm glad we didn't send the kids out alone."

Chapter 27

Reminiscing that evening, as they took in the last of the day's waning sunlight, resting on the cabin porch, Syl reached across the space between their two chairs and took Danny's hand. "That was a good day. Good in several respects. The food was truly great, and the kids enjoyed the wagon and convertible rides, as well as the trail rides through the bush. I think the rest of us enjoyed the visiting as much as anything else.

"Dad encouraged Aaron to dig out those old, typed manuscripts, telling him how much he enjoyed the two books. There is no doubt that pleased and, I hope, encouraged him to get back to his writing in a serious way.

"And Aaron and Belle seem to be really hitting it off.

"Maria says Box is going to hang around for a couple of days. She promised time for a visit before he leaves for home. and, although nothing was said, that came to my ears anyway, Box was friendly with Bo, although we all know how Box felt, back when the rustling was discovered. But the best, in my mind, was how Bo and Meg came to relax after a bit. I'm thinking they felt accepted. I admit the whole thing is really strange since it was Bo that rustled D-F stock, but there it is. We preach and talk about forgiveness, and then we were given an opportunity to truly practice it. Meg said this was the first time she had left the house, except for shopping, since the start of the deeply embarrassing incident. She was craving fellowship, and she found it there today. I'm hoping their kids felt welcome too."

Danny, as was often the case, found no words that needed to be spoken in reply. Syl carried on with her final thought on the topic.

"And surprise, surprise, when I asked Meg about their spiritual connections, she said neither her's nor Bo's families showed any particular beliefs, and she and Bo hadn't either, so far, in their marriage. I invited them to meet us at church in the morning. She hesitated, but didn't say no. I'll kind of hang close to the door to welcome them if they show up."

Danny said nothing for a moment, but he turned and looked at Syl, with a bit of a grin.

"It's amazing. I keep finding new reasons to be thankful for you and to keep you around a bit longer."

"I'm here for the long term, Buster."

On Monday morning Danny and Bo sat their saddles at the junction of the four quarters on the home place and discussed possibilities. Danny hadn't ridden the bush quarter for some time, but Bo had. He brought Danny up to date on the grass situation in that quarter. They could scan the other three quarters, in a general sense anyway, from where they were sitting.

"I'm thinking, Bo, that if we move them often enough, we may get through till fall on just the three quarters, leaving this hay land untouched. It isn't like spring's growth, but the rains have brought the grass on as much as we could expect, after the roots were starving for moisture for so long. We got the one small hay cut. But if we get more growth before freeze-up there may be winter graze, to offset our shortage of baled feed, if we end up having to hold these over and feed them out. As usual in this country, much would depend on the chinook winds. And at the least, we will have late fall graze.

"The market for feeders appears to be saturated. The feed lots bought light stuff early, falling for the temptation of stressfully low prices. We may have to take these all the way to finished weight and sell into the beef market next spring or summer."

Bo thought for a while and then responded, "We'll have to really watch the hay if the chinooks fail us. I thought I heard you say something about buying a few truckloads from Aaron's family, up north somewhere."

"I did buy it. But the fella that always takes the hay off this quarter was desperate. And he's been a good customer. We'll need him, come another year. I re-sold four semi loads to him. Got the trucking and the price out of him. And just a touch of profit for my trouble. That helped him and I don't think it will hurt the D-F. I counted our bales and did some calculations. With even a moderate winter we should be alright. Tight, with no room for waste, but alright.

"It's the bunch across the road that troubles me. The truth is, they'll either have to graze or they go to market. We'll keep a close eye on that situation. But your job will continue to be this bunch. You see anything I need to know, don't hold back."

With that agreed on, Danny traded his horse for the pickup truck and drove over to have much the same conversation with Aaron, about the six hundred animals under his care. Driving to the north ranch Danny was reflecting on the discussion about the bush quarter. What no one on the ranch knew, not even Syl, was that he had hidden the old pickup in the bush just off the county road and walked the trails leading to his fence line. He had done it three times during the summer. He had come to trust Bo, but the other rustler, plus the shirt tail rancher who bought the calves were out of jail and circulating somewhere. Danny wanted to be sure they hadn't circulated back to the scene of their original crime. He came away satisfied that if rustling was happening, it wasn't happening on the D-F. That didn't mean he wouldn't keep checking.

Box and Maria dropped in for coffee the evening before Box was to leave for home. They had set the date for a wedding. It was to be in late October, just a month and a bit away. Syl offered her congratulations. Danny nodded silently, holding back on his questions about Box truly giving up his noisy freedoms.

When the talk of weddings settled down, Danny changed the subject to horses. Maria slid her chair closer to Syl to continue the girl talk while Danny said, "Box, you did me a good turn last year when you picked out that pony for the kids to ride. You made a good choice. Now, I'm going to ask for another favor. Knowing you to be a better judge of horse flesh than me, I want you to find us two good, stable working geldings for the ranch. The K bar might have a couple they can part with, or you might know of some other source. Would you do that for me?"

Box, showing more enthusiasm than he had done with the wedding talk said, "Consider it done, old buddy. I've been working the kinks out of a small string down on the home place. Good looking animals. I could pretty much guarantee you good service out of four or five we have ready for use. Any two would serve you well. You could come get them if you wanted to see them, or I could trailer them up to you if you'll let me pick two out for you."

"Pick two out and bring them up when you're coming this way again. I expect that with so much to plan for the wedding you'll be here often."

Box kind of leaned back in his chair and studied his old friend. "I'd hate to come right out and accuse you of grinning at me, but I will say I'm suspicious. I'll let it go but you need to understand I keep a written record of these things. I'll put another tick alongside your name when I get back home. But you need to know that I'm having little input into the planning. Maria and her kin are doing it all. They're just going to tell me where and when and expect me to be there. And I will say, old buddy, that I picked that pattern up from observing you. Seems to me you let Syl put it all together except for that ride to the wedding in the old convertible, in the middle of winter yet. And here you are, just as married and settled down as you would have been if you were involved in all those tedious decisions."

When the two women turned their eyes his way, Danny felt he had said enough about both weddings and horses. It was time to go for the coffee pot again, his one long-proven escape from tight corners.

For his first real date with Belle, Aaron was in the process of trading trucks with Danny. He couldn't drive the unlicensed unit on the public roads, although he stretched that a bit when he drove from ranch to ranch. And he felt it would be inappropriate to drive up to Belle's house in a travel van. But Syl took a hand and said, "Here's the keys to my red truck. You can't pick Belle up in that filthy old pickup. I doubt if any self-respecting woman would step outside her door if she saw that rig sitting at the curb."

Danny looked up at Syl from where he sat in his personal 'office' on the cabin porch. As if he really didn't understand, although Syl knew he did, he said, "You rode in it often enough. Still do, for that matter."

"That was before it was loaded down with bits of old harness, two worn out hats, and several mismatched leather gloves, an old pair of rubber boots covered with who knows what, half a bale of scattered hay and several lumps of 'I don't want to know', scraped off your boot bottoms. And that's not even mentioning the dust perpetually in the air, and the grime that hasn't been cleaned from the windshield since the truck was built.

"And as for now, as an old married woman with a domineering husband, what's a girl to do?"

Danny waited a few seconds and then said, "Domineering?"

When Syl just grinned, Danny studied her for some time before saying, "Better take the red truck, Aaron," as if that solved the problem and eliminated the need to clean out the old truck.

When Aaron called the hotel dining room for a reservation, he had specifically asked for a private booth, if such existed. On their arrival, the young lady doing maître d' duty that evening directed them to an almost perfect place. They were able to see into the restaurant as well as enjoy the greenery of the garden outside the window, and yet it was as private as it could be in a public space.

They took their seats and made themselves comfortable. The server brought ice water and a crockery mug of black coffee for Aaron. In the camps where he cooked, Aaron had always insisted that coffee be served in crockery mugs, believing that porcelain enhanced the taste of the precious repast, while a glass mug tainted the taste, turning it bitter. He had never found a good reason to change that opinion. Belle was satisfied with the water.

The conversation began slowly and cautiously, dealing mostly with the happenings of the day. They scanned the menu as they talked. With his dinner choice made, Aaron slid his menu to the side of the table and bent his arms, placing his elbows on the table, and leaning his chin on his cupped hands. Within a half-minute Belle, too, slid her menu to the side. She sat primly and graciously, with her hands folded on her lap, beneath the table.

Aaron had thought for days about this moment. What would he talk about? Would he start the conversation or wait for Belle? He hoped the talk would be just serious enough to be meaningful but certainly not intense on a first date. How to accomplish that? And then the real question, 'was this, in fact, a date?'

Belle relieved Aaron of the need to sort it out.

"You've been alone for some years, Aaron. Where were you all that time and what were you doing?"

There it was. Right in front of him. The question that could carry the evening. It could carry the time to a happy conclusion or scare the lady off all together. And if he played it truthfully but well, there was a chance he could turn it back to her when the timing was right, asking for the same information. Proceed, but be cautious. That was his last thought before he said, "Well, I spent the first two years alone on the farm, slowly sliding further and further towards the inside of a bottle and feeling sorry for myself. The second year happened to coincide with a hail that took my crop. Being in a stupor, I hadn't taken out hail insurance. I had borrowed for a couple of pieces of new machinery and some operating capital. My brother, Adam, saw what was coming and managed to peel off two quarters for himself to add to his other two. Unfortunately, when Adam took his two quarters, that overbalanced my equity position and there was no recovery possible. The result was that I lost the farm my grandparents started, and my parents built up. Adam and Francie, his wife still live and farm there. The family downside is, unfortunately, that Adam barely talks to me. Doesn't want me around. I'm as sorry about that as almost anything else in my life. It's not right for brothers, but I feel I've done what I can do towards a reconciliation that Adam has no interest in.

"Anyway, to complete the tale of my failures, I also lost my publishing contract about that time. I had no idea where my wife and daughters were. Ex-wife I should say. She had managed a divorce by mail, somehow. I contacted her divorce lawyer and offered child support but never heard back.

"I didn't have to be a genius to figure out that the bottle wasn't going to bring back my family, my farm, or my publishing contract. A bit late, you might say, but I did finally figure it out. Obviously, I had to do something other than sink into a deeper hole and suffer in my thoughts. I saw an ad for beginner kitchen help in a construction camp up north. Isolated. Well paid. Dry. No booze. No drugs. Although I had never used drugs anyway. Inside, sheltered from the weather and the world. Warm kitchen to work in. Away from the northern winter. It was exactly what I needed, a place to hide and recover whatever was left of my life and my dignity. I called. They must have been desperate, to take a totally inexperienced man, but they hired me right away. They flew me into the camp, and I started out in a completely new life. Washing tables and scrubbing floors. Scouring pots and pans and endless mountains of dishes. I did that for several months. Dried out cold turkey along the way. Took the pledge. Not AA or anything like that. Just a pledge in my mind and heart. I was never going to allow myself to go that low again. And I never have.

"As time passed and I proved up, I was moved to salads and prep work. Within a year I was cooking under the direction of the chef. When that chef felt he'd been north long enough, he asked for his time, and I found myself with the responsibility of feeding three hundred men. I lost some sleep with worry, but I stuck it out. And, if you know anything about camps, you'll know that the happiness of the crew depends largely on the kitchen. I've heard of cooks desperate to escape in the dark of night just to save their skin when the crew got upset. I had no such happenings.

"Another camp offered me a higher wage, so I moved. Worked in three camps over six years. I met Danny in the second camp. He was just an eighteen-year-old kid doing labor work, driving trucks and making deliveries to the job sites and trying to write in the evenings. We kind of hit it off. I helped him a bit with the writing, but I didn't tell him about my own books that were, by then, off the market. I did tell him later on, but at the time I feared losing my publishing contract would show me up as another level of failure."

He sensed that he was still holding Belle's attention, so he carried on.

"Danny and I had a few other things in common too. Neither of us smoked or drank and neither ever went to town. Nor did either enjoy spending money. I wouldn't be surprised if Danny still has his first paycheck folded up in his wallet. There's no cost to living in camp and we both managed to save towards the future, although we had talked enough to know that neither of us knew what that future would look like.

"I finally tired of the north and the isolation. Drew my time and flew home. Adam didn't welcome me, so I stayed only the one night. Caught the bus to Calgary and went to the Stampede. There I smelled the wonderful spicy odor of well-prepared brisket and heard this sing-song voice of a man extolling his own virtues and the wonders of his food. Then he would break out in song before smacking the edge of his big flipper on his sheet-iron of his grill. Oh, he knew how to draw a crowd. He sure drew me. BBQ Barnes is the name he goes by. Big, jovial, wonderful black man. Not in the least inhibited about bragging up his grilling genius. We talked some as I was chewing my way through the most wonderful sandwich I had ever imagined. Long story short, he hired me. Took my cooking skills and expanded them into grill and broiler work.

"He travels the rodeo circuit. Outdoor all summer, indoor during the winter. I did the grill work for him for three years while he managed the broiler and the briskets. We served up thousands and thousands of burgers. Hot dogs for the kids. Tons of brisket went through his broiler, served up with home baked beans and sour dough biscuits done by his wife, with her own crew.

"BBQ is a thoughtful, devout Christian man. He's often been known to use his booming voice to get everyone's attention inside his big tent, drawing them away from the food lying before them, while announcing that it was time they all gave thanks. He would then shout out his thankfulness to the Lord, on behalf of himself and all those within ear shot. Which covered a considerable range, I might say. Then he might serenade the crowd of eaters with an old country song or a hymn. You never knew what's coming next. Great man, and a great woman who worked by his side."

Aaron paused and looked off towards the setting sun that was casting its final rays for the day, over the garden, before turning his eyes back to Belle.

"But I got lonesome for home again. I turned my van north and drove to the farm. Didn't last but an hour or so. Time for lunch was all. Adam may never get past his anger, but I no longer worry about it.

"So that's me. Pretty ugly in spots, but there it is."

Belle had paid careful attention as he spoke. Just as he finished the story their food arrived. Belle thanked the server and then turned to Aaron.

"I'm not sure it would be appropriate to include everyone in the restaurant the way your BBQ Barnes friend does, but perhaps you should give thanks for our food anyway."

Aaron's comfort zone normally closed up a bit before praying publicly, but he knew he couldn't refuse. He was sincere in the short prayer, but he still wondered if it was adequate. When Belle picked up her fork and proceeded to eat, he did the same, hoping he had found acceptance in the eyes of both the Lord and this lovely lady sitting across from him.

They ate in silence until perhaps half their dinners were consumed. Belle then lay down her fork, raised her head, and asked, "How did you find the girls again?"

Aaron gave a small laugh. "That's the wonderful part. I didn't. They found me. It's a story with several twists. It could easily be worked into a piece of fiction. I'll never write it, of course, it's too close to my heart, but someone could. I hadn't seen them or heard a word since they were little girls.

"But to explain that I have to go back to the camp. Danny had written two stories during his time in the camp. Well, one and a half really. He completed the second after he was settled into the Sugartown Road cabin as a bachelor rancher. He tried to keep what he called his hobby, secret. But Syl and her father backed him into a corner and got the truth out of him. That was before they were married. Turns our Syl's father had been the business administrator for a large publishing company. He read Danny's manuscript and liked it. After some massaging, editing, and re-typing, he sent it off to his old company, and it was accepted. All of that caused Danny to think of me and the writing we had done together. Thinking of what's happened since, I'm now glad I had finally told him about my books and the lost contract.

"He got what he thought was my phone number from our old employer. Turned out to be Adam's number. When he found out I wasn't there, Danny left his return number. It wasn't long after, that Clara phoned Adam, looking for me. Of course, he didn't know where I was, but he gave her Danny's number. They came for a short visit with Danny and Syl, got trapped in that snowstorm, met Syl's parents, who fell in love with the girls, and here they are."

Belle smiled and said, "I'm loving the story so far. How did all the pieces manage to fit together into the seemingly happy situation we see today?"

"When I arrived back at the farm, after leaving BBQ Barnes down south, I couldn't get past Adam's cold shoulder. But Francie gave me lunch and Danny's phone number. It's like a jigsaw puzzle that finally fell into place. And interestingly enough, it all centers around that little cabin on Sugartown Road.

"The girls like the town and have learned to love, and lean on, Danny and Syl. I've been saving money for years. When Danny didn't need that set of buildings across the road from the D-F, he cut off twenty acres and sold it to me. The old house had been remodeled and the water damage caused by freezing pipes during the power outage had been repaired. So, it was ready to move into. So far, the girls are fitting in nicely. I'm not naive, of course, given the ages of the girls they will be off on their own far too soon. But I'm determined to enjoy every minute until then. Sounds like a fiction story doesn't it. But it's true."

It both frightened and encouraged Aaron that Belle had asked so many questions and listened so carefully to his story. But her last question could mean just curiosity, and passing the time on a dinner date, or it may hold another meaning altogether.

"And have you not brought anyone special into your life over the years?"

He hadn't expected to talk about other women, but now that the question was on the table, he was glad that the answer was both simple and truthful.

"Never, Belle. I have to admit that my healing was slow, and I was cautious in the extreme. I have not so much as thought seriously about another woman until I met you. I hope that isn't too bold of me to say that. You might just as well know that I find you most attractive. Not just your obvious beauty. I feel I see something of beauty in your heart and I see it in your children and the way you interact with each other."

Again, afraid he had gone too far, or too fast Aaron chuckled a bit at his own embarrassment before saying, "And I had no intention at all of saying anything of the sort, or being that forward, when I invited you to join me this evening. Now, I'm hoping you don't take offence at my boldness."

Fortunately, he was still able to smile through

his nervousness after saying that, although he was wishing he could dig up a Danny type of disarming grin.

They ended what to Aaron was a wonderful evening with a short stroll along the river walkway. When Aaron made a brief mention of Belle's lonely years she answered, "Another time. We'll have to see. Perhaps another time."

Recognizing that so recently losing a mate to cancer was not an easy matter to deal with, Aaron smiled and nodded.

"Soon, I hope."

Chapter 28

Fall came right on schedule and the periodic rains continued. But now they carried a chilled feeling with them. The cattle were still putting on the pounds, but the market didn't loosen up for feeders. If Danny had second thoughts about wintering the herds, he said nothing about it.

Ace did a great job with the lacquer paint. The surrey was now a gleaming, gloss black. The spokes and wheel rims were lovingly hand painted a deep red. A small carpet Syl had found in a secondhand store, having an antique pattern on it, was cut and fit as a floor mat. The seat ended up being reupholstered when it was found there was no way to repair the original cracked and worn leather. Looking it all over, as Ace pulled it from the garage after painting, Danny and Syl were delighted.

Danny said, "All I can see now is that the fringe needs to be replaced. I don't think there's any hope for the old one. But I tell you what to do, Ace. There's a lady tailor down in town. She fit me up with a dust shield when I broke my leg last year and had to protect the cast. She acts as if she can do anything if it involves cloth and thread. Take that old piece of fringe down to her and see what she can do. I'm betting she'll find a way to fix this one or make us a new one. I can almost hear her saying, 'Ya, is goot, I'm fix.' And she will."

Turning to Syl he asked, "What do you think about colors, my love?"

"I'm good with a black band, with perhaps just a thin, red edging sewn along the bottom. If she could do gold tassels, that would set the whole job off."

A week later Ace had made a new friend of the tailor and the buggy was complete, gold tassels and all. After an appropriate number of photos were taken with the brushed and gleaming Toby in the shiny new harness Danny had purchased, with Danny and Syl taking turns at the reins, they rolled the buggy back into the barn stall and lovingly laid the tarpaulin over it. They hoped to get some use out of it the next summer, although judging by the few times the .32 was driven from its garage, the future use might be less than they hoped for.

Ace then pulled the cutter out and got to work. The instructions from Syl were to paint the box bright emerald-green with maroon fabric upholstery on the seats.

The third week of September, the early morning fall chill was a definite warning that winter was gearing itself up, back in those mountain valleys, just ready to pounce onto the flat land at the earliest wind driven opportunity. Giving way to the cool mornings, and somewhat abandoning their much-loved porch, Danny and Syl were taking breakfast inside, at the kitchen table when the phone rang. Syl looked on as Danny picked it up. They had just finished eating.

"Danny. Sol here. Got time to talk?"

"I could set a few minutes aside, Sol. What's happening?"

"I'm wondering if you want to sell some animals. I've got a new client and he's anxious to purchase."

Danny, knowing Sol was both a good broker and a wise businessman, needed to be careful. He trusted Sol but he trusted his innate caution more.

"You talk. I'll listen."

"Alright. The thing is, a big grain farmer down in the dry country named the summer for a total loss earlier than most of his neighbors did. Before his green grain stems started turning to straw, he took it all off as silage. He thought to sell the silage to other feeders this fall, but then he started asking himself why he didn't feed it himself. So, he and a couple of adult sons got busy and put up some corrals and feed pens and now they're in the market for yearlings. He'll take all you've got if you want to sell."

"What's he offering?"

"He'll offer market. I'm sure you heard the quotes at noon yesterday. He'll go with that."

"I'm sure he would Sol. But perhaps you also heard the end of that report. The price was followed by 'no feeders on offer'. I'm guessing that means the market is mostly settled for the winter. Now here's my deal. I'm going to keep the original herd. But the second bunch you got me is available. That's just over six hundred head. He needs to come up from yesterday's quote and understand that the price is at my farm gate. He does the trucking. We weigh them out here. I'll hold them off water overnight and weigh them as they're loading onto the truck. He'd be welcome to send a man to check the weights.

"He puts an irrevocable letter of credit into my lawyer's hands before we start. He releases the full purchase price the same hour the last load leaves here, allowing just enough time for both of us to calculate the weights and the end price. With that, he's in the finished beef business."

"He'll go with it. I don't know how much he'll bump the price, but I'll call him right now. Don't go anywhere. I'll be right back to you."

Danny set the phone down and looked at Syl, who had listened carefully to Danny's half of the conversation.

"Solves a problem for us, Syl."

"Yes, it does. But that isn't what I was thinking."

When Syl said no more for longer than Danny could wait, he asked, "And what exactly, my dear, were you thinking?"

Through a sly and loving grin, she answered, "Oh. I was just thinking how comfortable you have become with all of this. If we had a recording of you handling calls like that a year ago, I think you'd be amazed at the difference. It's a good difference, mind you."

Danny chose not to discuss the matter, so he

changed the subject.

"I see that roll of house drawings sitting out. I noticed it last evening and meant to ask but forgot. Are you thinking about it again?"

"Well, it was just a pipe dream for now. I knew we couldn't build until we got clear of some cattle, so I was just looking the sketch over and dreaming a bit."

"If Sol calls back with a deal perhaps you can realize on your dream."

"Perhaps."

Danny had the feeling that there was something not being said. That wasn't like Syl, and he wasn't sure how to proceed. Instead, he suggested they put on warm coats and have their second cups of coffee on the porch. He would take the phone out and wait for Sol.

They were no sooner settled in their chairs on the porch when Sol called.

"Up a nickel and take them all with your conditions met."

"Come get them. I'll see if the scale is available. We can be ready day after tomorrow."

"Done. You still using the same lawyer, Danny? Can I give him that name and address?"

"Same. No changes."

"Thanks, Danny."

Danny gently rested the phone in the cradle and looked at Syl. She returned the look with the comment, "There's sure a lot of money changing hands with a phone call and a promise."

Danny accepted that statement and turned his mind back to the house.

"We can build any time you wish, my love."

Again, Syl seemed to be a bit dreamy and slightly evasive.

"Is it wise to start in the fall? That would mean working through the coldest months."

"I'm not a builder, Syl. But I think it's safe to say that if building projects couldn't be done during the winter in this country, the builders would all move to a milder climate. How would it be if I call Willy and have him drop out for a visit. In the meantime, you can finish up sketching your ideas on that house plan. You were looking at them last evening, you say. Did you see anything you want to change?"

"Well, just one thing we hadn't thought of before, or at least neither of us mentioned it. I'm wondering if we could move things around a bit to make room for a nursery."

Danny, without thinking through the gravity of the question said, "I'm sure we could... Wait... Hang on. What are you saying?"

"I'm saying we'll need a nursery, perhaps sooner than we had planned."

"I wasn't aware that we had planned anything at all. Are you saying we're going to need it pretty soon?"

"Yes. That's what I'm trying to say."

Danny couldn't sort out the meaning of the look on Syl's face, but he asked the clear question.

"Is this a roundabout way of telling me that you are going to have a baby?"

Syl just nodded. The look on her face turned to something close to concern.

"Are you happy with that Danny?"

Danny stood and, smiling, took Syl by the elbows and, with just a bit of pressure indicated that she should stand. When she was on her feet, he wrapped his arms around her and said, "My love, I can't think of a single thing in the entire world that would make me happier. Can I assume you are happy about it too?"

"Oh, yes. I'm very happy. A little surprised but still happy."

Danny smiled down at her and said, "I'm thinking two happy people should seal their happiness with a hug."

Syl folded herself into his arms and said, "You're going to be a wonderful father."

"I'm not so sure about that, my love. I've no experience at all being a father. But I'm pretty sure you will be the best mother ever."

As they hugged, Syl seemed to melt into his embrace, savoring the closeness. Without moving from the embrace, she said, "We have to remember that this is how it all started."

Danny thought it best to allow that surprising comment to pass without any input from him.

After they took their seats again Danny enquired about Syl's health, which she confirmed was fine, no nausea or sickness. Or, at least, not enough to worry about. Just a bit of weakness. Some fatigue. Studying her, Danny wasn't convinced that was the total truth.

With just a bit more talk, Danny pushed to his feet with the announcement that they would find someone to draw up house plans for them and talk to a couple of builders, but right then he had to get to work.

Chapter 29

After a couple of evening hours scanning drawings with Willy and discussing the project at some depth and getting confirmation about Willy's experience with up-scale houses, they made a handshake agreement, 'until the final plans are in place'. Willy could then price it out and a final decision would be made. Danny was weary enough after the day's toil that he might have agreed to almost anything in order to bring the day to an end.

The day had been busy almost to the point of frantic. There were wooden fences to be built and at least one catch corral, two would be better if the work of building went quickly enough.

Ace was pulled off the cutter sleigh repair job and brought over to the Bradshaw west quarter. There, he and Danny and Aaron would get busy building the infrastructure necessary for the weighing and loading out of the animals. The rental company arrived with the scale. The lumber company from town delivered the ordered timbers and posts. Ace grabbed the post hole digger after Danny laid out the pattern to follow, driving short stakes where the posts were to be tamped in. Aaron started cutting timbers to size. By evening they had enough in place to do the loading job, but the few more hours before the first truck was expected would make it just that much better.

Graham Wills was hired again for the few days, and all the working horses, except Bo's pair were taken to the loading site. The two animals Box had delivered were trailed along with the rest but they wouldn't be used unless fatigue in the other mounts made it necessary. Danny hadn't tried them out yet and the last thing he needed was a problem horse while they were loading cattle. He had intended to have Bo take a few days with them too but that hadn't happened yet.

Ace was detailed off to handle the weighing and recording. Not worrying about the weights of individual animals, they would be weighed in groups, as many as the riders could direct that way, ten as a maximum on the scale at one time.

The purchaser was as good as his word. The letter of credit for the estimated final sale price was lodged with the lawyer. No one showed up to check on the weights. The trucks arrived with almost no gap between them, allowing the job to move ahead with little lost time. But there was also no down time for horse or rider. The two new animals were saddled and, in the first hour, proved their worth. By the end of the second day the job was complete.

Sitting their saddles together, as the last truck pulled away, the men looked across the empty grassland and then at the hastily erected corrals and loading chute, with each man feeling the satisfaction of a job well done.

Graham passed the reins to the horse he had been using to Ace. He then walked to his pickup for the drive home while Ace swung into the saddle and joined the other men for the ride back to the D-F. Out of habit, rather than necessity, as the fields were now empty of cattle, the men closed each gate as they rode slowly across the Bradshaw, and then the Kingsbury land. Men and horses, both were exhausted.

Since their marriage Syl had been handling the home finances, while the lawyer, together with an accountant who rented a one-man office in the same building, dealt with ranch matters, including, in this case, the calling-in of the letter of credit for the cattle sale, and paying out the expenses. With that done, he sent his secretary across the street to the bank with a large check to be deposited to the D-F ranch account.

Danny was a hands-on guy, content to let others push papers around their desks. That didn't mean he was careless of details. He carefully went over every penny of the transactions, after the two professionals sent him their report.

In the old Kingsbury home, the evening meal was completed, the dishes were done, and the girls had abandoned the kitchen, preferring their own rooms for the cool of the evening. Aaron was sitting at the table with the newspaper when the phone rang. He picked it up and gave the usual greeting. The line was silent, although he could sense that it had not gone dead. Finally, a hesitant female voice said, "Aaron? Is that you, Aaron?"

"It is. Who's calling?" he asked, although he was sure he already knew.

"Oh, Aaron. It's so good to hear your voice. But when I tell you this is Cookie, perhaps you'll want to hang up, but please don't, Aaron. I so wish to talk with you. For just a minute, I promise."

Raw memories. Memories Aaron might never find release from, came flooding into his mind. The same memories had visited him in the night hours as he lay awake in his construction camp bed or later, in his travel van. They never got easier. The pain had never ceased. His own sense of failure and weakness had never diminished. His sense of shame at not being able to hold his marriage together and of his failures after, and the high price of those failures; these things visited him over and over.

In a sense he blamed this woman who had now called, after all the silent years. But in another very real sense, he heaped blame and guilt onto himself. He really had nothing to say to his ex-wife. To acknowledge the hurts was to be honest. It was also honest to say he had become numb. Not uncaring. Not without the feelings of lost love. Just numb. There was no more anger. No more recrimination. No sense of wanting to lash out at this woman. And nothing to be gained now, by refusing to talk to her.

"I'm here, Cookie. Say what you have to say. I'm listening."

There followed a three-minute-long speech expressing sorrow and guilt. An admission of poor judgement. Of having stars in her eyes. And that even after the stars dimmed, she was too stubborn to go home. Or perhaps it was shame. But something held her back from seeking reconciliation. Nor was she seeking reconciliation now. Knowing it was years too late, there was no reasonable chance that Aaron would even consider... No, that wasn't going to happen, and she wasn't asking. She ended by saying, "Aaron, I don't deserve it, but will you forgive me?" She started to weep at that point.

"I forgave you years ago, Cookie. I either had to do that or drive myself crazy. Or back into the bottle. Yes. You can rest, knowing that much at least. And know this too. You somehow managed to raise three fine young ladies. So good on ya for that."

"Thank you, Aaron. It means a lot for me to hear that. I called my folks. We cried together and I apologized for my foolishness. They told me about your visit and gave me this number. Thanks for taking the girls up there. Mom and Dad greatly appreciated the visit. Do you mind if I speak with the girls now, Aaron?"

"Hang on, I'll get them for you."

Aaron called the girls and before they even picked up the phone, he had his jacket on and was out the door. He would walk the property making plans for the land, which had become one of his favorite pastimes.

An hour later, if he had made any plans at all, he couldn't have said what they were. His mind was an emotional blur.

Danny set his mind to renovating the interior of the barn hoping to make it more comfortable, and perhaps a bit warmer for the horses during a long winter. He found that Willy could spare a week or so and that Aaron was prepared to help him. Ace could also be called upon if need be. Bo would stay with the cattle.

"I want box stalls down both sides, fellas, with a wide runway between. Three to each side. Talk with Bo about the size of the stalls. He's the most knowledgeable about horse things here. I'm thinking of this as a permanent fix, so make them strong, with good gates and hinges. Secure. And we'll want a tack room and a feed storage room. Neither needs to be too large. Put the tack room tight against that small living space. Lace the loft with straw bales for insulation. There should be more than enough bales already up there for that.

"If your time holds, Willy, we'll cut a wide door in the back wall to make the runway a drive through. If we have time before freeze-up, but more likely in the spring, we'll move all the corrals away from the barn and put them to the west side so we can access them from the other side of the yard."

With a bit more discussion and a quick look at his pocket watch, Danny got into Syl's pickup truck and drove to the staff entrance at the hospital.

Picking Syl up at the end of each of her shifts was a practice he had no intention of changing. Rather than her usual, smiling self, chatting, and waving at her work mates as they all headed for their vehicles, she dragged herself out the door and groaned a bit as she lifted herself into the truck.

Danny studied her with considerable concern.

"You're tired this evening."

"Just a bit. I'll be alright."

"Rough day?"

"Not particularly. Just long. My feet didn't seem to want to do what I asked them to do, and the clock was moving slower than normal, I'm sure of that."

Danny waited until they were out of the jammed parking lot and onto the city road that would connect them with Sugartown Road, and home.

"Alright let's have it. You didn't sell me on that last bit of nonsense. What's going on?"

Syl had proven herself to be as stalwart as Danny, as they had worked together to move their ranch and their married lives towards success and fulfillment. She never complained and, from all outward appearances, was a healthy and contented young woman. But she could see she wasn't going to be able to hide what was happening from her observant husband.

"Just a bit of fatigue. Goes with the territory. This being pregnant changes some things in a woman's body."

Danny smiled across the cab of the truck. Syl had her eyes open, but her head was rested against the seat back.

"Alright. I understand. As much as I can without being pregnant, anyways. But the pregnancy has a long way to go yet. What's going to happen with this fatigue? And is there something causing it that isn't normal?"

"Perhaps you should have been a lawyer, cross examining someone on the witness stand. Or a doctor, insisting on more detail in the examination room."

Danny said, "Young lady, you will not recognize me without my white coat on, and that thingy I usually hang around my neck, but I am Doctor Framer. If I'm going to be able to help you, it will be necessary for you to tell me the truth, the whole truth and nothing but the truth."

"You forgot 'so help me God'. And you have your professions running together."

"Come on, Syl. The truth."

"Alright. It's nothing to be concerned about. I think I have a bit of anemia. Very common during pregnancy."

"Low on iron. That's what that means, is it not?"

Without waiting for an answer, he asked, "You're surrounded by doctors all day long. Have you consulted with anyone?"

"Not yet. It was too busy today but one of the ER guys will run a test for me tomorrow."

"Uh. Uh. Not going to happen that way. You are going to call in sick. Take a few days off. You're going to call our own doctor in the morning and have him check you out. Or call a lady baby doctor if you know one. This is my wife and child we're talking about here. Let's have no casual approach to things."

Syl dropped her hand onto Danny's arm.

"Alright. You convinced me. And you're right. I really am feeling tired."

By noon the next day they knew that Syl's self-diagnosis was correct. She was suffering from anemia, a common occurrence, but not common at the levels Syl tested at. She booked longer term sick leave and adjusted her diet to help her body produce the chemicals or whatever was required for it to heal itself. She felt sleepy and weary most of the next two days. Slowly, the rest and diet seemed to be improving her situation.

That evening, Danny asked if Syl had told her parents about the baby.

"I've invited us over to their place for lunch on Sunday. Until then, not a word. If Mom hears that I'm on sick leave, and why, she'll jump to conclusions. Her conclusions will almost positively be right, but I'd rather tell them face to face. I take it as a once in a lifetime thing to tell my parents that we are expecting our first child. I'm looking forward to it. We need to drive up to the city and tell your folks too."

"You're right again. We'll see how you feel in a few days. If you can't manage the trip, I'll phone them."

Sunday afternoon, Wes and Danny chatted in the living room while Syl helped her mother put the finishing touches on the meal. Syl was feeling better, but she knew she was a bit pale and perhaps, just a little unsteady on her feet. She sensed her mother watching her but could do nothing about it. A nurse is always a nurse. There's nothing to be done with that truth. When her mother caught Syl staring at nothing, while she slowly stirred the gravy with one hand and held the other hand gently on her tummy, the light came on for the retired, but still knowledgeable mother.

They eased their chairs from under the table, while Syl brought the gravy boat over. After they were seated, Mrs. Mabry said, "Wes, how about you give thanks and then Syl can tell us how far along she is."

Syl was thunderstruck, while Wes looked startled. Danny came close to bursting out in laughter but managed to hold back the impulse. But to Syl it was no laughing matter. She was deeply hurt that her mother would burst out with assumed news that she, herself was very much looking forward to sharing.

Through sudden tears Syl said, "Mother! Honestly, Mother. Sometimes you have just no appreciation of situations at all. I was so looking forward to telling you that you're going to be grandparents again. That news was ours to share Mother. Danny's and mine."

Syl, her hands shaking in anger and frustration, and with tears still dribbling down her cheeks, reached for the potatoes, but Wes laid his hand on her wrist.

"Let's still give thanks, Sylvia."

With her mother finally understanding what she had done, the meal was eaten in uncomfortable silence. Without even waiting for dessert Syl said, "I'm really not feeling well. You'll have to excuse us."

Her mother sat alone at the table while Wes walked Syl to the door. He gave her a peck on the cheek and quietly said, "I'm really very happy for you two."

With that Danny took Syl's arm and guided her down the stairs and across the driveway to the truck. Wes went back to the table and sat down, saying nothing. His wife was quietly weeping. They sat in silence for a half minute before she said, "I've done it again, Wes. I've hurt our dear Sylvia. You know I wouldn't do that purposely for all the money in the world. I fear I'll never learn. And now I don't know what to do.

"I'll clean up later. I'm going to lie down for a while."

Wes said nothing and offered no advice. He agreed with his wife. She did have a habit of bursting out with untimely words. When he heard the bedroom door close, he quietly rose from the table and began cleaning up the lunch dishes and putting away the uneaten food. When he looked at the untouched coconut cream pie on the counter, Syl's favorite, his heart sank for his two ladies. A coconut cream pie was a lot of work to make, and it had been made in love for their precious daughter. Now, how to mend the fence?

With Bo and Aaron each enjoying a day of rest, Danny was caring for the cattle on Sundays. With the second herd being sold off, there was only the home place to be concerned about. As long as no fences were down, and there were no sick or injured animals, checking on them didn't amount to much. Before dressing for church, he had done a quick ride through, earlier in the morning on the ATV. Now, for a more thorough check he would saddle one of the new horses. As the two new mounts appeared to be working out, they would take Syl's Boots' place as working ranch horses. Boots would be retired, leaving him for Syl to baby and ride at her convenience.

Idly, Danny wondered how much she could ride while she was carrying a baby. Perhaps the horse would see no use at all and that wouldn't be good either. A horse needs to be used to stay in shape and to hold onto its training in discipline.

There was an early fall nip in the air, but Danny liked it. They had seen the last of flies and mosquitoes for the year and the leaves were turning to their fall golden color, at least those that had held their green during the spring drought. There was a pleasant, pungent odor on the slight breeze, a product of wild cranberries ripening in the bush, falling aspen leaves, curing grass and whatever else was happening in nature.

Syl was resting and Danny was alone on the porch later that afternoon when Wes Mabry slowed the car to a stop beside the cabin. He looked at the visitors with some surprise. They had not phoned ahead. Danny knew, as anyone would understand, that the situation at lunch could not be left to stand, without an effort made towards reconciliation. But it wasn't his call. He understood that, too.

He knew Syl would get past her disappointment

and that her mother would offer an olive branch towards peace and forgiveness for her indiscretion. The only question would seem to be, 'when would that happen? And what, and how much, would be adequate? Were just a few hours, or a few words, enough to settle hurt feelings?'

Danny stood and waved the visitors to the porch. They had come dressed for an outdoor meeting, which was standard at the small cabin, where the covered porch was used almost as an extension of the indoor living room. Mrs. Mabry stood slowly from the car and then reached back in to retrieve the still uncut pie. As they were walking towards the porch Danny stepped inside to tell Syl they had visitors. She reluctantly rose, straightened her clothing, had a wash, combed her hair, and put on a coat. Wordlessly, she stepped onto the porch and over to her favorite chair.

Danny still hadn't sat down. Now he said, "Wes, I'd like to show you what the boys are doing over in the barn. Want to go for a short walk?"

"Good idea. I'd like to see how Ace is doing with that cutter too."

Neither man was fooling the women, but they said nothing, simply watching them walk across the yard. What happened after they left, or what was said between mother and daughter wasn't relayed to either man, neither then, nor later. Wes and Danny were both content to leave it that way.

When they returned from checking out the carpenter's work, there was a fresh pot of coffee ready, and plates and forks set out for pie.

The next hour of visiting lacked its usual jovialness and lightness of spirit, but clearly, the ladies had come to a point of reconciliation. The hurt feelings would just need some time to settle in behind them completely.

Syl knew she wouldn't be up to making a five-hour drive. Danny phoned his folks, told them the news, and at his mother's request, passed the phone to Syl. The two women talked for a couple of minutes before Danny's mother surprised Syl by asking, "May I pray with you now, my dear?"

Syl happily agreed. She sat silently with the receiver tight to her ear as her mother-in-law prayed for her health and for an easy pregnancy. She then prayed that Syl would grow in godly wonder at the things that were happening in her body, and the mystery of creation being replicated. She closed her prayer with thanksgiving for God's greatness and goodness before saying, "My dear, you are, like all mothers, greatly privileged to be a part of God's forever plan. I would ask that you remember that on the days when you are tired or sick or weary. And those days will come. But, as the saying is, there is great joy in the morning."

Syl then passed the phone to Danny so he could talk with his father. After just the briefest comment of congratulations on the expected addition to the family, he wanted to know all about the ranch happenings. Syl, tired of hearing the one-sided conversation since she knew all the facts Danny was relaying, went inside. Since the evening had taken on a distinct chill, she kindled a fire in the wood stove, the first of the fall season. For a young woman who had never dreamed of building a wood fire until a bit over one year before, she did an admirable job. The room was soon filled with the pleasant and mind calming crackle of burning poplar. Stove warmth was radiating into the kitchen in a matter of minutes.

The day ended on a better note than Danny had anticipated as they drove home from Syl's parents after lunch.

With fall firmly in the air and with the summer's work behind them, Danny was determined to get as near to full time on his writing as possible. He would keep Bo on to feed cattle. With the weather making further work on the cuter sleigh difficult, if not impossible, Ace had decided to fly home for the winter months with the promise to return at the first sign of spring. He left with a handshake and another 'thank you', and the promise, "If something should come up that's of an urgent nature and where I could be of assistance, you call. I'll be on the next plane."

The ground was not yet layered with snow. The pastures were providing adequate feed for the growing yearlings. With the loss of Ace, Danny arranged for Graham Wills to help with the feeding, mornings and evenings, when that became necessary.

As the bus that would take Ace to the airport drove away, Danny and Syl looked at each other. Syl wrapped up their feeling with, "I'm not sure I ever really believed someone could change their actions, if not their basic nature, but there it happened, right in front of us."

With the biting fall wind tumbling fallen leaves along the city streets, they hugged their coats tighter around their necks and hurried to their warm truck.

That evening Wes phoned with a message from the publisher.

"Danny, I don't know how I'm going to convince these people that I'm not your formal agent. It appears they're pretty stuck in their ways."

Wes was interrupted by Danny saying, "Well, you've proven that you're good at it and it's not really that much work, an hour or two here and there in the evenings. Why not take it on and let me pay you for it? And you could add Aaron into the mix. It would keep you from wandering the streets, wondering what to do with yourself."

"Yes, I can see your point, but wandering the streets isn't one of my larger life problems."

When Danny didn't follow up with any new thought, Wes said, "Anyway, what they want of you is a book tour. They promise it will only be short and quick. The book is selling well, and they feel this is the time to jump on it with some further, very targeted promotion. Just four stops. Not much more than a week, with the travel. They want you in Calgary, Denver, Houston and Amarillo, all oil cities where they have solid book retailer contacts. They may want another tour after the new year but that's not set yet."

Wes said no more, leaving it to Danny to respond.

"Give me the exact dates and let me talk with Syl about it. If she can get her feet back under her and get to where she's feeling stronger, I could probably get away."

"Good. I'll tell them you'll get an answer out in forty-eight hours. Now, is Aaron over there?"

"Haven't seen him all day. Is he not at home?"

"He didn't answer his phone. If you see him, have him call me."

When Aaron showed up at coffee time the next morning, the porch was vacated. A light tap brought Syl to the door. When she saw Aaron through the window, she simply waved him in. Danny was seated at the table with the typewriter before him.

Aaron stepped into the comforting warmth of the small cabin and was going to say something about Danny wimping out with the slightest hint of winter in the air, but Danny didn't give him a chance.

"Wes wants you to call. Give him a ring after he gets home from work this evening."

"Don't have to. He called this morning early. Outlined what next steps I have to take before he shows my writing to the publisher."

Danny laughed and responded, "Let me guess. Self-edit with a red pen, send to professional typist, wait, rewrite again after you receive the document, re-type, send to editor, wait..."

Aaron laughed and said, "That about sums it up. Sounds like a lot of work, but if that's what it will take to get the books back onto the market, I'll get it done."

Syl said, "Along with the new story you're put-

274

ting all your free time into, right?"

He laughed and looked at Danny, sitting behind the table with the typewriter in front of him and the ubiquitous coffee cup steaming beside the stacked paper.

"That's a demanding woman you're tagged onto, my friend."

Syl had no answer, but Danny said, "You wait, give Belle a bit of time to start feeling comfortable. Whether you're dealing with the writing or other life matters, when she gets up to pace, I have a feeling she might have an idea or two her own self."

Chapter 30

The second time Aaron and Belle were alone together, she had invited Aaron and the three girls
for dinner on a Friday evening. After a delicious, if
noisy, dinner the five young people decided to go for
a walk along the river road. Clara really didn't want
to go with the younger ones but, seeing the mental urging in her father's eyes, she smiled a small
knowing smile and put on her coat. Aaron grinned
inwardly at the wisdom his eldest daughter was
showing, and at the interesting reversal of roles.

There was a comfortable sitting room with soft
seating, but for some reason, Aaron and Belle remained at the dinner table. Belle talked Aaron into
another small piece of chocolate cake. They visited
about nothing important while they finished their
cake and coffee.

As Belle took the empty coffee cups to the cupboard Aaron said, "Why don't we clean up the kitchen
while were talking? Won't take but a few minutes."

"The kids usually do that."

"I know. But let's give them a break just this once."

Belle piled the dishes into the soapy water and washed while Aaron dried. Laughing, he said, "If I told you how many mountains of dishes I've washed in the construction camp kitchens, you might not believe me. Try to picture three or four hundred hungry men three times a day with just two of us bussing, scraping and loading the big dishwasher. And then unloading the cleaned dishes and resetting the places on the tables, ready for the thundering herds again, in just a few hours. I still cringe when I think about it. The day I graduated to salads and prep work was a happy day."

With the kitchen cleaned, they again sat at the table, almost as if moving further into the home was a commitment, or a freedom, or a familiarity of some sort that neither really wanted to enter into quite yet.

Aaron had poured himself the last cup of coffee and sat sipping it, waiting. Hoping that Belle would indicate where she wanted the conversation to go.

Before the silence became uncomfortably heavy Belle said, "Aaron, you told me your story. Mine is much shorter and less exciting, in a sense, but if you'd like, I'll share it with you."

Aaron put the coffee mug down, folded his arms on the tabletop, smiled, and said, "I'd like."

"Well, it's a simple story. Hurtful at all levels, but simple. I studied for an arts degree at the community college. Now, we have to understand that millions of people have arts degrees. It really means nothing unless the student moves on into a particular discipline for another bachelor's degree on takes a masters. What I'm saying is that my degree prepared me for exactly nothing in the real world.

"I didn't worry about that. I took it mostly for general knowledge, waiting for when I found that perfect man. My main goal in life was to have a long and loving marriage and to be the best stay at home mom ever. Well, I had all of that for a few years. Short years as I think back on them now. And far too few. But as it has often been said, cancer is a cruel disease and no respecter of persons."

As Aaron listened intently, she told him of her job and how she had found herself a widow with no marketable skills. Knowing she had to support the kids on her own, she took whatever she could find, which turned out to be a clerking job in a real estate office. The pay was minimum but steady, and it covered their expenses. Barely. She had family who would back her up if the need should arise but so far, she had managed.

"When Walt took out the mortgage on this house, he added life insurance. That gave us a debt free home that I am very thankful for. He had another small policy that I used to purchase a new car. The old one was showing its age and I wasn't up to pulling wrenches the way Walt did.

"So financially, we're secure, but things are tight. We control our spending and we're doing alright. The kids and I have been alone for about five years now. I'm already up to the point where I don't think about Walt every night. Just most nights. So, you see, you are way ahead of me in healing. The rest of the story is simply one day after another. Nothing exciting. Everything pretty steady. The kids take the extra lessons they want, Steve with his guitar and Olivia with the art. I try to encourage them in that.

"And to answer the question for myself that I was forward enough to ask of you, no, I have no other special friends, and never have had. The future? Well, who can answer that? Quite frankly, the biggest fear I have in the family right now is that Steve is growing up with no, or little male influence."

There could have been a question or a comment or an enquiry, or nothing at all, in that last statement. But silently, Aaron was hoping it was an invitation, a lead in, to some kind of an offer from him. To do exactly what, he dared not guess.

After just enough of a pause, Aaron said, "Belle, I've not had a son. And for the most part I haven't had my girls either. They only came back into my life a few months ago. So, I know a lot more about bachelorhood and cooking for crowds than I do about life with children. Of course, none of our kids are really children anymore. I'm neither a hunter nor a fisherman. And sleeping in a tent I see as only for desperate situations. But I know a bit about farms, horses and cattle. And I'm a fair to middl'n carpenter. I can fix simple things on cars and old trucks, and I enjoy driving and exploring new country. I played the guitar a bit as a kid but I'm sure Steve will be way past anything I ever did or knew.

"I can't be the replacement for his father, Belle, but if Steve wanted to learn to ride, either for pleasure or to work cattle, I'd be honored to get him up to speed on that. We could probably find opportunity to get behind the wheel of the pickup, out on the pasture too. Or pull a wrench, to keep those old trucks operable, when the need is upon us. Sometimes I'm not sure what keeps those antiques running. They remind me of a poem I read in school years ago. You're a reader. Do you remember 'The Wonderful One Horse Shay'"

"Ran for one hundred years and a day? Oh yes. I remember it. Funny how a person can almost recite word for word, poems learned in school years before. The modern educators cast a jaundiced eye at the concept of memorization, claiming it's not the same as learning concepts, or whatever it is they say. But I can remember several poems from years ago. To say nothing at all about the times tables."

"Alright, what's twelve times twelve?"

"One hundred forty-four."

They both broke out laughing, lightening the evening and the visit considerably.

Aaron returned to the idea of spending time with Steve.

"There's the tractors and the ATV over at the D-F. Danny is generous with his equipment as long as it isn't abused. And Steve is old enough to put in some hours of paid work in season. That could be snow removal with the tractor and front-end loader, or it could be in making hay.

"Making hay. Building stacks. Handling bales. That kind of work would put some muscle on his frame, perhaps better that any other activity, certainly better than any gym workout. There's lots of things we could do together. Some for pleasure, some for work."

When he saw that Belle was holding her attention on what he was saying he continued.

"I'd be pleased if Olivia wanted to ride also, but I think one-on-one time with Steve, at the start, would be the ticket. We could arrange some one-on-one time with Olivia too but at a different time from Steve. As far as that goes, you could climb onto a horse and learn at the same time."

Belle appeared to take all of that in, but she had little response, and they turned to other subjects to keep the conversation light.

All too soon the kids returned from their river walk. Steve said nothing when he saw Aaron and his mother still sitting at the kitchen table but Olivia, reminding Aaron of his own Abby, also fourteen years of age, said, "What? You'd rather sit on hard kitchen chairs than move into the living room?"

Aaron, striking up some boldness himself, said, "Well, when we finished up all the cleaning and washing, we were too tired to move."

Abby, twirling her fingers like a phonograph recording said, "Here we go. Story time again."

With that bit of sarcasm still floating in the air, Aaron said, "Yes, well don't sit down, girls. It's time you took this old guy home. And since we came in Clara's car, I guess we'll all have to say thank you for the great meal and good evening."

Chapter 31

The building of box stalls in the barn wasn't quite completed, but Willy had another contract that he needed to act on. He had everything laid out in a way that allowed Aaron and Graham to complete the work. With Ace having flown for home, the work was now left to just the two of them.

Ace had regretted dropping the cutter repair task, but he had to face the facts. Any repairs requiring gluing or forming curves into the light plywood were greatly complicated with the cold weather and would be best left until spring. And it was already far too cold for painting. He had carefully covered the cutter with the canvas tarpaulin and put all the tools away before leaving for home.

The grass was holding up well in the pastures in spite of the cold nights. Bo had little to do except ride the land, checking fences and watching for problems with the animals. When he was confident the herd was well cared for, he found time to help with the building project.

Danny was back at his winter venture, the writing of a new story, although he was often distracted by the thought of over-wintering the herd. Aaron had promised that he would be writing also, but Danny didn't feel it was his place to question or push. Wes might question if the publisher turned out to be as impressed with Aaron's old books, after their revisions and re-typing, as Wes had been. Wes certainly wouldn't want to promote an author that wasn't going to follow through on his commitment. But Danny would leave that between Aaron and Wes.

Syl was almost back to her old self and was beginning to question whether she ever wanted to return to nursing and the shift work that was such a big part of it.

The wedding of Box and Maria was imminent. Ab and Mrs. Kane had insisted, at first, that the ceremony and dinner to follow would be held at the ranch. They would rent a big tent and welcome folks from miles around. Have a real old time ranch wedding.

Halfway through the explanation, Maria simply said 'no'. The living room at the big ranch house fell to silence. Mrs. Kane finally said, "What do you mean no? And what would you prefer as an alternative?"

What followed was reminiscent of the conversation between Syl and her parents, although Syl had never spoken to anyone about that, and Maria had no way to know what took place. In one way Maria was ahead of where Syl had been. She had found and purchased her dress weeks before.

"I would prefer that you remember two things, Mother. One is that it will be the third week of October. We could be in the midst of a raging blizzard and snowstorm…"

Her father jumped in with, "Or we could have a beautiful fall day with the sun shining and no more than a slight chill in the air."

"Yes, Father, that's true. Would you like to guarantee the latter?"

After father and daughter studied each other in silence for a few seconds, Maria said, "I didn't think so." But just to drive the point home she continued, "And have you forgotten that it was in October that I came close to death on a cold gravel road with the rain and snow pounding my back?"

Both parents sat mute.

With that point made she moved on, "The second thing, Mother, is that it is to be my wedding. Not anyone else's, except, of course, Box. We prefer to not have a great extravaganza. We'll invite family and friends, of course, but not ranchers from all over southern Alberta.

"There are a couple of halls in town, as well as the hotel facilities that would suit just fine. And people would not have to drive thirty miles of gravel road to get there."

That discussion had been in mid-August, still allowing time enough for hall rentals, caterers, etc. Now, with the wedding just two weeks away, all appeared to be in readiness. Without saying anything about the idea, Maria wondered about borrowing Danny's surrey buggy for the occasion.

Having loved the way Syl arrived at the church in the .32 convertible, she wondered about something similar, but again, her fear of the weather forced her to stroke a line through that notion.

Box had been acting like a drop of water splattered into a pan of hot grease, but he assured Maria that all was well, that he would be fine. Maria figured that if she could ease him through the next two weeks he would settle down and realize that he had made a good life decision.

Aaron was strolling through the neglected and overgrown yard around his old farmhouse, new development and landscaping plans growing by the minute, when Clara came out to talk to him.

"Hey, Clara, what's up? You're dressed like you're going into competition with Cinderella at the Princess ball."

"Well, perhaps not quite that, Father, but I am going out. A fella I met at the store is coming over. We're going out for dinner and maybe a movie or maybe just a walk along the river if this threatening rain holds off."

In the short few months the girls had been with him, Clara had not been out on a date. Neither had Becky, for that matter, although both girls were of dating age. With the girls living apart from their father for most of their lives, he felt he had little to say. Or at least what he said had to be carefully worded and gentle.

"Well, Babe, in the short time we've been together you've shown character and good choices. I'm trusting that will be the pattern tonight and for life. Do you know anything about this fella?"

"I know he's a rancher's son. They have cattle but they also have a large flock of chickens. Buzz works with the chickens. They sell eggs. They purchase their feed from our bulk processing plant, but the orders and invoicing are done in the store, so I've seen him several times. He's perhaps a bit shy in a crowd. It took him forever to get the words out when he was asking me for a date, although I knew what he was trying to do. The store is usually pretty busy. There's seldom a chance to talk one on one with anyone without others overhearing. Buzz hung around after placing his order until the store cleared out. It was kind of cute really, him standing on one foot and then the other and glancing at me from across the room. After all that, I just couldn't play the hard to get game. In fact, I almost had to help him ask me. But don't ever embarrass him by repeating that. He's actually very nice. I think you'll like him."

"If you like him, Babe, I'll like him. If he turns out to be less than you thought, you get shut of him. If you have to phone for a ride, don't hesitate."

"There's one other thing, Dad. The girls and I have been talking. We enjoyed meeting the grandparents. We all liked them, although Grandma's menu wouldn't be found in anyone's good food guide. How would you feel if we invited them down here for a few days? There's nothing I saw that's keeping them on that old farm. I'm sure they could get away."

Aaron nodded his head, smiling, while he answered, "That's a great idea. But one of you girls should make the call."

Just then a well-washed pickup made its way down the lane. Clara looked towards the noise coming from the gravel driveway and said, "I've never seen what he drives, but that's probably Buzz. Come over and meet him."

Chapter 32

Off the streets, away from public view, and known only to those in the chosen circles, there exists, for many trades and industries, and in many towns and cities, an informal, inner meeting spot. A place to share industry news. A place to recruit new workers. A place for the workers, to seek out new positions. Or sometimes, just to sit around visiting and shooting the breeze. This meeting place is often at the back table of a local diner or working man's café, if the industry in question is of the hands-on nature. For white collar industries it may be at a bar or club.

The small group of men dressed in khaki work clothes and crude-oil stained boots, at the large table butted against the rear wall of the Black Gold Café, told anyone observant enough to notice that these were oil workers. If anyone not of their tribe were to approach the big table, conversation would stop as all eyes turned to the intruder.

"Morning, men, may I join you?" The man was taking a seat even as he asked the question. The conversation fell to silence. The visitor had picked up a mug of help-yourself coffee on the way to the table, and now made himself at home. Seven heads turned his way, but no words greeted him.

Any observant working man would quickly guess that this fella had never climbed the steel ladder to the top of a drill rig. But they would also notice that there was nothing soft about him. Slim and wiry, he stood about five foot ten or eleven, with not a sign of fat anywhere. He wore boots and western garb naturally enough to tell anyone looking on that this was not for show. A knowledgeable observer can quickly tell a town cowboy from the real thing. This man was the real thing.

He took a sip of coffee as he cast his eyes around the staring circle, smiling and nodding at each man in turn. Inwardly he was grinning. He was totally familiar with private trade group meetings, meetings where each one present shared a common work history and view of the world. That his familiarity was totally unconnected with the oil industry didn't really matter. The men were all holding to type, as did the visitor's more familiar group.

When the scan of the group was completed, the visitor gently laid his coffee mug on the counter and eased his Stetson back a bit with the tip of his thumb, allowing a wave of light brown hair to escape.

Through a small smile that never seemed to fade, he said, "Name's William. Or Bill if that rolls out easier."

The silence continued around the table. No questions were asked by either the visitor or one of the group. Bill had no need for questions. He had already chosen his man. He turned and looked to his right, to the older, yet still not old, man who sat alone at the end of the table, like a natural born leader, one set apart from his lessors, with the younger workers arrayed along each side of the table, like devotees. The targeted man sat a half step away from the table, slightly sideways on his chair; his long legs crossed at the knees. His hair was longer than most, with a compacted ring of hair just above his ears, where an oil worker's aluminum hard hat was designed to grip and press, securing it against wind, rain, and gravity, for when the worker bent over his task. But instead of the hard hat so familiar to his industry, there was a well-cared for, tan colored Stetson resting, saddled on the man's knee.

Even a quick glance had told Bill that there was steel in the man's grip and in his mind. He felt his eyes boring into him, as if trying to get a jump ahead, to figure out this intruder. His shoulders were wide but slender, as if everything but bone and muscle had been burned off. His very appearance spoke of knowledge. Perhaps not general knowledge, of world events or history or literature. But knowledge of the industry he had spent a working lifetime in.

Demonstrating, perhaps, the man's single vanity, he had the name 'Topman' professionally embroidered on the pocket of his khaki work shirt. It wasn't really a title, as no such position as topman existed in the industry, as far as Bill knew. But the name fit. Nor did it seem to scream of arrogance. It was as if it just was. Something earned and accepted. Unquestioned. Like a mountain, needing no proof or explanation of its existence. It just is. Bill could respect such a man.

"Like to talk with you."

"Alright."

Saying nothing to the group, Topman glanced around the table. Getting the hint, one man stretched, looked at his watch, and said, "Time I got home. Myrt will be wondering. She might have even found time between her soaps, to rattle some pots and pans."

As if by magic, the others pushed their coffee mugs aside, reached into their pockets, and laid the price of the coffee on the table, and stood. Bill and Topman were soon alone.

Topman, showing just the slightest grin, growled out from his much-abused voice, "You're a buck and a jump off your home range here, Rowdy."

Bill burst out laughing., before saying, "Figured it out, did you? Those others showed no sign."

"Those others ain't from around here. Oil business draws them in like flies to honey, from all over the country. Not a rider or a rodeo man among them. Spotted you when you walked in the door."

Bill extended his hand with a smile.

"Not hiding anything. Just don't want to be seen as making my way into the business world on the strength of something done in the past, in another vocation. Another world."

"Well, son, with the gap you left in the Rodeo world with your early retirement you've proven your worth more than just the once. Ain't no one come'n even close to trailing you these past two years. What you up to since you quit?"

Rowdy stood and picked up both coffee mugs. He said, "I'll get some fresh. Then we'll talk."

Two or three diners took long looks at him as if they, too, recognized him. He was careful not to look their way. A waitress who was cleaning up around the big coffee urn said, "You're getting some attention, Rowdy. Sorry to have to advise you that ignoring it won't make it go away. You're looking at the rest of your life here, Pal. Just the price you pay for fame. Just the price you pay." She walked away laughing quietly.

He was almost getting use to the attention after two years away from the chutes and the bucking horses. Almost, but not quite. He had hoped it would fade, but there was no sign of that. His face was constantly before the public, as he was almost forced, by reputation and tradition into doing promotions for rodeo.

His fame had risen, if anything, since his retirement. When he was actively competing, the public was content to watch from a distance. Now, there were far more demands for public appearances than he was happy with.

Setting the clean coffee mug before Topman, Rowdy said, "Do you want to tell me what all you've done in the field, or should I ask questions?"

"Done about it all. You want specifics, you lay

'er out."

With a nod Rowdy said, "My business doesn't work the rigs or the seismic trucks. I do a little with pipeline valving, pumping stations, and control. But mostly I'm into gas plants, sulfur extraction, small mixing plants and the like. I do flow control valves and actuators of all kinds. Design, supply and installation. Servicing when it's needed. Specialize in central control systems. That mean anything to you?"

Topman took a sip of coffee, making Rowdy wait. He then said, "Best man ever stood on the top of a rig, fighting wind, rain and snow, danger and the stink of crude. Moved on and got my pipefitter's ticket. Worked the lines all over the nation, building and maintenance. Pushed pipeline jobs couple of thousand miles, I suppose. In charge of diggers, cats, pipe layers, welders and pumping station construction.

"Work slowed down. Moved on into building the small units you're talking about. Foreman mostly. Site super a couple of times, working to keep the engineers from making too many mistakes. You lay er out, I can do it."

As with the embroidered name on his shirt, Topman somehow managed to say all of that without sounding arrogant, yet in a way that made the listener believe, and take note.

"Question, Topman. Busy time right now. Yet here you sit available for work. Want to explain that?"

"Easy to explain. Own a ranch southeast of town a bit. Brother and I own it together. Not usually enough work for two owners. My brother and three hands handle the work. Leaves me free to get away. Of course, I haven't exactly figured out yet what's the most miserable, and potentially dangerous to work with, a horned beef critter on the prod or an oil worker in the morning. Don't always smell all that different either. Been doin' it a long time though. Found it kind of slow on the ranch once I'd been away from it for a while. Not much excitement, so I stuck with the oil."

"Brother took sick a while back. Called me home. Been here three months now. Brother's back in the saddle, time to move out."

Rowdy phrased his next question carefully.

"Are you looking for adventure and excitement or would you be content with a position here in town if there was just a bit of travel to it, time to time?"

Topman ran his hand over his face and then through his graying hair, before smiling and saying, "You can see I've got some miles on me. Wife, she lives on the ranch in our own house. I've been away too many months over the years when they're all added up. Missed a lot of my kids' growing years. Time to pull in my horns. Yes, I'm ready to talk. What you got in mind?"

Rowdy started in with what almost sounded like an apology.

"I fell into this business. It's a good business. But that's no thanks to my efforts. The business was owned and built up by a bachelor uncle of mine. He knew the industry inside out and came up with a few new ideas too. But he went and grew old.

Knowing he had no one to pass the business on to, he looked around the family. I'm not exactly sure why he picked me over a few other cousins, but there it is. He made an offer that was hard to refuse. That's only one of the reasons I hung up my saddle.

"He took me under his wing and, almost as if he was frantic to get everything transferred from his head to mine, we practically lived together the first months. He had always held the information under his hat, but he knew he was failing. After examining the old man's heart, his doctor told him to sell out immediately and get rid of the stress. He didn't do that, choosing to bring me into his circle, instead.

"He lasted just over one year. Then I was on my own. Two old timers who had stayed on just because of loyalty to the old man, took retirement when my uncle died. I've stumbled a few times along the way, but I kept it going. Now the business is thriving and there's new things coming along that will do nothing but good for the industry, and my business along with it."

"I probably knew your uncle and the business both. Are we talking about Bow Valley Flow Control?"

"We are."

"Met your uncle several times. Fine man. A gentleman, and trustworthy."

"Thank you, Topman. That's a compliment he would have appreciated hearing, and I appreciate it too. I hope to hold up his long record in the industry."

"Today is Friday, Rowdy. I'm expecting someone here any minute to give me a ride home. I'm interested in what you have, but we don't have time right now. How about coming out to the ranch on Sunday afternoon if that suits you, or Monday morning if that sounds better?"

"What I'm looking for can hold for that long, Topman. I don't like to tie up my Sundays though. But I can set aside Monday morning. Just give me directions and I'll be there around nine."

Topman sketched on a paper napkin and pushed it toward Rowdy. With both their heads bent to the table while Topman explained his sketch, they failed to see anyone approaching. Just as Topman was finished with his explanation a female voice said, "Am I interrupting something, Topman?"

Rowdy looked up, quickly rose to his feet and removed his Stetson.

"Sorry, Miss. I didn't see you coming."

She smiled a bit and looked at Topman.

"Uncle, have you sunk so low that you're reduced to spending time with worn out rodeo riders? Bucking horses, no less?"

Topman laughed and said, "Rowdy, I want you to meet my very outspoken and opinionated niece, Josie Greenwood. She's pretty much harmless unless she finds cause to bite or scratch. Should really get a vaccine put up or an antidote of some kind for when she takes a notion. Got her practice at misery, training riding horses for other folks. Never much liked the taste of horse ear my own self, but she seems to have grown into it."

"Why thank you, Uncle, for that generous introduction."

Turning to Rowdy she held out her hand, "It is a pleasure to meet you, Rowdy. I've watched you live, as well as on TV many times. You were one of a kind. The rodeo world is poorer for your retirement."

She extended the handshake for longer than most women would have, boldly keeping eye contact the entire time, but finally pulled away. She then said, "In spite of that introduction, Rowdy, and what my uncle would have you believe, I really can be kind and considerate. When I really have no other choice, is what I mean to say."

Holding her eyes on Rowdy she said, "If you two are talking business I can wait in the pickup. I've only come to give Topman a ride home since his unit is in the shop."

As she talked, Rowdy couldn't be blamed for noting that, although she wasn't truly beautiful, she was certainly attractive, slim and strong looking, like most ranch girls that have been riding all their lives. Her hands were a bit chapped and callused but stronger than many men's hands. At about five-and one-half feet tall and very nicely shaped she couldn't help it if she drew attention wherever she went.

Topman said, "We have laid our business over till Monday morning. Do you have time for a coffee or are you anxious to get back?"

"I'll have a coffee."

Topman, who hadn't left his chair since Rowdy's arrival, sat like he expected someone else would see to getting the drink.

Still on his feet, Rowdy said, "I'll have another if you don't mind the company, Josie."

"I'm fine with the company."

"Then I'll get the coffee. You, Topman?"

"No. I've had more than enough."

Rowdy was soon back with two fresh mugs.

After both Rowdy and Josie had taken a sip, Rowdy said, "So tell me about this horse training business."

"It's more of a hobby really. I'd never make a living at it. Dad lets me use a couple of stalls in the stable, although we're always short of space. Then I just use a fenced-in bit of pasture set aside, away from ranch use. We don't have an indoor arena or anything like that. Dad wouldn't hear of it, and I'd probably agree with him. The business of the ranch is cattle. Not pleasure horses.

"I'm just doing this to keep myself busy and make a bit of spending money until I'm discovered. You know, like those Hollywood starlets who sit on soda fountain stools until some big producer comes along and is instantly mesmerized. Of course, nothing like that ever happened in real life but it's a good story and one I hang on to."

"What are you waiting for? What do you hope will happen?"

"Oh, you know. Young man. Handsome. Rich. Drives a gold-plated pickup truck. Wise beyond all measure. Star struck at first sight of me. All the standard stuff."

"Well, I'm still reasonably young but not handsome. Certainly not rich and I don't drive a gold-plated pickup truck, although, by the price of the things you would think they should come gold plated. If I was wise, I would not have been riding bucking horses. But I am just a bit star struck and mesmerized, although sharing dinner this evening might help me figure out just how star struck I am."

Topman was grinning inwardly although no one looking on would ever see it. It wasn't often his niece was bested in verbal games. He was also wondering if either of them was really playing a game or was there the very small beginnings of something more, some opportunity best taken, and a potential loss if ignored.

Josie sat wordlessly, never taking her eyes off the speaker. Rowdy appeared to be perfectly comfortable with the unspoken probe. Silently, he was counting, six-seven-eight. His rides were always timed to eight seconds before the horn blew, signifying it was time to reach out to a pickup man and get gone from the bucking horse.

He started wondering if there was a mounted pickup man hovering in the café wings, waiting to rescue him from his own folly. Josie had gone past the magic number eight, but finally, in a much-subdued voice she said, "Mr. Benson. Are you inviting me to join you for dinner this evening?"

Rowdy grinned a bit and answered, "Well, I was talking about dinner and you're the only one here except Topman and has already said he has to get home. So you could be safe in making an assumption."

Josie turned her head to study her uncle, hoping for a voice of wisdom. He returned the look but offered no wisdom or opinion, one way or another.

She finally gave it up and turned back to Rowdy.

Studying him the entire time, but still saying nothing, she reached into her oversized shoulder bag that was now lying on the table and without looking at the bag, fished out her truck keys. She lay them on the table and pushed them towards Topman. He wrapped his big, work hardened hand around the bundle and stood to his feet. He left with no words of either caution or encouragement. With just a slight full-handed touch on Rowdy's shoulder as he walked past, he was gone.

Rowdy sat for another few seconds before rising also. He walked around the table and held out his hand to Josie with a smile

"I'm new here. You will have to suggest a nice place for a long, quiet dinner."

Chapter 33

Aaron and all three of the girls rushed from the house and stood in thinly veiled excitement as the grandparent's car rolled along the dusty gravel driveway. After living long without grandparents, uncles or aunts or cousins, or, of course, their father, the idea of meeting their often-longed-for family and getting to know them in some intimacy, was creating within the girls a sense of expectancy.

Clara was the first to speak, loudly offering a welcome as soon as the driver's door opened. Nick and Anna each swung their legs out and, holding onto their doors for balance slowly stood, almost like a duet of travel weariness. Grinning at Aaron, Nick said, "Long time for these two old folks to sit in one position. Good to be here though, and good to see you all."

Aaron stepped forward to receive a firm handshake from his long-estranged father-in-law.

When Grandma Anna found her stability, Abby,

the youngest at fourteen years, rushed into her arms. Judging by the mutual reactions, the child and the grandma were both ready to start making up for all the growing up years they had missed.

Clara, again acting as the eldest and responsible hostess said, "It's chilly out here. Come to the house. Lunch will be ready in a few minutes."

Nick stood looking all around the small holding while Anna walked to the house with Abby hugged tightly under one arm and Becky under the other.

Aaron, who had come outside with no coat on, stood wishing Nick would head for the house where it was warm. Instead, the old man studied the farmyard with care, noting, it seemed, every building, every fence, every overgrown shrub, and the long unused corral. Finally, with just a lift of his chin as he looked across the yard, he asked, "Find any use for that barn or is it as empty as mine?"

"Nothing in there but an old pickup I hope to keep running through the winter. That and an equally old three-ton grain truck."

"Just an old tractor I use for snow clearing in mine. Old buildings like these have fallen on hard times all over the country. Hundreds of them. Maybe thousands."

Aaron, entering for just a moment into Nick's nostalgia, answered, "Yes. But they gave good service in their day. And when you consider that most of them were built by men who knew more about teams and plows than they did about carpentry and construction, and engineering, they've stood the test of time remarkably well."

Nick looked at Aaron and simply nodded before turning to the house.

In the big kitchen Anna was marveling at the beautiful, nickel trimmed and decorated wood stove.

"I still use my wood stove every day. Always have. But it's no such beautiful thing as this. I'm so glad someone thought to hold it back from the scrap dealers."

Clara said, "We're all trying to learn how to use it, Grandma. I've made lunch on it. We like the warmth it radiates into the kitchen. Perhaps while you're here you can explain what all the levers and cranks are for and help us to understand how to cook better on it."

"I'd love too. I'm looking forward to that."

Over lunch, which the girls worked together to prepare and serve, Abby asked, "How long can you stay, Grandma?"

"Well, I'm not really sure, honey, a few days anyway if that works for all of you. There's really nothing calling us home quickly."

"How about forever?" burst out Becky.

No one answered, as everyone cast eyes around the table, waiting for someone to speak.

When no one voiced anything, either for or against the thought, Aaron studied his in-laws. He saw nothing to indicate that it was an out of the way suggestion, unworthy of consideration. It made him wonder how lonely the old folks had been with two sons in the city showing little interest in the old farm, or in the elderly parents.

The time for Box and Maria to stand before the altar, with the pastor waiting to declare them forever one, forever tied to each other, finally arrived. There was some doubt at first whether Syl would feel up to attending. Her anemia seemed to have taken a tight grip and was showing considerable reluctance to let go. But by resting for the couple of days leading up to the date, she managed to convince Danny that she was strong and fit enough to attend. Neither wanted to miss the celebration, or as Box had called it, his surrender, but they finally decided that no harm would come to either the baby or the mother if they were careful, watched what Syl ate and forgot about dancing at the reception.

Box, who had never found himself to be short of words and a verbal sling or two, was amazingly subdued. Danny suspected that Maria had laid down the law, the first of what would probably turn out to be a considerable list of rules before the happy-go-lucky cowboy and the head strong rancher's daughter celebrated their golden anniversary.

With the news of Syl's questionable health being spread freely at the reception, there was an almost unbroken string of wedding guests that found their way to the table for four that Danny had pushed into a corner, a bit out of the way. Box brought his parents over while Ab and Mrs. Kane broke away from their families and came for a short visit. Somehow, keeping in the spirit of the happy day, those who were aware of the cattle rustling managed to dance around the subject of Bo's employment on the D-F.

Danny was reasonably certain Ab Kane hadn't yet gotten around to forgiving the rustler, but even he said nothing.

Mose and Cable, the two riders that rescued the summer when Danny broke his leg, found time between dances to say hello.

When the other two chairs at Danny and Syl's table became empty, Maria walked their way with another young couple in tow.

"Danny and Syl, I want you to meet Rowdy Benson and Josie Greenwood. Rowdy and Josie, this is Danny and Syl Framer. You will remember the story of my rescue from the storm, Josie. Danny was the hero of the day. I owe him my life, something I will never forget, or be able to repay. As it happened, Syl was my rescuing angel nurse. So, Danny really owes me for unwittingly and unknowingly setting up their initial meeting."

Turning to Danny and Syl she said, "Josie is an old school and riding friend. She somehow managed to get herself picked up by Rowdy, just yesterday. They can tell you how that happened. There could be some discrepancy in their stories. Which one you believe is totally up to you. Rowdy has something he wants to talk about with you, Danny. I'll leave them with you, I have to get back."

With a smile and a wave at the two empty chairs, she was gone. By that time Danny was standing. He spoke first to Josie, and then shook hands with Rowdy. The two visitors spoke to Syl, and then took their seats.

After a few seconds of uncomfortable silence,

Danny said, "Well there was a lot in that brief introduction. Might be best if we forgot about most of it and just say Syl and I are pleased to meet you."

Rowdy smiled and came back with, "Pleased to meet you as well. There's probably a couple of things that need a quick explanation though. First, while it's true that Josie and I only met yesterday she actually did not manage to get herself picked up, as I believe the bride called it. Actually, we were properly introduced by her uncle. I, of course, was smitten from the start and here we are. And yes, if it is not intruding on your celebration, I do have a small piece of business I would like to put on the table. It was actually the groom who mentioned your name when he asked what I was up to after my previous ventures came to an end."

Danny caught the words, 'previous ventures', but decided not to pursue the matter. But he did say, "Your timing is good here, folks. We were just going to find our coats and head home. But we have a few minutes to talk."

"Then I'll be quick," responded Rowdy. "What I'm looking for is stable space and some attached workout acreage. And a man who knows horses and is prepared to oversee their breeding and foaling when the time comes. Then work with the foals, bringing them along safely to adulthood.

"I have a stallion and three mares I intend to breed and train as bucking horses. Rodeo stock. They will have to be held apart from other horses and it wouldn't be good if there were other mares around. The stallion will mix alright with geldings but, still, they shouldn't be penned together. Of course, I expect to pay for the boarding and wages for the attendant. The groom, I think they said his name is Box, a most unusual name even for a nick name, said you run only geldings and may have some space you would rent out."

Danny studied the man before he said, "That's an interesting situation. But I'm not your man and the D-F is not the right place. I don't have the knowledge of horses required for the job or the training skills you're looking for, but I may have a suggestion for you. First, tell me a bit more please. And understand, I don't know the first thing about bucking horses. But I have to assume you do."

Josie held up one hand like a school crossing guard and laughed.

"Everyone, stop. I can see I have to come to the rescue again. It's clear Danny that you're in the dark here. Perhaps you're not a rodeo fan. This guy, whose nickname Rowdy is at least as unusual as Box's, was the two-time world's saddle bronc champion. Retired two years ago and is now in another business that keeps him too busy to care for his horses. So obviously, his previous ventures as he called them, was practically owning the world's rodeo circuit. And yes, he knows bucking horses."

Turning to Rowdy she said, "Now, please continue quickly. I believe I can see that Syl is feeling the need to be at home, probably where she should have been the entire evening."

Neither Syl nor Danny responded to the veiled invitation to explain Syl's weakness.

Rowdy was going to continue, but Danny spoke first.

"While I can't accommodate you, Rowdy, I have a friend that you should meet. His name is Aaron. He lives right across the road from us. He's not at the wedding but you could probably talk him into meeting you for lunch tomorrow. We're all out of church by about twelve-thirty. I'll write his phone number down for you. It's not too late to call this evening. He has the space and the land, although he may have to upgrade some fencing and find some hay for the winter. What his knowledge of horses is you can discuss between you.

"A few folks often go for lunch after church. Perhaps you'll be invited to join the group. We plan to be at church but not at the lunch. We'll be going straight home."

Danny tore a page from his daybook, wrote simply Aaron, and the phone number on it and slid it across the table.

"Give him a call. You'll find him receptive, I'm pretty sure. And folks, while it's been good to meet you, we must head for home. I apologize, Rowdy, for not being a rodeo fan or knowing your name, but I'll remember it now. Perhaps we'll meet again soon."

As the two men stood and shook hands Danny was surprised to hear Josie ask, "When is the baby due, Syl?"

He didn't hear the answer.

Chapter 34

The next morning, church felt almost like a gathering of the clan. Aaron arrived with the girls and then waited beside the open door, waiting for Rowdy. He hadn't told the cowboy his last name when he invited him to join them at church and lunch or admitted that they had been friends for years. He chose to hold that surprise for when Rowdy arrived and placed eyes on him.

Danny and Syl were in the foyer saying hello to a couple of friends before moving into the sanctuary. Looking over the heads of the crowd Danny was surprised, but pleased to see Bo and his wife, Meg. The kids were not with them. From his position beside the door, Aaron greeted them first before he walked them over to where Danny and Syl were standing. Syl was needing to sit down so the greetings were friendly, but short.

Bo, feeling totally out of place, cautiously followed Danny down the aisle until they found space enough for four. Danny ushered Bo in first so that the ladies could sit together, with their husbands at their sides.

It wasn't long until Aaron, with Belle walking beside him and with Rowdy and Josie, the couple from the wedding reception following close behind, took their seats.

Following the service Danny kept the comments to Bo to a minimum, simply saying it was good to have them there. Saying anything more might overwhelm them, leading them to hesitate about coming again. But he did manage to gather the group close enough to introduce Rowdy and Josie. Unlike Danny, Aaron and Bo, as well as Meg, his wife, were rodeo fans and were well familiar with the exploits of the saddle bronc star.

Laughing at the coincidence after a couple of years of separation, Aaron said, "Thanks for giving Rowdy my name, Danny. We go way back. Back to my grill and broiler days, following the rodeo circuit all over North America. I always felt it was a tossup for Rowdy. Did he crave the brisket and beans the most, or was it my scrumptious burger and beans, liberally laced with red chili? Of course, there was no going wrong on either one. I'm thinking of writing a recipe book featuring those two items and their many variations. May even start a new trend, adjusted good food guide and all, with Rowdy's picture on the cover."

No one seemed willing to pursue this thought. So, Aaron grinned and said, "Bo and Meg are joining us for lunch. Will you two come along?"

"No. You rodeo folks will have lots to discuss, and we need to get home."

Danny and Syl made their quick departure while the rest of the group were still visiting.

The next morning, after listening to the grim, long term weather forecast, Danny walked out to the hay yard to count bales once again. Bo was out with the cattle so wouldn't be aware of Danny's actions. Danny had counted so often he started feeling as if he could identify individual bales as they were removed from the stack when feeding time came. The fact that he was concerned was obvious to Syl, who watched, and mentally marked down her husband's every move and unspoken thought. When she was able to discern his thoughts, at least.

His feelings and concerns regarding the winter's feed had been clear to her for some time. There was a long winter ahead of them and the herd represented more money than either Danny or Syl had ever dreamed of in their most optimistic moments. That much of it would be needed for the next spring's calf purchase, only added pressure on them. They couldn't afford to lose even a small portion of their working capital.

Holding his worries tightly to himself, Danny had said nothing to either Aaron or Bo.

That they hadn't been forced into feeding yet was a bonus, but would it be enough of a bonus if cold weather and heavy snows proved to be a part of the next few months?

Reentering the cabin, he poured another cup of

coffee and joined Syl at the table. Without lifting her eyes from the book, she was reading, she surprised him by asking, "How many bales this morning?"

After Danny got over the shock of the question a small, surprised laugh escaped his mouth

"Is it that obvious?"

"Well, let's just say that when the stoic Danny Framer is pacing the floor at three in the morning, when he thinks I'm sleeping, looking at the calendar and counting the days till spring, as if their number was going to change for their frequent counting, and studying the hay stack regularly, although Bo hasn't had to begin feeding yet, any observant person with a minimum of calculation might come to the conclusion that there is a problem. Or at the very least, a potential problem. So lay it out, my worried husband. You've come to the conclusion that holding the herd over till spring might be a mistake. Am I correct in this guess?"

"Can you imagine. I used to believe I would be able to hide a few things from my wife if I should ever get married. You know what I mean? Have a secret or two. Always believed a man deserved at least that much in life. Now I find that was totally naive.

"But you're right again. It's tight. We knew it would be, from the start. I maybe should have kept more hay back instead of selling so much off and hoping for an open winter, and an early spring.

"I'm afraid I may have listened too well and too long to Murphy when he was begging for hay. But he's been a good and faithful client since I first moved onto the place. I'll still need him for a client in the good years, when the country is awash in hay, so I wanted to keep him happy."

Danny took a big drink of his coffee, then cradled the mug in his hands while he thought through his options again before saying, "But here's the thing. Sol phoned again yesterday. He's begging for animals for that same feed lot down south that bought the other herd. But his offering isn't all that attractive. It's even down some from before."

Syl, with her eyes still firmly glued to the page of her book said, "I called the bank manager yesterday. He checked for me. There's still room enough in the account for more money, if you should sell."

Danny smiled at his seemingly nonchalant sounding wife, although he knew she was anything but casual in her attitude to ranch, cattle and business.

"He said that, did he? I'm glad you thought to call. The main reason I didn't sell last month is that I feared there would be no place to put the money. You know, like I'd have to stow it away in the barn loft or something, and then find out in the spring that the mice had built their nests out of it."

Syl simply lifted her eyes for a flash of time and grinned. "Everyone has problems to solve, my dear."

The room fell to silence while Danny lifted his coffee cup. Syl seemed to have one final thought.

"Sell or feed, it's your choice. I can't offer to throw bales, but otherwise I'm with you, whatever you decide."

She went back to her book as if they were talking about nothing at all, when in fact, there was a great deal of money on the table. Picking it up now would not mean a loss but it would mean a drop from the hoped-for gains.

Danny refilled his mug and pushed his arms into a warmer coat before taking his seat on the porch. He had some thinking to do. An hour later, he went in search of Bo. He was in time to see the cowboy riding towards the barn as he came in for his noon change of horses. He waited until the horse was unsaddled and cared for before saying more than, "How are they?"

Bo was almost equally sparing with his words.

"Cattle looking fine. Grass is still holding up but not for much longer. Five hundred beef critters do a lot of eating."

The wind howling around the eaves of the little cabin woke Danny. He rose from his bed and glanced at the clock radio on the headboard. 2:30 a.m. The calendar, if he should take time to look at it, would confirm that it was early November.

He stepped into his slippers and hung his robe across his shoulders without bothering to slip his arms into the sleeves. While he carefully crossed the bedroom floor, Syl's eyes followed him.

He pulled the cabin door open with the intention of stepping outside to get a read on what was happening. A quick peek and a thrust of wind told him there was no need to leave the warmth of the cabin to know what the ranch would face in the morning. Although the deep darkness was barely penetrated by the yard light, he could see large snowflakes forced almost sideways by the howling wind. As he watched, the table on the porch slid to the far end of the floor and tipped over onto the grass of the yard. A coffee mug he had left there the evening before fell but didn't break. Both his and Syl's chairs were moved out of position, but they were too heavy to be upset, although the seat cushions were picked up and flung off into the darkness.

He gave momentary consideration to going to the barn to check on the horses, but quickly thought better of the idea. They were safely housed in the new stalls and would be fine. But what the cattle were doing was a whole other question. He wouldn't know that until the morning light showed the way.

Even as he watched, the wind seemed to drop enough to give a better idea of the snow fall. Instinctively he knew there would be several inches on the ground by morning. Where the snow would gather when the wind finished having its way with it was an unknown.

Slowly he closed the door. As quietly as he could, he built up the fire in the wood stove and again checked the furnace thermostat. With that done, he quietly made his way back to bed. Syl kept her eyes closed, leaving her husband to his own thoughts.

What the newly breaking dawn showed him in the morning was even worse than he feared. The mercury had plunged into the seriously cold range and the snow lay heavy between the house and barn, sculpted in places where the wind wound around the power pole and a few other small obstructions. Studying the buildings, including the power plant shelter and the new house that was under construction, Danny saw drifts two feet or more deep, showing the pattern the wind had followed. But the wind was gone, for the moment at least. A quiet calm had fallen over the ranch yard. Danny figured it wouldn't last.

Not bothering with breakfast or coffee, he pushed his way through the snow and opened the barn door. With a flick of the light switch all the horses turned their heads his way. His mind was on the cattle, but he managed to say, "Good morning, boys. Be patient. I'll get to you, bye 'n' bye."

With hopes that the battery still held a charge, Danny made his way down the center aisle to the stall that held the small tractor. It hadn't been driven for some time. He checked the oil and the antifreeze level, mostly out of habit, climbed to the seat and turned the key. With some reluctance, the starter kicked in and with a minimum of delay, the engine started. He drove outside and backed under the wagon shed.

With the barn closed up again and the wagon hooked up, he pushed through the snow to the hay yard. He had twenty bales loaded on the wagon when Bo came around the corner. After a brief greeting, Bo said, "I thought Graham was coming down to feed."

"Called last evening. The whole family's down with the flu."

With that simple explanation, the two men went to work, loading the wagon with enough bales to last the day's two feedings. Danny was hoping the cattle would use it as a supplement while they continued grazing what little grass still protruded through the snow.

Danny drove the tractor slowly down the pasture while Bo dropped bales off each side, hanging the twine over a post built into the rear rack. The cattle quickly gathered along the trail of feed and dropped their heads, tonguing their first mouthfuls of cured grass. Bo counted as he unloaded, working on the estimated feed requirement he and Danny had calculated a few days before. Just as they were finishing for the morning the wind whipped up again, lifting snow and hay, both, off the ground and twirling it across the pasture. Knowing there was nothing to do about it, Danny, with a sinking heart, turned the wagon back to the shed. The morning had turned ugly in the past hour. Danny went for breakfast while Bo saddled a horse and rode out to look for lost or down cattle.

The official weather forecasters had shouted loudly and clearly that the present mild westerly winds and pleasant fall temperatures would last at least another week, and probably more. But as so often happens on the northern grasslands that close to the high-up Rockies, and perfectly timed in accordance with the warnings in the Farmer's Almanac, nature proved the weatherman to be wrong. Again. Or, perhaps still, depending on which cynic a person chose to side with.

Each and every opinion was voiced over multiple cups of coffee down at the Crossroads Café, by men wearing bib overalls and John Deere hats, or, in the case of the ranchers, jeans, high heel boots and Stetsons. These various opinions were, from time to time, articulated with considerable vigor and emphasis among the old friends and neighbors, so much so that the waitress finally walked over and said, "Now, boys." That was enough to settle the bunch down.

Wiley Hamilton, local rancher and amateur historian, a quiet, thoughtful man, said, "She's going to be a tough one, men. Not the worst this land has ever seen but maybe close to it. Ain't ever known the Almanac to be far from the truth when it's all added up. You're going to see a record snowpack in the hills before spring and even for this windy country, we're going to set records. Or come close. The snowpack will drive the moose and elk and deer onto the flatlands, where they'll compete with the cattle, for what grass remains available among the drifts."

"How do you know that, Wiley, other than the Almanac, is what I mean to ask?"

Wiley looked down the table to a man he'd known all his adult life. A man he called friend. But, in Wiley's mind, a man who knew no more, nor had any deeper understanding now, than he had fifty years before.

"You got to learn to observe, Clint. See what the land is telling you. There's been messages in those high-up wisps of clouds drifting over faster than a horse can run, these past few days. Then, the wind changed direction again yesterday. There's been other signs as well. You got to see the warnings. What we've seen the past few days are the signs that caused the Indians to gather their buffalo robes close and drag their dried firewood inside the wigwam."

"You know about Indians, do you, Wiley?" grinned a man who was new to the country, and the coffee group.

Wiley's answer was friendly to this newcomer, but serious.

"Know enough to keep my wood box full and prepare for what's coming."

Someone else at the end of the big table laughed and said, "Why don't you tell the story of John Ware's big ride during his first winter on the Bar U, Wiley?"

Someone else groaned, "You really want to hear that tale again?"

"It's a great story, and a true one, mostly."

"Who really cares? That was near enough a century ago. New way of doing today. Most everything's different."

Wiley had heard about enough of what he, privately, considered to be ignorance.

"It's all new and different. No question of that, boys. But you think on it, you'll know that most of the young men today couldn't or wouldn't do what it took to build this great country. Most men today ride only for pleasure or show. Work their herds from the seat of a pickup truck or an SUV.

"Some of you know this, some don't. My grandfather knew John Ware. Knew many of the other early greats too. Knew and worked with him in the years after that great ride of John's, where he never gave up on the Bar U stock during that terrible October blizzard of 1882. Thousands of animals died on the grass that winter, but John did the almost impossible, following the drift and gathering them together when the storm finally broke. The Bar U lost fewer animals than the Cochrane, by a long shot, even fewer than some of the small outfits, although there weren't more than a handful of herds on the grass at that time.

"In later years, my grandfather was one of the cowboys that trailed John's herd from his place on Sheep Creek all the way east to the Red Deer River country. Drove them right through Calgary after the constable warned them not to. But Ol' John he was a man to get things done so he bided his time and then pushed on through. Great story. But that's not what we're on about this morning."

He looked around the table, sizing up each man, friend and neighbor alike.

"If we're going to learn from history, we need to know the weather signs, because so much of what happened in history on this grass happened because of the weather. We need to know what and who's gone before us too. A personal account of that great storm should have been wrote down by those who lived it. That first great ride should have been wrote down, too, at the time. Oh, she's been wrote down alright, but not by those who were there. It was wrote down years later by the academics, the boys that care more about grammar and commas than they do about the soul of the story. Or the hearts of the men and women who lived it. Right around this table boys, and all around this country, there's living history. Old timers whose eyes have seen things that will never be seen again in this changing culture. And much of it has to do with the hardships of bitter winters or summer droughts, where the cattle had to be brought to feed and water or the ranch would go bust. Things that should be wrote down. History should be kept by those who can do 'er up proper, telling the story firsthand.

"Unless you've settled into a rock-hard saddle, leather frozen stiff at thirty below, your Stetson tied down with a scarf. Another scarf wound around your ears and nose. Your feet and hands so cold you're near to tears with the pain. Each cold breath you take feeling like a razor blade slicing down your throat. Unless you've experience all that, you can't really write it. Oh, the academics, the educated boys, will try. Try from their nice warm offices, in their nice comfortable, tax paid colleges. Even the storytellers will try. But they don't know the whole of it. They don't know the feel of it. They'll leave out the heart of the man. Or the woman.

"Who can describe the long days in the saddle in scorching heat, pouring rain or winter's blizzards? Who can describe the hopelessness of a cowboy, walking because his horse is done in, leading the poor brute, to who knows where, lost beyond hope in the dark of night, the wind swirling the blinding snow until he finally spots a lit lantern hanging from the house eve?"

The speaker let that thought sink in while he lifted his cup again.

"Who can describe the soul quenching loneliness of a woman on a frontier ranch, miles from the closest neighbor? Who can tell of a woman, alone but for her clumsy husband, giving birth in the back bedroom of their small shack with neither one knowing what they were doing or what to do next? And who can tell of that same woman a few weeks later as she holds her little one while he breathes his last, after losing the battle to pneumonia. Or of her rancher husband trying to hack a three-foot grave out of frozen ground with pick and shovel, while tears froze on his cheeks. And neither of them not yet twenty years old. Recording that is a job for those that lived it, boys."

While most had heard these sentiments from Wiley before, still they listened.

"Now you look out that window. We've pretty much got tame cattle today, too much beef on them to care for running. But imagine chasing an ornery, half wild Longhorn on the open range, not a fence anywhere to control the drift, trying desperately to save it from its own stupidity. They'll turn tail and drift with the wind and sure enough fall off a cliff or bunch up at the bottom of a draw, dying in the cold. But it's your job to prod him out of there and get him to shelter. To save his miserable life for the ranch. And do it all for small enough wages and questionable food when you finally get back to the bunkhouse.

"No, boys. The educated fellas can't write that up. That's your job. And mine. Men who've experienced the country."

The table had become quiet as the waitress refilled the cups and the men mulled over what Wiley had said. After that short silence Wily pointed his finger across the table.

"Dusty, you've had a clear half century up in those hills, off to the west. Made friends with the Blackfoot. Came near enough getting et' by a cougar. Broke your leg miles from the cabin when that fool grey went down under you. Those things and many more. And all the time sided by a better woman than you deserved. That should all be wrote up."

"I ain't no hand to write more than my name and a number on a check, Wiley. Wouldn't know where to start."

"Well, I'll tell you where to start. You know the old Mulholland place, out along Sugartown Road. Young fella named Danny something or other has it now. Runs summer calves. Grows a bit of hay for sale. They say he's a writer. Has a book published and all. Just as quick as we're finished up sharing wisdom here you get yourself out there. It's on your way home anyway. Talk with him. See what he has to say. He can't do more than sic the dog on you."

A man sitting to Wiley's right said, "I've been there just a few weeks ago trying to buy hay. He ain't got no dog."

Clint laughed and said, "Well, that clears that up."

With the unrelenting wind and the steadily falling snow making the feeding of cattle a miserable job, and with Danny watching in despair as so much of his precious hay was lost to the wind, the first week of feeding had seemed like a month. Both he and

Bo had red, chapped cheeks and frost puffed ears. Their fingers, almost frozen into a permanent curl from tossing bales around by their tie twine, remained aching and curled even after they warmed themselves by the stove.

When Aaron walked out to the feed area and shouted, "Are we having fun yet?" Danny had to hold back an uncharacteristic comment. He said nothing as he turned the tractor back to the barn. Aaron hopped onto the wagon with Bo.

After putting the tractor in the barn, Danny said, "Bo, if you'll feed and water these horses, and take a quick scan of the pasture to look for downers, I'd like if you'd go home for the day. There's nothing at all to be gained by standing around here. Come back for afternoon feeding and then we'll have to develop some different kind of a plan."

Bo nodded in silent agreement. Danny and Aaron walked up to the cabin. Along the way Aaron glanced over at the partially built house and asked, "The men able to work at all?"

"Haven't been here for a week."

Aaron joined Danny and Syl for a coffee. In the middle of a conversation about nothing of importance, the phone rang. Danny didn't even have the receiver all the way to his ear yet when Sol shouted out, "How about now, Danny? The offer still holds."

"Bring 'er up two nickels, Sol, and we've got a deal."

"Done."

When he hung up the phone, he glanced from Aaron to Syl and back again.

"Having to admit you're wrong just never seems to get any easier."

The others at the table remained diplomatically quiet.

Danny had never liked it when the time came to tell a man his work and wages were ending. But it had to be done. After the phone call from Sol, Danny waited until the evening feed time to speak with Bo.

"Here's what's happening, Bo. No matter how many times I count the bales there's never going to be enough. And then, with the wind blowing a good chunk of it into the next county, the feed just gets tighter and tighter. And then, the broker hasn't left me alone for weeks now. I've paced the floor at night and prayed for wisdom. I finally had to make a decision. Either gamble and take a huge risk or take what we're offered now and play it safe. At the end of the day, after all the deliberations, there was really only one decision I could make. I accepted the sale price, and the herd will be gone by the end of the week. I know that's hard on you. Perhaps there's a place for the winter for you on one of the big ranches. You can feel free to give my name for a reference, and perhaps we can do this again next spring.

"I'm sorry to not be able to follow through on the original plan but sometimes we just have to admit the truth and go with it. I'd like if you would stay until we're loaded out though."

Bo lifted his hat off and ran his fingers through

his hair and grinned.

"Danny, my friend, you promised me only a summer's work and we've done that. The wintering-over idea was really lost the minute the price of feeders and the price of hay got into competition with each other. So, in fact, you have more than kept your word. And you've done more than pretty much anyone else would have done, giving me a chance. Don't ever think I've forgotten, or that I don't appreciate. I'll stay and see the cattle weighed out and off the property. And we'll talk again come springtime."

Four days later, the pasture was empty, the rental scale returned and somehow, the bank, faithful to their word, found somewhere to put another large amount of cash to the credit of the D-F Ranch.

When the last truckload cleared the driveway and swung onto Sugartown Road, Danny, Bo, Aaron and Graham Wills watched its dual-wheel blown snow cloud up and then slowly settle, no one knowing exactly what to say. Bo finally broke the silence.

"I'll get the shovel and wheelbarrow and clean the barn. Then I'll tie a lead to my two animals from the back of the pickup and take a slow drive home. Should get there just about in time for supper."

Danny responded, "Leave the barn. I'll find it good therapy sometime in the next day or two. Anyway, the day is far advanced. You'll already be pretty late getting home."

The men all shook hands and went their separate ways. Three days later, the sale check was deposited.

Danny and Syl looked at the balance in the checking account and had nothing to say. Danny finally folded the printed sheet he had brought home from the bank and slid it across the table it to Syl.

"Here, Mrs. Bookkeeper. This is yours."

Chapter 35

Willy, the building contractor had managed to get the foundation for the new house formed and poured before the first serious frost. Within another week, the floor was on, and the framing was well advanced. Danny found his view from the porch chair interesting and informative. He had promised himself that he would go no closer to the project than his chair on the porch, remembering the time Willy had offered to buy him lunch if he would go somewhere else and let him get on with the work.

He spent hours observing during the first week of the building, but then he started to become bored, knowing there was an entire winter's work ahead for the building crew.

Syl had gone back to work for almost one full week before she recognized that she couldn't continue. While overall she didn't feel really sick, the remaining anemia was sapping her strength. She found herself looking for opportunities to sit down even for only a minute or two.

She reluctantly signed on for a long term, unpaid sabbatical and settled back in at home. Her baby doctor, as Danny described the obstetrician Syl had chosen for her care, was fully in favor of the decision although she cautioned Syl to get lots of gentle exercise and to be careful with her diet.

After the cattle were sold and trucked off, Danny had cleaned out the barn, making it as comfortable as possible for wintering his own horses, and repaired a broken manger. The crew quarters in the barn had been winterized weeks earlier.

With little to keep him busy, Danny visited Aaron across the road as he was preparing for the delivery of Rowdy's stallion and the three mares. When he returned from that visit and entered the cabin, Syl was at the kitchen sink peeling potatoes. The wood stove had warmed the room and the coffee, as always, was ready. He hung up his heavy jacket and turned to pick a porcelain mug off the shelf, when he noticed the typewriter and a stack of paper sitting on the table. Laughing, he said, "Now, that wouldn't be a hint would it."

"It's more than a hint, my multitalented, but humble and somewhat evasive husband. The world awaits your next fictional output. People are calling for information. Book stores keep having to make excuses to their many enquiring customers. Libraries are concerned. The professional reviewers and critics twiddle their thumbs in anticipation. The publisher's accountant has a check with your name on it, just waiting for the amount to pen in."

"And my wife, who has never before shown any tendency towards creating fictional accounts, just might be doing that right this very minute."

Danny poured the coffee and set it within reach from the typewriter. He then squeezed behind the table and took his seat. He adjusted the papers into their appropriate stacks of blank pages, and already typed on pages, took another sip of coffee, chaffed his cold fingers, and asked, "Have you forgotten the book tour next week?"

"I haven't forgotten it for a minute, but this is only Tuesday. You can get several days of writing in before the weekend."

Danny hunched his shoulders and resigned himself to Syl's oversight.

"It's too bad they don't make you the hospital administrator. Why, you'd have that place humming like a high voltage wire on a country road."

Syl chose to ignore the comment.

A Sneak Peak At Danny Book 3:
The Truth of the Story

Belle stood outside the new, white painted 2 x 6 in. training corral behind Aaron's barn and wrung her hands in worry as her seventeen-year-old son, Steve, prepared to mount his first bucking horse. Aaron stood beside her, wishing he could hold her hand as he did on their long river walks. But her hands were pretty busy, and he wasn't at all sure she even remembered that he stood there. The early spring sunshine was adding just enough warmth to the day to make the afternoon enjoyable without wearing the heavy coats of the winter months.

In the corral with Steve stood Rowdy Benson, the recently retired two-time world's saddle bronc champion rider. Rowdy had borrowed the gelding from a friend after he noticed how quickly Steve caught on to riding, and his many questions about rodeo. Without comment, he acknowledged to himself that he was looking at a natural rider. He was also wishing the young man was even younger.

Most professional riders had been on horseback all their lives. If Steve chose to compete, he would be at a distinct disadvantage, but perhaps Rowdy could guide him through, and over, that learning curve.

"Now Steve, this ol' horse, Bandit he's called, on account of he slips clean away from most riders, isn't any way a mean bronc. The mean ones might toss you against the fence and then come after you, teeth bared and hind hooves at the ready. Bandit's nothing like that. He just doesn't like to be ridden. He'll carry your pack into the mountains and happily haul your venison back out for you, but for some reason he doesn't take well to having a human on his back. There's not a truly mean bone in his body. He'll toss his head and hump his back, then kick out his hind feet. Maybe twist and turn a bit. But you can handle him. Remember, it's only for eight seconds.

"We're going to get Aaron in here to hold the horse down while you climb aboard. I'll be riding the pickup horse. Josie is going to time the eight seconds and blow the air horn when it's time to bail off. I'll be right beside you. Like I told you before, when you hear the horn, you drop the bridle rope, kick your feet clear and slide off onto my horse. You take a hold on me, my shirt, my belt, whatever you can grab, and I'll take you to the fence and drop you off safe and sound. If you feel yourself going over Bandit's head or off to the side, let him go and try to land on your feet. There's near enough a foot of wood shavings under you so the landing will be soft.

"Are you ready?"

"About as ready as I'm likely to get."

As Steve spoke, Aaron had walked away from Belle's side and was quietly approaching, leading Bandit, who was showing a bit of uneasiness at the feel of the saddle belted around him. Arrayed outside the fence were four girls, Steve's sister, and Aaron's three daughters. They had all been learning to ride but only Steve had shown the kind of natural talent that caught Rowdy's eye.

Belle, who had taken her first ride in the fall, before the long, cold winter had settled in, wasn't at all sure she wanted her son mounting a bucking horse, but she held her tongue, knowing Steve was old enough to make most of his own decisions.

Aaron held the horse while Steve carefully put his foot into the left-hand stirrup, while his right hand held the thick bridle rope and the saddle swell, at the same time.

"For better or worse," he said to Aaron, as he put his weight on his left foot and quickly lifted onto the saddle. As soon as he hit the seat of the saddle, Aaron turned the animal loose. Steve had barely found the offside stirrup before Bandit lowered his head, putting a strain on the rope held in Steve's hand. Bandit lifted enough to throw both hind legs out and lowered his head even more.

"Spur him good," Rowdy hollered. "Let him know who's boss."

Steve leaned back, putting pressure on the rope and encouraging the horse to lift his head, while he raked both sides of Bandit's neck with his boot heels and the small set of spurs Rowdy had produced from somewhere.

The next eight seconds would never be counted as a winning ride, but Steve stayed with the animal through all its twists, kicks and turns. When he heard the air horn and knew the ride was over, he pulled his feet free, dropped the rope, swung his left leg over the saddle and slid to the ground, landing on his feet on the offside. He had somehow forgotten about Rowdy and the pickup horse. As Bandit lunged across the corral and Steve marveled that he had successfully completed his first ride, he heard cheering and shouts of encouragement from the gathering outside the wooden rails.

When the back slapping and additional congratulations were ending, another car drove into the yard. Ace, or Phillip, as his parents had named him, who had just that day arrived after the long drive from the east, stepped out and joined the group. A couple of people recognized the arrival with a nod of the head or a quick, "Hi", or "welcome back", but Steve remained the center of attention.

When things quieted down, Aaron said, "I'm wishing Danny had made it over. He would have enjoyed this. And he would have been so proud of you, Steve."

Into the silence that followed that comment Ace said, "I'm thinking his mind might be on things other than rodeo rides right at this very minute. Danny just became a father an hour ago."

Watch for Book three of the Danny series,
The Truth of the Story available soon.

About the Author

Reg Quist's pioneer heritage includes sod shacks, prairie fires, home births, and children's graves under the prairie sod, all working together in the lives of people creating their own space in a new land.

Out of that early generation came farmers, ranchers, business men and women, builders, military graves in faraway lands, Sunday Schools that grew to become churches, plus story tellers, musicians, and much more.

Hard work and self-reliance were the hallmark of those previous great generations, attributes that were absorbed by the following generation.

Quist's career choice took him into the construction world. From heavy industrial work, to construction camps in the remote northern bush, the author emulated his grandfathers, who were both builders, as well as pioneer farmers and ranchers.

It is with deep thankfulness that Quist says, "I am a part of the first generation to truly enjoy the benefits of the labors of the pioneers. My parents and their parents worked incredibly hard, and it is well for us to remember".

CPSIA information can be obtained
at www.ICGtesting.com
Printed in the USA
LVHW100342050222
709876LV00005B/7

9 781639 774081